Life and Death on Siesta Key

Sheila Marie Palmer

www.sheilamariepalmer.com.

ISBN: 1484988515

ISBN-13: 9781484988510

Library of Congress Control Number: 2013909639

CreateSpace Independent Publishing Platform

North Charleston, South Carolina

Also by Sheila Marie Palmer

Life and Death on The Tamiami Trail

As always…for my Harry

Chapter 1

Early Tuesday Morning

Freezing, I wiggled my hands and feet in an effort to stimulate circulation, but my arms and legs felt stiff and heavy from the cold, and the movement made little difference. My body shook with terror at the thought of freezing to death. My heart pounded in my ears and echoed in my head.

My eyes snapped open, every molecule in my body instantly alert. Several moments passed before I realized I'd awakened from a nightmare. It felt nice and warm in my bed. Familiar objects gradually took shape as my eyes adjusted to the dim light. My husband's head rested on the pillow next to me, his handsome face looking peaceful in childlike repose. I wanted to nestle into his arms, where I always felt safe, but it would have been unkind to wake him so early. The clock on my nightstand indicated it was 4:00 a.m. I didn't want to go back to sleep for fear of returning to the dream, so I got out of bed to continue the work I'd left unfinished the previous night.

After a long and difficult day, I had been glad to see the windows of our house aglow as I drove down the long driveway, because it meant my husband had arrived home before me. During the two months of our marriage, I'd grown accustomed to the quiet of our remote ranch house, but its vastness made me feel lonely when I was home by myself. I was rarely alone on the property, but "lonely" wasn't the same as "alone." The bunkhouse, home for thirty ranch hands, was a short sprint away and even closer by intercom phone. Still, the hired help rarely came over to the main house, so there was seldom any sound inside.

I'd been too tired to park in the barn, where we usually housed our vehicles, so I'd edged my Crown Victoria along the side of the house. I grabbed my purse and pulled a bulky, over-stuffed file box from the trunk. I was glad I didn't have to unlock the front door. I turned my body sideways as I approached the house, pressed the latch with my elbow, and pushed the massive oak door open with my hip.

The rustic chandelier in the foyer emitted a warm yellow glow that reflected off the cream-and-tan marble floor tiles. A narrow cypress table ran the length of one wall; an elaborate mirrored coat rack opposed it. A variety of outerwear hung from the rack: my heavy camel's hair coat; Buck's denim jacket; and two rain slickers, one in size small, lettered with the words SARASOTA COUNTY SHERIFF, and another in size extra-extra large, lettered, DESOTO COUNTY SHERIFF. Wooden pegs held hip holsters and hats.

As I pushed the door closed with my hips and back, Buck appeared. "Charlotte Bernadette Davis, what are you doing? Give me that box," he scolded as he lifted the heavy cardboard carton from my arms. He cleared a space on the cypress table and deposited the box on it. Then he turned and wrapped his powerful arms around me. I melted into his embrace. I felt the soft beat of his heart as I rested my head against his broad chest.

"Hey, house rules—no heavy lifting by the womenfolk," he said with a grin.

"OK," I answered quietly. "I'm just used to doing things for myself. It's hard to break old habits, you know." I had always been stubbornly independent. When Buck and I formed our liaison three months ago, and later married, both of our lives changed. I had not quite finished my adjustment period.

"I know, honey, but I don't want you to hurt yourself. Why did you bring that thing home anyway?"

"It's full of personnel files. I have to read all the evaluations and calculate raises so I can get the payroll changes processed this week. If I don't finish, there won't be time to do all the data entry for next payday. I was too busy to work on it today, so I figured I'd do it tonight."

"You look as tired as I feel. Can't that wait until tomorrow?"

"I've already put it off for a week. If I don't finish, everyone will have to wait another full month for raises."

Buck released me from the hug and kissed the top of my head. "I've started dinner. Why don't you slip into something comfortable and relax for a while?"

"Good idea," I murmured. As I walked from the room, I glanced back at him. Not only was my husband kind and loving, he was movie star drop-dead gorgeous. A six-foot-six-inch frame supported broad shoulders, a narrow waist, and lean muscular legs. His rugged face was clean-shaven; his black hair was stylishly cut; and he wore an air of casual confidence. Fate had certainly smiled upon me.

I made my way down the long hallway that led to our massive master suite, threw my purse and shoulder holster onto the bed, and entered a walk-in closet that was bigger than the living room in my first house. The designer had maximized the use of space and arranged all the storage elements efficiently. Drawers along the walls held bulkier clothing items and shoes. Wooden bars supported clothing on hangers. Hats fit into cubbyholes along the top. An island in the center contained smaller drawers for underclothes, socks, and sundries. A safe was cleverly disguised in the island cabinetry; we stored papers, weapons, and my valuable jewelry there. I undressed hastily, threw my clothing into laundry bins, and grabbed a warm terry-cloth robe. Full-length mirrors along both sides of the closet door allowed us to check our appearances before exiting, so I stopped in front of one to assess my body. I'd been in good shape most of my life, but now I looked frumpy. My waist had thickened, and my legs weren't as toned as they should be. As I examined the dark circles under my ice blue eyes, Buck appeared at the door.

"Yes, you're beautiful, Bernie," he said.

"I was thinking the opposite. Look at me! I'm so fat!"

Buck smiled a tolerant smile, his bright-green eyes sparkling as he wrapped his arms around me again. I loved his touch. His manly scent made me feel warm inside.

I knew my exhaustion was making me a little bitchy. *Calm down, Bernie,* I told myself. *You're home now. Take it easy. Enjoy this time.*

Buck grabbed my hand and led me toward the living room. He had started a fire in one of the two stone fireplaces that dominated opposite walls of the great room. The fire's light gave the space a pleasant glow, without any need for artificial lighting. The dry oak sputtered and popped as the flames licked the logs. We gravitated toward our usual seats on the couch in front of the fire. On the table next to me was a fine-crystal goblet filled with milk. I smiled as I saw Buck had included "milk cubes" in the glass.

We both had grown up in the sweltering, damp climate of coastal Florida in the 1950s. As children we didn't yet have the luxury of home air conditioning. Even Ca' d'Zan—John and Mable Ringling's fabulous mansion on Sarasota Bay—had been built without AC. Homes were cooled through the use of ceiling fans or box fans, though most of the time they just circulated hot air. A glass of milk sitting on the dinner table would warm quickly and spoil soon. Postwar housewives learned to freeze milk in ice cube trays and added the "milk cubes" to the glasses to keep drinks more palatable. Buck had placed a small dish of Oreo cookies next to the goblet. I often said the only good use for a glass of milk was to dunk Oreos. Tears stung the corners of my eyes. I couldn't begin to count the kind acts Buck performed for my benefit.

I left the milk and cookies untouched and slid across the couch into his arms. I lay my head on his chest and felt the crisp, starched fabric of his heavy oxford shirt against my cheek. Buck stroked the curly blond tresses that cascaded across my shoulders and down my back. For many minutes we sat quietly, wrapped in each other's arms, enjoying the warmth. A gust of howling wind and a barrage of heavy rain broke the spell. I jumped at the sudden sound of rain pelting the windows. Florida winters aren't particularly cold, but the winds can be harsh, and rain is commonplace.

"I'd planned to grill steaks," said Buck, "but that wind will stir the charcoal ash, and the meat will be covered with it. Guess we'll have to settle for indoor cooking." Since we lived on a cattle ranch, we always had plenty of beef in the freezer and ate some type of it three or four times a week.

After we finished the meal and cleaned the kitchen, we returned to the living room. I had drunk the milk with dinner, but the Oreos still sat on the table. I grabbed a light blanket, curled up on the couch, and nibbled a cookie as I read an employee file. The first one in the stack was that of Isaac McDuffie, one of my detectives, whom I'd known since seventh grade. We'd met on the long bus ride home from school and eventually found ourselves sitting together during every trip. Our paths seldom crossed during the school day, as I attended accelerated classes, and Ike wasn't interested in studying, but we became good buddies just the same. I soon realized I had a crush on him, but he didn't notice my adoration, so I curbed my feelings and settled for friendship instead of romance. We remained friends until our bus-riding days were over; I rarely saw him after that.

In high school Ike's size and bulk made him a natural for the position of center on the football team. He spent his free time on the practice field, while I spend mine tutoring math to students who had little knowledge of the subject. I'd heard he had joined the sheriff's department after high school but didn't think about him until I joined the department after college. Even so, I was a patrol officer on the graveyard shift, and he was a detective on the day shift, so our paths never crossed.

In January 1981, when I'd been sworn in as the elected sheriff of Sarasota County, I held three employee meetings, one for each shift. At those meetings, I swore in each deputy. That was the first time I'd spoken to Ike since high school, but he just smiled and executed his oath without saying anything further. I held employee meetings every year just to keep in touch with everyone. It was now December 1985, and I'd been sheriff for nearly five years, but Ike never once had made an attempt to speak to me.

Ike was known as the department's goof-off and party guy. Even with a hangover, he was a good detective, and his arrests were usually airtight, but his irresponsible attitude had impeded his advancement. I turned the pages of Ike's file, trying to evaluate his performance objectively. I was tired, and my mind kept drifting to those long-ago days when we had chatted happily on the bus. I was jolted from my memory trance to see Buck standing before me. He took the file from my hands and placed it on the table.

"You're asleep, you know. You need rest. Let's go to bed."

Chapter 2

Early Tuesday Morning

It seemed like only moments had passed since Buck had herded me to the bedroom the previous night. I donned my robe and tiptoed from the room. The central heat purred as it pushed warm air through the house, but the tile floors still felt cold under my feet. Figuring coffee would warm me, I switched on the lights in the kitchen and placed water and coffee in the pot. Before I pushed the "brew" button, the phone on the wall next to me rang loudly. Startled by the noise, I almost dropped the mug I'd removed from the cupboard.

After Buck and I had married, we realized we needed to rearrange the phone lines in the house. On one wall of the kitchen was a large multiline panel for the phones on the ranch property. The bunkhouse, barn, line shacks, and main house were all connected via an intercom system. There were also several outside lines we used to conduct the ranch's business and a couple for personal use. Extension phones were located in bedrooms and our library/office. Since we both were sheriffs, either of us might receive calls from our respective offices at any time of the day or night—an inconvenience that came with the territory. Buck's office used one single-line phone to call him. Since my office was in another county, we'd installed a second toll-free phone line for calls from my office. It rang with two short bell tones to distinguish it from Buck's office line. The sound that broke the silence of this early morning chimed two short bell tones, meaning the call was for me. I hurried to answer it before the noise woke Buck.

"Sheriff Raines. I mean, Sheriff Davis," I said into the handset.

"I'll never get used to your new name either, babe," the voice on the other end said with a chuckle. It was Lieutenant James Kenwood, my booking officer and ex-partner.

"Good morning, James," I said. "This can't be good news."

"You'll never guess who we have as a guest this morning."

"It's four o'clock in the morning. Much too early for guessing games. What is it?" I snapped.

"You sitting down? Well, it's none other than your old flame, Danny Dean, county administrator."

"For crying out loud, he is *not* my old flame. I can't even believe I let him talk me into going out with him. What did he do this time? Run his county vehicle into the ditch again? You don't have to call me every time Danny Dean gets drunk, you know."

"Ooh, did we wake up on the wrong side of the bed this morning? You know I wouldn't call about something like that. We have him booked for murder one."

I nearly dropped the phone in surprise. "Uh-oh. Are you sure? Danny doesn't seem the type to plan to kill someone. Who's the victim?"

"His longtime mistress, Sally Keith. Did you know he had someone else?"

I'd gone out with Danny four months ago, right after his divorce was final. To say we didn't hit it off is an understatement. "No, I didn't know he had a girlfriend, but there's no reason he shouldn't have one."

"Well, he won't talk to anyone but you," James said. "We booked him around one a.m., and three hours was as long as I could postpone making this call. I know you need your beauty sleep."

James's smirk appeared in my mind's eye. "I'll be there as soon as I can."

I placed the handset into its cradle and leaned against the wall. This was going to be a difficult case.

Anything involving a political figure had to be handled with kid gloves. Justice was my primary objective, but maintaining the integrity of my office also was important. I wished I could ask Buck for help, but since I'd dated the county administrator, that liaison would probably be uncomfortable. I needed a partner for this, but I had no idea whom I'd select.

Buck's voice greeted me as I walked into the bedroom. "What's up, honey?"

"We have a high-profile guest in the jail this morning. County Administrator Danny Dean has been arrested for murdering his mistress, or I should say his girlfriend, since he's no longer married."

"Sounds like a tough one. I know you dated him for a little while."

"I'd hardly call our outings 'dates.' We attended some civic functions together, but that was about it. We really didn't hit it off. James said Danny won't talk to anyone but me, so I have to go in."

"I see," said Buck quietly.

"Hey, now," I said as I sat on the edge of the bed. "Don't be jealous. He meant nothing to me. You know that."

Buck sat up and kissed me. The warmth of his touch was inviting, but I resisted his efforts to pull me back into the bed.

"I have to go, Buck."

"I know," he said with a note of disappointment.

I showered quickly. When I returned to the bedroom, Buck wasn't in bed. I heard him in the kitchen, and I smelled coffee, so I knew he was making breakfast for me. I slipped on my underclothes and socks then pulled a white cotton blouse from the rack. Although I no longer wore a uniform, I usually wore the same clothing combination each day—white long-sleeved blouse, gray slacks, navy blazer, and black shoes. I fastened the first button of the blouse, but I was unable to fasten the next two. I pulled the garment more tightly across my back and tried again to fasten the buttons, but I couldn't close the opening. I supposed the cleaners had shrunk it. I removed the garment, tossed it to the floor with a whispered curse, and pulled another blouse from the rack, but I couldn't button the placket closed on that one either. I had the same problem with the third blouse. Finally I found a white turtleneck knit top and pulled it over my head, but it was so tight I could hardly move. I added it to the growing pile on the floor.

Next I stepped into a pair of gray slacks. I forced the zipper up and fastened the button with difficulty. As I walked across the closet to find something else I could wear as a blouse, the button popped off, and the zipper inched its way down. I pulled off the slacks in frustration, uttered another curse, and threw them into the "discard" stack. Hot tears trickled down my cheeks as I stood in the closet staring at the long rack of clothing. I simply had nothing to wear. Nothing fit. Sweatpants might fit, but they weren't appropriate for the sheriff to wear to a high-profile interview. I sat down on the closet floor, crossed my arms across my knees, put my head on my arms, and cried.

"What's the matter?" Buck asked from the closet doorway.

"I'm so fat that none of my clothes fit! They fit yesterday, but they don't fit today."

Buck grabbed my hands and lifted me from the floor. Then he walked to his side of the closet and removed a Maas Brothers department store garment bag. "Try these," he said softly.

I unzipped the bag and removed a dozen garments. They were maternity clothes.

"It's time, Bernie. It's time to give in and wear these. I bought white tops and gray slacks. The slacks have been hemmed to the same length as the ones you usually wear. Your navy blazers probably will fit for a while, as long as you don't try to fasten the buttons."

Buck was an angel to put up with me. I stood on my tiptoes, and he bent down so I could kiss his cheek. "Thanks, my love. You always know what to do to make me happy."

I joined him in the kitchen as he finished the breakfast preparations.

"You're so beautiful," he said with a slight catch in his voice.

I couldn't help smiling. I felt much more comfortable in these clothes and could have kicked myself for not accepting this sooner. Dukker, the king of the Gypsies and my childhood friend, had foretold our union and the children it would produce, so I knew this was inevitable. One can't change his or her destiny once the cards have been dealt.

Chapter 3

Tuesday Morning

It was pitch-black dark and raining as I inched the Crown Vic down the long driveway. An hour later I parked in my reserved slot, pulled my raincoat more closely around me, and sprinted in the rain toward the jail. The first-floor office hummed with activity.

"Mornin', Sheriff Davis," the desk sergeant greeted me. He pushed the button to release the electronic security latch on the door so I could enter.

"Mornin', Dooley," I mumbled as I passed through the steel door and into the booking department.

James, who was seated at his desk, rose as I entered his office. I closed the door, hung my dripping raincoat on his coatrack, and turned toward him. He was silent as we faced each other across his desk. His lips had parted to speak words of greeting, but no sound came from his mouth. After a moment of awkward silence, he stepped from behind the desk and wrapped his arms around me.

"Oh, babe," he said softly. "I didn't know."

"Didn't know what?" I asked as a smile crept onto my face.

He released me from his embrace and stepped back, his eyes sparkling with warmth. James had been my supervising sergeant and partner on the night-shift patrol when I'd first joined the department in 1973. He was a tough, opinionated, hardheaded cop and fifteen years my senior. We'd butted heads often, but enduring tough times together had made us inseparable friends. Department regulations prohibited intimate relationships between partners. We had purposely avoided casual sex, knowing it eventually would destroy our friendship, yet we remained as close as two people could be without being lovers. James sat down, leaned back in his seat, put his feet up on the desk, and peered at me over his reading glasses. I sat down in the chair opposite him. I smiled to see James wearing glasses. He needed them at forty, but had finally given up his fight against wearing them when he turned fifty. Age had greyed his curly, brown hair and dulled his eyesight, but he was still as fit and trim as the day I had met him. As a lieutenant he wore a uniform, but his shirts were white instead of the usual light green of the line officers. He always had his county-issue shirts tailored to be more form fitting. Though he tried to pass off the tailoring as an effort to give the perps less cloth to grab in a fight, I knew that he liked his muscles to push the limits of the fabric.

"Love the new wardrobe, Bernie," he said with a laugh. "Congratulations. When are you due?"

"About six months."

He placed his feet back on the floor, sat upright, and raised his eyebrows as he stared at me. "Six months?" he repeated.

A blush rose on my cheeks and spread to the roots of my hair. "Yeah, well, I don't want to pin it down too closely. Buck and I have only been married two months. I'm just hoping no one starts counting days. And before you ask, no, we didn't get married just because I was pregnant. In fact, I didn't even know then."

"You two are a perfect match, Bernie. This is right for you. Your answer to the question I just asked needs to be 'seven months.' Two plus seven is nine, but if the baby arrives a little early, so what?"

"I don't tell lies, James."

"I know that, babe, but your political enemies would love to make a big deal about the state's first female sheriff getting pregnant out of wedlock. The people in this county love you, or they wouldn't have elected you to a second term, but there are power brokers out there who'd love to have someone pliable sitting in your chair. You won't be lying—you're just bad at estimating time. Do it. Trust me."

"OK. I don't want this to turn into something negative."

"Good. The kid'll call me 'Uncle James,' won't he?"

"You bet he will, even if he's a she."

James chuckled then shifted the conversation back to business. "Let me tell you what I know so far about the murder," he began. "A security guard at one of the condo buildings on Siesta Key called us around midnight. He said he heard what he thought was a gunshot at the house next door. There's one single-family residence wedged in among all those high-rise buildings out there. The victim, Sally Keith, lived in that house. The patrol officers found Danny Dean sitting on the stairs leading up to the deck at the residence. He was holding a pistol in his hand. The girl's body was lying across the threshold. There was a single bullet wound in her head. The forensic team is still there, so we don't have any details yet, just the initial report made by the patrol officers. Dean won't say a word. As I mentioned, he said he wouldn't talk to anyone but you, so I made the call."

"Is he in a cell or one of the interrogation rooms?"

"I put him in a cell since I knew I wasn't going to call you right away and it would take you a couple of hours to get here."

"Good thinking. Call up and tell them to put him in room six."

We sat in James's office for a few minutes to give the guards time to move Dean from his cell to the room.

"Don't let that asshole give you any crap."

"James, please don't start. I know how to do this."

"Well, you of all people ought to know what an idiot he is."

"Tell me how you really feel about him."

"Humph," James snorted. "Want me to go with you? I could punch his lights out if he starts in on you."

"Oh, that's just what we need—a police-brutality lawsuit."

"Well, it might be worth it if I could connect this to his smart mouth," James said as he punched his right fist into his left palm.

I heaved a big sigh as I rose to leave. James chuckled, knowing he'd been able to aggravate me. He took pleasure from yanking my chain, and I was equally adept at ignoring him.

I took the elevator to the second floor and walked to interrogation room six. Deputy Higgins, who was stationed at the door, stood at attention as I approached. I acknowledged him, took a deep breath, and opened the door. Room six was just a little less dingy than rooms one through five. The floor was a little cleaner; cigarette burns and graffiti hadn't yet scarred the table; and the chairs weren't bent. Fewer interrogations had been held here, so blood, sweat, and tears hadn't completely worn it out. County Administrator Dean sat at the table with his folded hands resting on top. Danny was the king of polyester fashion. He wore a three-piece, brown, windowpane plaid suit, a creamy yellow shirt, and a coordinating handkerchief. The open jacket and vest revealed over-forty tummy bulge. His sunlamp-tanned face took on a greenish hue in the harsh light of the fluorescent ceiling bulbs. Deep, dark circles lay beneath his watery blue eyes. As I walked closer, I could see tiny beads of perspiration coating his forehead. Bits of grey were visible near his scalp where dye had not fully covered his aging blond hair. He smiled his leering smile when I entered but didn't stand.

"What the hell happened to you?" he said. "You look like shit. No one would know you were only thirty-five years old by looking at you."

"It's great to see you too, Mr. Dean," I responded with a forced smile, resisting the urge to punch him.

"I apologize, Bernie. That wasn't very nice of me."

"Tell me what happened last night, Danny," I said, as I pushed a button on a cassette recorder and sat across from him at the table.

"I swear I didn't kill her. She was dead when I got there."

"Let's start at the beginning of the evening. What did you do last night?"

"I worked late. There was a public hearing at the planning commission meeting. It started at seven. I was there the whole time. You can ask anyone at the meeting. None of us left until after ten." Danny stood up and began to pace back and forth in the small room.

"Sit down, Danny. This interview is being recorded and if you wander too far away the tape recorder won't pick up your voice."

"So what? So what?" he ranted and as he ran his fingers through his thinning hair. "Do you know that your minions took my tie and belt when they booked me? Took all of my cash and wallet and keys too. That cash had better be there when I get out of here, Bernie. Heads will roll if it is a penny short!"

The door opened and Deputy Higgins poked his head inside. "Everything alright in here, ma'am?"

"Yes, Higgins. Everything is fine. I'll call if I need you."

I waited for the deputy to close the door. "Are you finished?" I asked. Danny's melodramatic episode was his typical reaction to a situation he could not control. "Where did you go when you left the meeting?"

"The Tiki Bar." He sat down hard in the chair and slumped against the back.

"Is that the one near the hospital?"

"Yeah, Sally and I went there often. She got off work at eleven."

"Where did she work?"

"She was an ER nurse at the hospital. Worked three to eleven."

"Did she meet you at the Tiki?"

"Yep, she came over right after the shift change."

"How long did you stay there?"

"I left around eleven thirty."

"Did Sally leave at the same time?"

"Yeah. I followed her. I stopped for gas, so I was a few minutes behind her. When I got to her house, she was dead."

"How do you know she was dead?" I asked.

"The house was dark when I arrived, which I remember thinking was odd. Sally was afraid of the dark, so she always turned on all the lights as soon as she got home. The lights on the deck weren't on, but I made out a white object on the ground near the door. As I got closer, I saw it was Sally. Her uniform was white. I knelt beside her and saw that half her head was gone. There was blood everywhere, Bernie!"

Danny began to cry. It started with a few tears and gradually escalated to sobs of grief. "She was so pretty. Why would anyone want to kill her?" he wailed.

"What did you do next?" I asked softly. He wasn't putting on a show for me this time. The man was in obvious distress. I felt a bit sorry for him.

"I saw the gun lying on the deck, and I picked it up."

"Why in the world did you do that?"

"It was my gun."

"How did your gun get there?"

"Like I said, Sally was afraid of the dark, so I gave it to her for protection. She said she heard noises outside all the time. Between the noises and the dark, she was scared."

"I assume she was your girlfriend, since you gave your gun to her?"

"Yeah, I was seeing Sally for a while. I'm not married, you know. Nothing wrong with me seeing someone," he responded defensively and sat up straight in the chair.

"Yes, I know there's nothing wrong with that. Did you see anyone else when you arrived? Did you see other vehicles on the property? Did a car pass you as you approached the house?"

"No. No people. No cars."

"Did you hear anything?"

"The west wind was fierce last night. All I heard was the surf pounding the sand."

"You realize you're the obvious suspect, don't you? Two deputies found you at the scene holding what appears to be the murder weapon."

"I know it looks bad, but I didn't kill her! I need your help, Bernie. No one else will listen to me. Look, I know I can be difficult at times, but there's no law against being an asshole. I shouldn't be convicted of murder just because people don't like me."

Danny reached across the table and attempted to take my hands into his. I averted his action by standing up from the chair.

"I'm going to investigate your case myself, Danny. I don't know what skeletons I might find in your closet during the process, but after everything shakes out, I *will* know the truth."

"Thanks, doll. I knew I could count on you. I know we didn't exactly hit it off when we dated, but I knew you wouldn't hold that against me. Heard you got married a while back. I guess this is your matronly look?"

"I'm pregnant, Danny. These are maternity clothes."

"That's too bad, doll. You used to have such a good body."

I gritted my teeth and bit back the nasty retort that sat on the tip of my tongue. Then I turned and left the room.

Chapter 4

Tuesday Morning

My next stop was the detective division. I strode directly to Captain Jackson Stone's office. Jack was a veteran officer and former Marine. He was tall and thin with deep brown eyes, a swarthy complexion, and cheeks that dimpled when he laughed. Though he did not seem to know it, half the women in the courthouse had crushes on him. He was known for being a stickler for detail and did everything by the book, yet he was tolerant of human error, and as a result had earned the admiration of those who worked for him. He smiled and stood up when he saw me in the doorway. His eyes drifted to my abdomen, but he made no comment.

"Jack, anything in on the Sally Keith murder yet?"

"All we have is the patrol officers' report. The crime scene investigators haven't returned, and neither has the medical examiner. They're all still out there, ma'am. The techs might take a couple of days to process the scene. Considering Dean is a political figure, they'll have to be as prepared as possible when they take the witness stand."

"I just talked to him," I said, leaning against the doorframe. "He swears he didn't kill her. He also won't talk to anyone but me, so I'll oblige him and investigate this case myself. I need a partner, though…" My voice trailed off as a commotion distracted us both.

A large form danced from the elevator into the division office. His hands waved in the air, and he sang in a cadence, "Sheriff girl is prego. Sheriff girl is prego. Sheriff girl is prego."

Ike McDuffie stopped his dance and song when he saw Jack and me staring at him from the doorway. He gave us a sheepish grin and a short salute before sitting down at his desk.

"Looks like I just found my partner for this case," I said with a wry smile.

"Don't do this, ma'am," Jack warned.

"Got to. By the way, there's something else we need to talk about." We moved into Jack's office, I closed the door behind me, and we both took seats. "It'll be seven months before I deliver this child, but we need to plan ahead for the event. Realistically I'll be out for six weeks after the birth, but I may not be able to work every day up until that time. I just don't know. I do know I need someone I can trust to fill in when I'm not here. You are that person, Jack. I'd like to promote you to the position of chief deputy sheriff. You'll be authorized to act in my absence, and of course there's a pay increase too."

Jack was speechless for a few moments, but then he smiled. "I'm flattered, ma'am. I won't let you down...and congratulations.

"I'm counting on that. We'll announce this at the monthly department-head meeting."

I stood up, and Jack opened the door for me to leave. I tossed some words over my shoulder as I crossed the division office. "McDuffie, come on. We have work to do."

Chapter 5

Tuesday Morning

Ike didn't utter a word as he followed me from the detective division to the parking lot. I made my way to the blue four-door assigned to him and climbed into the passenger seat. He started the engine but made no move to leave the lot.

"Head for Siesta Key," I ordered.

We rode in silence for twenty minutes. During that time, I took a long, hard look at him. His sandy blond hair was shaggy and long. The pants and sport jacket he wore were mismatched. His tie had an orange stain on it—probably catsup or barbecue sauce. His shoes hadn't seen polish since they'd come out of the box. His shirt hadn't been ironed. His lips formed a thin, hard line. His brow was knit into a scowl.

I turned to face him, but he didn't acknowledge me at all. "What's wrong, Ike?"

"What do you mean, Sheriff?" he asked sarcastically.

I ignored his disrespectful attitude. "I mean, what happened to you to make you stop caring about everything?"

He was silent.

I waited several minutes before I continued. "I'd like to help if I can, but I can't force you to tell me what's going on. You and I are going to work the Sally Keith murder together. Media coverage will be intense. It's bad enough that I have to show up at the first press conference in maternity clothes. It'll be like chumming the sharks. I need my partner to be well groomed and carrying a determined, professional look on his face. We're going to the crime scene now. We'll look around to get the lay of the land, so to speak. We'll also talk to the crime scene guys and the ME. Perhaps we'll interview some neighbors. Then you'll drop me off at my office. You'll get a haircut. You'll also buy a new sport coat, slacks, shoes, and shirts. Charge them to your clothing allowance. Then meet me back here tomorrow morning at eight a.m. sharp. Am I making myself clear?"

He only said, "Yes, ma'am."

**

Patrol officers guarded the entrance to the Keith driveway to keep members of the media and nosy gawkers from contaminating the crime scene. Press vehicles lined both sides of the road. News reporters surrounded our car, clamoring for tidbits. Ike was only able to drive part of the way down the driveway, as official vehicles already filled most of the narrow lane. I had radioed ahead and asked the crime scene deputies not to move the body until we arrived. I walked up the steps to meet the ME and deputies, while Ike skirted the house and headed toward the water. The Gulf of Mexico appeared grayish green as it reflected the remnants of the stormy sky. Breakers crashed on the soft, white sand. Gulls squawked as they hovered in the stiff thermals and scanned the water for morsels of food. Except for the grisly scene here, the setting was beautiful.

The back deck was crowded with people from various government agencies. My eyes wandered across the group and spotted a head of unruly carrot-orange hair. Dr. Montague "Monty" Merrimac, the medical examiner, was sitting on a bench making notes. He looked up as I approached, and a smile broke his freckled face as he peered at me thorough horn-rimmed glasses. He rose to his feet and extended his hand in greeting but then thought better of it and gave me a quick hug instead.

"Congratulations, Bernie. Give my best wishes to Buck too. This is a wonderful surprise."

"Thanks, Doc. I appreciate that."

"Are you the lead investigator on this one?"

"Yes, Dean will only talk to me, so I'll be the contact on the case. McDuffie is my partner for this one. What do you see?"

The body was covered with a lightweight plastic sheet. Doc gently lifted the plastic as he spoke. "She was killed by a single shot to the head. Died instantly. The angle of entry is downward, so the murderer most likely was taller than her. I found powder burns at the entry point, so she was shot at close range. See, there—the hair is singed at the entry point. I imagine she was coming home from work when she was killed, since she's dressed in a nurse's uniform. As you can see, the body is partially inside the house and yet much remains outside. She was standing at the door when she was killed. Time of death appears to be about midnight. Can't tell you much more until I get her back to the morgue."

I looked down at the deck beneath the girl. Blood was congealing in reddish brown pools around her broken body. Her life force had seeped out onto these weathered boards. Before long, pounding rain and intense sun would remove the last remnants of her existence. "What's wrong with us, Doc?" I whispered.

"What do you mean, Bernie?" he asked. A look of surprise covered his face.

"How can someone do this to another human being? We are supposed to be civilized, yet we take life as if we were barbarians. It tears at my heart."

"I don't know why people do evil things, Bernie," Doc said with sadness in his voice. "All we can do is try to stop them from doing it again."

I turned away from the gruesome sight. I suddenly felt very cold. A shiver ran down my spine. My mother would have said that someone was walking on my grave. I leaned my elbows on the wooden porch rail and looked down at the sandy yard. Doc joined me.

"You can't let it get to you, Bernie. You and I chose our professions hoping we might help stop some of the evil in this world." He gestured toward the corpse of Sally Keith, which was again covered with the plastic sheet. "But, if you let things like this destroy you inside, then evil wins."

"Thanks, Doc. Thanks for understanding." It was several minutes before I spoke again. "I probably don't need to tell you that this is going to be a hot one. I'll check with you later, or give me a call when you finish the autopsy."

"Sure, Bernie," he said as he made his way down the stairs. I watched until his car disappeared from view, then stepped over the body and entered the house.

The crime scene deputies were still gathering evidence and would continue to do so for some time. I wandered from room to room and spoke with each of them briefly, but I knew it was too soon for them to answer specific questions. The home was a typical Florida beach house built in the 1950s. The rooms were small, with the largest being a twelve by fifteen foot living room. The décor was casual and "beachy." Dried starfish and sand dollars were clustered on the whitewashed walls, baskets of seashells adorned the tables; and shelves displayed vases filled with seabird feathers. A large conch shell, probably used as a doorstop, rested against a screen door facing the beach.

I saw for myself that the murderer had made no effort to clean up the crime. Blood spatter marked the walls, door, and floor. The victim's unopened purse lay on the deck next to her body, so robbery wasn't a likely motive. Those were the only details I'd give the press for now. Once the techs had time to analyze the data, something else might come to light. Danny Dean's future rested in our hands at this point.

Where was Ike? I looked around to see whether anyone was available to go down to the beach to find him, but all personnel were busily working. I crossed the deck, retraced my path down the stairs, and walked onto the beach. Ike stood midway between the house and the surf on the north side of the property. I spotted his footprints in the sand. He had first walked to the south then back to his present position. Apparently that was all he had done so far. He was looking up at the condo buildings, but my movement caught his attention, and he retraced his steps toward me.

"See anything?" I asked him.

"Maybe. The view of the gulf from these high-rise condos must be fantastic. I wouldn't know since I've never been in one. Remember when we were kids and that three-story hotel opened on Lido Key? Everybody in town went to the open house to look out over the water. I saw you there. We all thought that was the tallest building we'd ever see on the beach. Boy, were we wrong."

Ike glanced at me expecting a response. When I didn't say anything, he continued with his report.

"The Australian pines block any view from the north," he said as he gestured toward the towering dark green trees, "but the building to the south should offer a pretty good view of this house. Maybe someone up there saw something. Did you notice that my footprints are the only ones in the yard? That storm last night washed or blew everything away. A member of this team probably will make any other marks you'll see. I'm going to go up there." He pointed to the upper floors of the condo complex. "I'll be back in a little while." With that he was off.

I wandered toward the house and sat on a wooden bench near the edge of the yard. It was beginning to warm a little, and people had just started to venture onto the beach. Dogs accompanied several of them. Maybe one of these folks had been walking the beach last night.

I introduced myself to an elderly woman walking a tiny white poodle on a rhinestone-studded leash. "Were you walking your dog last night by any chance?" I asked her.

"Oh, no, dear. Bitsy goes to sleep at nine o'clock. We go out to the grass by the pool at seven for her to do her business before we take our bath and lock up the condo. We never walk on the beach at night."

"Do you know anyone who walks on the beach at night?"

"Oh, yes. Mr. Edwards jogs at night. Mrs. Edwards walks their terrier, Griffin, while he jogs. They aren't in town, though. They're up north visiting family. There's an elderly gentleman on the fifth floor who walks his bulldog at night, but I don't know his name." She stopped for a moment, pulled a plastic bag from her pocket, deftly folded it to form a glove, and scooped up a deposit the tiny dog had made on the sand. "And then there are those young people who come down here to go out on the jetties. I'm not sure what they do, but my friend Mable says they're witches who worship the moon. She lives in a building filled with them."

"Oh, really?"

"Yes," she said, then paused to pull the little dog toward her. "They sneak down the property line right here and go out on the rocks. They can't access the beach through any of the condos because we have fences and security guards. The young nurse who lives in this house doesn't have a fence or a guard or even a dog, so they come through here."

"Very interesting. Thank you. What's your name, ma'am?"

"Rose…Rose Ermine. I live on the third floor, number three-oh-two, right there," she said as she pointed upward.

I walked toward the water and stopped a middle-aged man. He'd been jogging in the hard-packed sand near the water's edge.

"I only jog in the mornings now," he said. "Don't see well enough to run down the beach in the dark anymore."

I thanked him then approached a young female surfer who had just come from the waves. "Were you out surfing last night by any chance?"

"Are you kidding? There are sharks off that sandbar. None of us surf at night. Sure are some good waves this morning after that storm, though."

As I thanked her, I spotted Ike coming from the condo building and made my way to him. "Anything?"

"Not yet. It's possible to see Sally Keith's house from the fifth floor and above, but the fifth floor is probably our best bet. People on the ground are as small as ants when you get too high." Ike turned toward the condo, shielded his blue eyes from the sun, and looked up. "No one on that floor was home. I got names and phone numbers from the manager, so we can call to see when they'll be available for us to interview."

We walked slowly through the sandy yard and down the driveway toward Ike's car.

"Many people walk and jog on the beach," I said. "Some of them come out at night. Might be worth it to come out here after dark. We might find someone who was out here last night. We'll also need to talk to Sally Keith's coworkers, the bartender at the Tiki Bar, and the planning commission members. They may be able to help us piece together Danny Dean and Sally Keith's movements last night."

Ike inhaled and opened his mouth as if to speak, but apparently changed his mind and remained silent, so I continued to outline the tasks we needed to perform.

"I know the patrol officers interviewed the security guard, but we need to talk to him again. Add to the list a man on the fifth floor with a bulldog and a woman named Mable who claims there are witches on the jetties."

A small smile tweaked Ike's lips at my last comment.

"That's about all we can do here for now," I continued. "We just need to prepare a preliminary press release. An overview should be adequate. Without forensic data, we can't provide any details. It would be better to have some evidentiary facts before we go out for interviews."

Ike and I traveled along the two-lane road that ran the length of the island. He was heading for the larger of two bridges that linked Siesta Key to the Sarasota mainland.

As we passed through Siesta Key Village, shopkeepers were beginning to open their doors. Modern times had brought skyscraper condos, four-star restaurants, and trendy bars to the key, but old-timers and locals still traded with the shopkeepers in the village. I wondered whether Sally had frequented any of these establishments. She wasn't an old-timer, but she might have wandered around her neighborhood a bit.

"Wait, Ike. Let's stop and talk to a few of the business owners. They aren't too busy yet and probably will have time to chat. They see things other folks might not notice."

"OK, ma'am," he said as he pulled into a space along the curb.

An elderly gentleman dressed in well-worn shorts, a T-shirt, broad-brimmed fishing cap, and sneakers tended to a deep heavy aluminum pot on a propane cooker outside a fish market. His gnarled hands were dry and calloused. Leathered skin, dark as mahogany, covered spindly legs and strong arms. When we walked up and peeped into the pot, his broad smile revealed false teeth that were too big for his mouth. "Hi, Sheriff Raines. Don't believe I've had the pleasure, young man," he said as he held out his hand to Ike. "You remember me, don't you, ma'am? We met when you came out to interview Bill Needles a few months ago."

"Of course I remember you, Mr. Rotella," I said with a smile as I remembered our encounter. Bill Needles, a retired police officer, known to friends as “Zebco,” had provided valuable insight into a murder investigation. Bill’s collection of fishing buddies had hung on every word we spoke. “I’ve married since I last saw you, so I’m ‘Sheriff Davis’ now.”

“Congratulations!” he said. “Call me ‘Sam.’ Mr. Rotella was my dad. Ha! Come to think of it, seems like I remember hearing something about your getting married. I bet your husband is that big, tall drink of water you brought with you to the cove. You and he looked sort of close.”

I couldn’t help but laugh at Sam’s comments. I had no idea my relationship with Buck had been so obvious to casual observers. “I didn’t know you owned a seafood store, Sam. I thought you were retired.”

“Oh, I don’t own this place,” he said as he glanced over his shoulder at the shop. “Just work here a few hours a day. The boys and me go out fishing as the sun comes up, and I bring whatever I catch here. Old Jumpin’ Jimmy buys my fish and lets me help out in the back. I clean the fish, boil the crabs and shrimp, and keep all the ice fresh. I do simple things for a little spending money between pension payments.”

“What’s in the boiling pot?” Ike asked, as we both looked back into the pot. The gray-colored water was covered with a bubbling layer of scum and didn’t look appetizing.

"I've been gettin' a bunch of these big conchs in my cast net lately. Can't eat the damn things since they're fishy as hell and about as tender as a bunch of rubber bands. So I boil out the animals and sell the shells. The tourists love these big ones," he said as he dipped a large pair of tongs into the pot and pulled out a seashell that measured a foot in length.

A blackish-brown mollusk was hanging from the opening. Indeed, it didn't look like something I'd eat, but the shell was beautiful. Delicate spines, arranged in concentric rows, accented the tip. The opening surrounding the mollusk was bright pearlescent pink. I'd noticed a similar shell propped against the screen door in Sally Keith's living room. "Sam, do you remember selling any shells to a pretty blond woman?"

"You must mean Sally. Sure, she has a couple of these. I gave them to her. She didn't want to take them, but I considered her paying attention to an old fart like me payment enough," Sam said with a sparkle in his eyes. "You never get too old to look, young man," he said when he noticed Ike's smile.

"She's quite a looker, that one," Sam continued. "Poor thing. She's sort of messed up in the head. Reminds me of my granddaughter. My girl got into those drugs, like kids do nowadays, and I'm pretty sure Sally's involved in that too." Sam put down the tongs, turned the valve on the propane tank to stop the flow of the gas, and picked up the tongs again. "She's such a moody girl," he continued.

"One minute she's happy and laughing; the next she's crying. It's a shame to see someone act like that."

"Sam, we have bad news about Sally," I interjected as the old man fished into the pot to pull out another conch shell. "She was murdered last night."

Sam looked up with tears in his eyes. "Such a waste," he said in a quavering voice. "Sometimes I'm glad I'm old and don't have many years left on this earth. It's not a nice place anymore."

"Did Sally say anything about being afraid of anyone? Did she seem frightened or distraught lately?"

"Actually I'd say she was happier the past couple of weeks than she normally was. She had sort of a glow about her. She giggled all the time, and I noticed a spring in her step that hadn't been there before. I was glad to see it."

Ike had wandered toward the front window of the fish shop while Sam and I talked. I could see him out of the corner of my eye, and knew he was listening to Sam's comments. He was purposely trying not to appear interested. Odd behavior for a detective on a murder case, I thought.

"Did she say why she was so happy?" Ike interjected.

"No," said Sam, turning toward Ike. "We usually just chatted about what was in the fish case that day and how to cook it. She was a good cook, but being from the North, she didn't know much about the seafood here. Halibut is a lot different than flounder or snapper. I'd tell her what she could do with the fish or shrimp, and she'd write everything down on little cards she carried with her. She always was cooking dinner for someone or having parties, so she needed lots of new recipes."

"If you think of anything—anything at all—will you call me?" I asked as I handed him a business card. "If I'm not in, ask for Ike or leave a message. We need clues, Sam."

"Sure, sure," he said as we walked away. He was obviously distressed, and I felt bad about bringing sadness into his life.

An ice cream parlor/snack shop stood next to the seafood market. An elderly gentleman was sweeping the walk in front of his shop but stopped as we approached. He was dressed all in white and sported a flat cloth cap atop his grizzled hair. He appeared to be dressed for a game of cricket.

"I say, didn't want to sweep dust over your shoes," he said in a proper British accent. Ike and I introduced ourselves to him and flashed our ID badges. "I'm Kendall Smythe-Furman, proprietor. What brings coppers to the village at this hour? Can't be good news then, can it?"

"Unfortunately, that's correct," I began. "We wanted to know if you were acquainted with a young woman who lived in a little house down the road. Her name was Sally Keith."

"Of course I know Sally. Everyone in Siesta Key Village knows that girl." He propped the broom against the doorframe and motioned for us to come inside. "Would you care for a spot of tea? The kettle's hot." Mr. Smythe-Furman busied himself with the brewing of the tea. He poured hot water into a glazed blue ceramic teapot, swirled it around, and emptied it into the sink. He then measured loose tea leaves from a tin box, popped them into the pot and added more hot water. "She'll be ready in a jiffy!"

"Where were we now? Oh, yes, we were talking about Sally. She doesn't seem to have too many friends out here, so she spends quite a bit of time poking around the shops. She comes in for ice cream a couple times a week—always chocolate. She once said my shop reminded her of one she and her pop used to visit when she was little. She misses her ole dad. Don't know what happened to him, but he isn't around anymore. I noticed you said 'was'—'Her name *was* Sally Keith.' Did something happen to her?"

"Yes. Someone murdered Sally last night," I told him. "Can you think of any reason anyone would do that? Was Sally upset about anything you know of? Was she afraid?"

"Oh, my word. How awful. Who would want to harm that girl? Don't know of a soul who didn't like the poor thing. Most felt sorry for her. She was troubled, that one. But she seemed happy the past few times she came to the shop. Big smile plastered on her face. Bought two scoops of ice cream in a sugar cone. Oh my, to think she's dead. This is simply terrible!"

"If you think of anything, please call us, Mr. Smythe-Furman." After I gave the man a card, Ike and I walked down the sidewalk toward the next shop.

"I'll be back in a minute," Ike said as he retraced his steps into the ice cream parlor. He came out a moment later with two cones and handed one to me. "Butter pecan, your favorite," he said with a grin.

I raised my eyebrows. "How in the world did you know that?"

"Oh, I just remembered that you liked it."

I was still trying to remember how Ike knew my favorite ice cream flavor when we came to a gift shop. A set of wind chimes, placed in line with the doorframe, announced our arrival. A spry, gangly gent dressed in khaki shorts, a thin, yellow nylon shirt, knee socks, and sandals emerged from a back room to greet us. His face was soft and lacked the wrinkles that time should have etched there. He was obviously balding and had made a vain attempt to disguise his lack of hair by combing strands from the side of his head onto the top. A strong wind would surely uproot the entire mass.

"Welcome, welcome, early birds," he chortled. "How can I help you? We have some great bargains today. Do your Christmas shopping a little early and save a bundle."

Shelves of greeting cards lined most of the walls. Sales gondolas near the front windows were piled high with Christmas gift selections, all with nautical or beach themes. Toys, plush animals, and beach equipment were neatly arranged on low shelves so children could reach them. Food items made from citrus fruit were nestled in colorful baskets. Missing from the gift selections were the tacky tourist items made from seashells and coconuts.

"Our visit is strictly business," I said as I offered my identification badge to him. Ike did the same.

The gentleman looked at our faces, glanced at our IDs, and then introduced himself. "Nick Flores at your service, officers. How can I help you?"

"Are you acquainted with a young lady named Sally Keith?" I asked.

"Sure, we know her."

"We?"

"My wife and I. We both know her. Mama, come out here. The police are looking for Sally."

"I knew something would happen to that girl," a voice said from a place behind the wall. Within a few seconds, a short, round lady waddled into the shop. She was dressed in a brightly printed Hawaiian-patterned muumuu and flip-flops. Hair that had probably once been dark brown was dyed a brassy auburn. Black eyebrow pencil defined her brows; peach lipstick covered her ample lips; and bright patches of blush powder accented her pudgy cheeks. "Did she disappear? I wouldn't be surprised. She's one troubled girl."

"Good morning, Mrs. Flores. Why would you think Sally Keith might have disappeared?" I asked her.

"She's so skittish, like a little rabbit, waiting to dart into her den."

"Now, Mama, you yourself said she looked happy the last time she came in here."

"I'll grant you that. She seemed much happier. Don't know how long that'll last," she muttered.

"Sally hasn't disappeared," I said matter-of-factly. "She was murdered last night."

Mr. and Mrs. Flores's faces registered looks of shock then sadness.

"That troubled child. She was always—" Mr. Flores began.

"Who would do such a thing?" his wife interrupted.

"That's what we're trying to find out, ma'am, I said. "Is there anything you can remember about your conversations with Sally that might give us clues as to who would want to kill her?"

"She was receiving a lot more mail than usual," the lady said, almost to herself.

"How would you know that, ma'am?" Ike interjected.

"Vandals have been knocking down Sally's mailbox. Each time it happened, the route man left her mail here for her to pick up until she could fix the box. She also left him a note when she went out of town so he could leave her mail here for her to pick up when she returned. Many of the residents near the village use us for mail delivery. We're an authorized postal service center. You can buy stamps, mail packages, and pick up certified or registered letters here," Mrs. Flores said proudly.

Ike pressed her a little. "Do you happen to remember what type of mail Sally was getting?"

"She had a couple bills from doctor's offices, greeting cards, junk mail, magazines, and a few small packages. Some of the cards and gifts could have been Christmas items," Mrs. Flores commented. She absent-mindedly removed bits of dust from a shelf and then wiped her hand on the muumuu.

"Do you remember any of the return addresses on the cards and packages?" I asked.

"Sure. They were mostly in Minnesota, but a few had local postmarks. If I had to guess, Sally had a sweetheart who liked to send her cards. They were definitely addressed in a man's handwriting."

Sometimes it's a good thing to be nosy, I thought. *Maybe those cards were the reason Sally was so happy.* Ike and I thanked Mr. and Mrs. Flores and asked them to call if they remembered anything else about Sally.

"We'd better head back to the office," I commented as we exited the shop.

We'd spent longer than I'd expected talking to the shopkeepers. I had to do some PR work before the day ended, and there was not much of the day left. Ike and I drove back to the jail building in silence, but his grim attitude had softened somewhat. During the drive to the crime scene, he had clenched his jaw so tightly that I thought he would break a tooth. His knuckles had been white from the strain of gripping the steering wheel. Now, he relaxed back into the seat with his left elbow resting on the window frame. His right hand was on the wheel, but it pounded out a rhythm of some song that must have been going through his head. He dropped me at the door and sped off. I hoped he was heading for a barbershop.

I passed through the jail, picked up my raincoat from James's office, and made my way to my office in the courthouse building. Once there, I unlocked the door, threw my raincoat down, and plopped into my chair. I looked at the second hand on my watch. Eighteen seconds ticked away before Dottie, the office manager, appeared at the door. She was impeccably dressed, as usual. Her white long sleeved blouse was starched so stiffly that it could probably stand by itself. The forest green of the uniform skirt and vest suited her dark coloring. Though well into her fifties, her skin was flawless and her hazel eyes were dazzling. A bit of lipstick accented her full mouth, which, at this moment, was smiling. Office staff members were issued smaller versions of the sheriff's star. She was proud of the badge and wore it pinned to her vest with honor.

"It seems congratulations are in order, Sheriff," she said.

"Thanks, Dottie," I said with a smile.

This woman definitely would be classified as a busybody, but she ran a tight ship. She kept my entire business office running smoothly. All deadlines were met. The finances were balanced to the penny every day. She intervened in office squabbles like a pro. And most important, no one was better at massaging the multitude of egos that existed in the criminal justice system. Every office needs a Dottie.

"Can I get you anything? Have you eaten lunch? Are you feeling OK? You look very tired."

"I'm fine, Dottie," I said but couldn't stifle a yawn.

"Go home, Sheriff. You need rest. You need to take care of yourself now," she said in a motherly way.

"I'll go home after I prepare a press statement and contact the media."

"Oh, by the way, you have a thick stack of pink message slips," she said as she handed me the squares of paper. "They all called."

After Dottie went back to her desk, I quickly wrote a press statement, handed it to a typist to prepare the document, and began to return the calls. I advised each media contact that the printed statements could be picked up in my office or in the public relations office and that I'd provide more information after the forensics team had analyzed the data. They all knew we had to wait for that, but each one wanted to scoop the others for the hottest story.

I sat back, pulled out the bottom desk drawer to use as a footstool, rested my head against the high back of my chair, and closed my eyes. Every muscle and bone in my body ached from exhaustion.

"Sheriff," Dottie said from the doorway, "are you OK?"

"I'm fine. Why do you keep asking me that? I'm just resting for a few minutes. I've been up since four."

She entered my office and sat down. I opened my eyes to find her brow wrinkled with concern.

"I'll go home in a little while, Dottie," I told her before she could ask again.

"Is Mr. Dean going to bond out?"

"I imagine he will. There won't be a bond hearing until the arraignment tomorrow. I don't believe he's much of a flight risk, so the judge probably will set bond. It'll be high, but I think he'll do it. I'm working this case myself. Dean won't talk to anyone but me, and we'll need to handle this one very carefully. Ike McDuffie's my partner." Interested in seeing Dottie's reaction, I dropped the last sentence like a bomb. She pursed her lips and scowled but didn't comment.

"Ike can do this," I continued. I didn't need to justify my actions to her, but I valued her insight and needed her support. "All he needs is a good kick in the ass and a push forward. He'll be fine." I didn't know whether I was trying to convince Dottie or myself. "OK, Dottie, that's all for me today," I said as the typist poked his head in and handed me copies of the press release he'd just prepared. "I'm going to take a few copies to Tom, and then I'm heading home."

I put on my raincoat, grabbed a few copies of the press release, and made my way down to the PR office. Sergeant Tom Jensen, my liaison officer to the media, the county commission, and civic organizations, was handsome, likable, literate, and smart enough not to be conned. His tall, powerful frame was a sharp contrast to a personality that was as gentle as a kitten. Tom's thick blond hair had grown longer than was typical for a law enforcement officer. His uniquely colored azure blue eyes drew the attention of everyone he met. School children called him "Officer Friendly" but his fellow officers on the SWAT team rarely teased him about it. He seemed surprised to see me and rose from his chair even though he was on the phone.

"I gotta go," he said into the handset then hung up.

"Here are some press releases on the Dean/Keith case, Tom. No other info goes out except this for now." I pushed the door shut and sat across from him. "We'll schedule a press conference for sometime tomorrow, after McDuffie and I have had time to review the evidence gathered at the scene."

"You're working this with McDuffie?" he asked with surprise in his voice. I could sense that he had more to say. Tom's fair complexion colored when he realized that he had spoken out of turn, but he took a deep breath and voiced his thoughts. "Is that wise, ma'am? You know this case will require finesse and diligence."

"Ike can do it," I broke in before he said something he might regret later. "He's not as stupid as he acts. There's more you need to know." I stood and opened my raincoat so Tom could see my new attire. "They'll make more of an issue about this than they will about the murder case. I wanted you to know so you wouldn't be blindsided tomorrow."

"Whew. Thanks for telling me, Sheriff. Tomorrow should be interesting. By the way, congrats!" He extended his beefy hand toward me and I shook it warmly.

Chapter 6

Tuesday Afternoon

My eyelids felt so heavy that I barely could keep my eyes open on the hour-long drive home. While our ranch encompassed thousands of acres in three adjoining counties—Sarasota, DeSoto, and Manatee—the house itself sat on land in DeSoto County. Buck's wedding gift to me had been an official opinion from the attorney general of the State of Florida, who opined that I could remain the elected sheriff of Sarasota County yet live with Buck on his ranch property since so much of the property was located in my county. My office was an hour's drive from the house, but I happily drove that distance twice a day.

It would be some time until Buck returned home from work, so I decided to take a nap. No sooner had I climbed up on the bed than the doorbell rang.

"Madame Bernie, you're home early," said the wiry little Cajun who was the ranch foreman. Maurice Devereaux wore his usual jeans and white T-shirt along with a saucy bandana around his neck. His speech was heavily accented in Cajun French, remnants of his roots in Thibodaux, Louisiana.

"Yes, Devereaux. Come in," I said as I opened the door.

"Madame, what is this?" he whispered as his gaze rested on my abdomen.

"Buck and I wanted to tell you together. We were going to drop by the bunkhouse tonight."

"This is a joyous moment for old Devereaux," he said with tears in his eyes. "I remember the day Monsieur Buck was born. He was named after his papa, you know. Madame Josephine swapped the words and named him 'Charles Bennett.' His papa was Bennett Charles. It was such a wonderful day on the ranch." He was silent for a moment, and from the look on his face, I could tell he was revisiting that happy time again. "Madame, is there anything you require of old Devereaux?"

"No. I'm going to take a nap until Buck gets home. I'm really tired."

"Is Madame well?"

"I'm fine. Just tired."

"Drink some orange juice. It is full of vitamins. It will give you energy."

"You sound like an advertisement for the Florida Growers Association," I said with a laugh. In addition to raising cattle on the ranch, we had hundreds of acres of citrus trees. Devereaux was right to promote the benefits of orange juice.

"*Oui*, Madame," he said. His black eyes sparkled with warmth as he bowed and kissed my hand.

**

I was still sleeping when Buck arrived, but I woke up when he sat next to me on the bed.

"Is anything wrong, Bernie?" I heard a note of concern in his voice.

"No. I'm fine. Everyone keeps asking if I'm OK. I only meant to rest a little, but I really zonked out."

"I brought home Chinese food for dinner. I even got dumplings."

"That's great! I love those things. It's been ages since we've eaten Chinese carryout."

While we ate I filled Buck in on the progress of the case. I also told him how I'd come to select Ike as a partner.

"Sounds like trouble to me," he said. "Hope he won't be detrimental."

"He'll be OK once we get more involved in the case. By the way, Ike and I may have to work a couple of nights. The vic worked three to eleven in the ER, and we need to talk to her coworkers. Danny met her at a bar shortly after eleven, so we'll talk to the bartender. I might need to see who visits the beach at night too."

"Take care of yourself, Bernie," Buck urged. "You know I won't interfere with your decisions, but you shouldn't work all day and all night anymore."

"I'll be fine. Please don't worry."

"I know you, my love. I know how stubborn you are." Buck said firmly. He paused for a moment, smiled his "little boy smile," and continued with a note of humor in his voice, "I also know how aggravated you are going to be the next time I remind you to take it easy. Are we clear?" he said with a wink.

"Yes, sir," I said with a mock salute.

Chapter 7

Wednesday Morning

I arrived at my office early. The rain had stopped; the front had passed; and a high-pressure area brought air that was crisp, cool, and dry. The change in the weather and a long night of sleep had invigorated me, and I was champing at the bit to get started. Ike arrived fifteen minutes after I did, which was probably the earliest he'd ever entered the building. The man who came through my office door was different than the one I'd seen the day before. The flattop crew cut he'd worn in junior high had returned. He wore a navy blazer, a crisp light-blue shirt, khaki slacks with a starched knife-blade crease down the front of each leg, and spit-shined shoes. I smiled my approval.

"Today's going to be a busy one, Detective. Let's get to it."

We left my office in the courthouse building and made our way to the crime scene lab in the jail building. The lead analyst, Joe Cameron, greeted us. Joe had worked for the sheriff's office since he was sixteen years old. He was a quiet man with a quick mind filled with knowledge gleaned from many years of experience. In the early years, he was the only analyst in what we now called the crime lab, and he remembered more about investigative technique than most people ever hoped to learn. Joe was tall, as were most of the deputies. His shoulders were stooped from many years of working hunched over a lab table. His dark hair was straight, as were the fine hairs of his little mustache. I noticed a dark grey stain on his hands as he handed us a stack of papers. It was probably the result of a mishap in the dark room. We sat at his desk to review the files.

"Tell me what you know, Joe," I said.

"First, someone surprised Ms. Keith at the door as she was entering. The door was open; her keys were still in the lock; and she was shot at close range in the back of the head. The murderer probably had been waiting in the shadows on the deck. We found scuffmarks on the boards in the corner, most likely made by black soles. Second," Joe continued as he ticked off the item on his fingers, "the weapon was a Smith & Wesson Classic forty-five Long Colt, registered to Danny Dean. The only prints on it were his. We swabbed his hands for gunpowder residue and sent the samples to the Florida Department of Law Enforcement. It'll take a while for FDLE to process those. Third, there were lots of prints in the house. We can match the ones from Ms. Keith and Mr. Dean, but we found many others, including a number of prints from someone with large hands. Here, look at these," Joe said as he placed cards on the desk in front of us. "See how big the surfaces of these prints are? We're working on all of them, but it'll take time to make positive identifications. Fourth," he continued, "Ms. Keith had at least two regular male visitors. We found men's clothing in the closet and dresser as well as men's toiletries in the bathroom. Sizes and styles of the clothing indicate two people. We also found two brands of condoms in the medicine cabinet, so she was probably sleeping with both men."

Ike and I reviewed the crime scene photos while Joe spoke. The living room had a lived-in look but wasn't messy. The kitchen and bathroom were spotless. The bedroom was in good order, with no clothing scattered on the floor.

"Did you open the drawer on the nightstand?" I asked.

"We opened everything, ma'am," Joe said. "Why do you ask?"

"See this drawer? I want to know if *you* opened it."

Joe walked around the desk and looked over my shoulder at the picture in my hand. "The photos you're viewing were taken first, before anyone else went in, so that drawer was open when we got there," he said. "After we shot the first group of photos, we examined everything more closely."

"Everything else looks so neat in this house. I find it odd that one drawer was open," I commented. "What did you find in the drawer?"

"Let me check my notes." Joe flipped open a spiral notepad and thumbed the pages. "Let's see…a phone book, address book, memo pad, pens, pencils, cassette player and earphones, and a box of forty-five caliber shells."

"Was there room for a handgun in there?"

"Yes."

"Do you have any close-up shots of the clothing in the closets as well as the toiletries?"

"Those are in the second set of photos." Joe sorted the stack and handed me two pictures. "From the lengths of the sleeves on the shirts and jackets, it looks like one really big guy and one normal-size guy."

I picked up a magnifying glass from Joe's desk to examine the items on the medicine-cabinet shelves. "Looks like Old Spice aftershave and Aramis cologne," I said. "Danny Dean uses Old Spice." *I wish I didn't know that*, I thought. I saw Ike and Joe make eye contact after my comment, but I continued as if nothing had happened. "There are probably twenty thousand men in town who buy Aramis. Our big guy probably uses that."

"We lifted prints from both bottles and both boxes of condoms, but we haven't had enough time to compare everything. All of that's here in evidence bags," Joe said as he gestured toward a stack of cartons in the corner of the room.

"Did you bag the clothing?" I asked him.

"We took one of each of the jackets but left the rest in the closet. The shirts and slacks were freshly laundered, so there's little chance of finding hair or skin particles on them. The jackets had been worn and are more likely to contain forensic evidence. Do you think we need all the items in the closet?"

"Probably not. I was just asking." We had finished reviewing the photos, so I gathered them into a neat stack and pushed them across the desk.

"Did you see any footprints around the house?" Ike asked. "There was nothing on the beach when we got there."

Joe sat down at his desk again. "Near the house we saw nothing. The rain and the wind had leveled the surface of the sand. Closer to the street, we found lots of indentations in the sand. Those were probably footprints at one time, but nothing was distinct. Too much rain." Joe stifled a yawn with his hand. "Sorry," he apologized. "Long hours, you know."

"Any sign of forced entry?" I asked, while resisting the urge to yawn back at Joe.

"No. All the doors and windows were secured and locked from the inside."

"Any way up through the floor from underneath? That house is up on pilings."

"We checked every inch of floor, inside the house and underneath. Nothing. Sheriff, Ms. Keith was killed outside, and we believe the killer was waiting for her. Why are you interested in how someone might gain access to the house?" Joe asked as he leaned back in this chair and crossed his arms.

"Danny Dean said he gave the pistol to Sally Keith for protection. I don't think she'd take it to the hospital with her, so she probably kept it in the house. I think it was in the drawer by the bedside. How do you think the pistol got outside?"

"Maybe Mr. Dean got there before her, grabbed the pistol, and waited outside for her. He may have had a key to the house."

"If he had a key to the house," I said, "why wouldn't he just kill her inside?"

"You've got a point," Joe admitted. His brow creased in thought, but he made no further comment.

I scratched my head. "I can't figure out how the murder weapon got outside. If it was indeed stored in the nightstand, someone had to get it and bring it out to the porch. But how did they get into the house? Why kill her on the porch where there was more exposure?"

"I don't know either," Ike piped in. "Anything of interest in her purse?" he asked Joe.

Joe stood up and walked to the stack of evidence cartons. He retrieved a plastic bag and placed it on the desk. “Typical stuff: wallet, makeup, hairbrush, notepad, pen, tissues. There also was a letter from somewhere in Minnesota. No return address, just a postmark. It was signed ‘Mother.’ We dusted these and photographed them, but I don’t want to take them out of this bag quite yet.”

“Any photos in her wallet?” Ike asked, as he picked up the bag.

“Not a one. Odd, isn’t it?” said Joe. “All women carry photos. Well, all women but Ms. Keith, that is.” He snickered at his own generalization.

“We’ll need to find the mother,” I said. “Is she listed in Sally Keith’s address book?”

“Not that I could see, but most people know their parents’ address by heart. There are several persons listed with Minnesota addresses in there. One of them probably knows the mother.”

“I’d like to look through the address book later,” I said. “Anything in her car?”

Joe retrieved another bag from the carton. It contained a set of keys and items that were found in the car. “Nothing out of the ordinary in the glove box or trunk. There were lots of short reddish-colored hairs. I suspect they belong to a cat or a dog. Humans don’t drop that much hair all at once. We'll analyze them. Didn't see any sign of pets at the victim's home."

"I know it's still early in the case, but is there anything else you can tell us?"

"We still have a lot of work to do, Sheriff. I don't have anything else right now, but I'll keep you posted of course."

Chapter 8

Wednesday Morning

Ike and I headed east on Ringling Boulevard toward the health department. Doc's secretary had advised us that he was in the morgue, so we rode the elevator to the bottom floor. A foul wave of vapor assaulted us as the elevator doors opened. It smelled like a mix of formaldehyde, bleach, and ammonia. I gagged at the stench.

"You OK, ma'am?" Ike asked with concern in his voice.

"Whew, it's that smell. I don't know if I can do this without vomiting, Ike. I'll try, but I may have to leave."

"I can do this alone, you know."

"I'd like to be there," I said.

Doc glanced up from his worktable as we entered. "Bernie, you look green. And you don't look so good yourself, Ike."

Ike's face had blanched at the sight of Sally Keith's body on the table.

"Looks like you have a couple of wimps on your hands today, Doc," I said with a weak smile.

"It's never easy, Bernie. Let's do this quickly. You know she was killed with a close-range shot to the head. Bullet was a forty-five caliber. There were no indications of a struggle or any defensive wounds on her arms. The bullet entered the back of the head and exited through the jaw. She was probably a gorgeous girl. Her body is in great shape. She was healthy and well nourished. In my day people would call her a 'real looker.' This may be important to you as a possible motive—she was pregnant. I estimate she was three months along."

My eyebrows shot up. "I wonder if the father is Danny Dean. Anything in her stomach?"

"Orange juice and pretzels."

"That's all? No alcohol?"

"None. Why?"

"She may have gone to a bar after work that night," I explained. "I expected to find alcohol in her system."

"Her clothing smelled slightly of smoke, so I figured she was a smoker, but her lungs showed no evidence of that. I guess the smell came from the bar. She probably consumed the orange juice and pretzels there too. The stomach contents had hardly begun to digest."

"That's odd," I commented. "I'm hungry all the time. You'd find a lot more in my stomach any time of the day or night." I fought the urge to vomit as another whiff of the vile chemical odor reached my nostrils.

"C'mon, Bernie," said Doc as he tore off his gloves and coveralls. "You need to get out of here. Inhaling too much bleach isn't good for you or the baby."

Doc led us into a file room. He guided me into a chair, disappeared down the hall, and returned a moment later with a paper cup filled with cold water.

"Drink this," he urged. "Then we'll go upstairs." He bustled around the room gathering bags of evidence and stacks of photos, which he deposited into a carton. After he handed the carton to Ike and helped me to my feet, we all escaped to the elevator.

"Sorry to be such a pain, Doc," I said when we were all seated at his conference room table.

"I have five kids, Bernie," he said, to explain his understanding of my misery.

I removed the evidence bags from the carton. The white nurse's uniform was a sharp contrast to the red and rust colors of the blood, but besides that, we saw nothing significant on it or her shoes. We scanned the autopsy photos one by one but found nothing of any more interest than we had when we'd viewed the body.

By the time we reached Doc's office, the color had returned to Ike's face, but he paled again while we reviewed the close-ups of the girl's head and torso. I made no mention of it there, but as we returned to the car, I asked, "You OK, Ike?"

"Yup."

"You seemed a little shook up in there."

"She was so beautiful," he whispered, almost to himself.

I didn't see how he could tell that from the photos or the corpse, since a good part of her face had been blown away, but maybe he saw more than I did.

Chapter 9

Wednesday Afternoon

Ike parked in the jail parking lot. We agreed to meet again at 3:00 p.m. in the meeting room, as he had other cases he was working, and I had some administrative duties that required attention. I also needed to prepare for the press conference. I called Tom in the PR office to fill him in on the little bit of data obtained from the ME and the crime scene crew. His job was to call the members of the press to advise them of the time for the conference. I spotted Dottie hovering near my office door, so I called her as soon as I finished talking to Tom.

"Sheriff, Mr. Dean bonded out this morning," she said.

"What was the amount?"

"Two hundred fifty thousand. Two of the county commissioners posted cash."

"You're kidding!"

"No, ma'am. Mr. Torrino and Mr. Ruskin each posted one hundred twenty-five thousand each."

"Wonder what he has on them," I muttered.

"Sorry, ma'am. I didn't catch that."

"Nothin', Dottie. Will you call Tom and tell him?"

"Already did, ma'am."

"Thanks."

I waded through the stacks of reports on my desk. After thirty minutes, a knock at my door interrupted me.

"Hey, babe, it's lunchtime. My nephew needs food," James said with a chuckle.

I smiled at his nickname for me. He had called me "babe" the first night we'd met, and it had stuck. He was the only person who could call the elected sheriff by a name like that and get away with it. "I *am* starving," I said. "OK, let's go, but it has to be quick."

We walked a half block to Geschepe's Sandwich Shoppe. A tinkling bell attached to the door announced our arrival. I paused for a moment to breathe in the delicious smell of garlic, salami, olive oil, peppers and tomatoes. The tiny lunch counter was filled to capacity and most of the tables were occupied, but we were able to find a booth in the back of the dining room. All tables were covered with red and white checkered cloths. Cruets of olive oil and red wine vinegar, as well as empty bottles of Chianti topped with candles, added to the Italian atmosphere. Mama bustled out of the kitchen, drying her hands on her apron. She was clothed in a printed cotton dress, support stockings, and sturdy laced pumps. Her grey hair was drawn back into a neat bun. Brown eyes were flecked with bits of gold that sparkled in the dim light of the room. An ornate cross set with precious stones, hung from a chain around her neck and rested on her plump bosom. I wondered if she ever took it off.

"Oh, Bernie, Bernie, Bernie," she cooed as she deposited kisses on my cheeks. "Welcome, bambino," she said as she bent over to direct her words to my midsection. Her round, angelic face smiled as she set the table. Without a word she disappeared into the kitchen and returned with a huge glass of milk and her husband. Mr. Geschepe, known to everyone as Papa, was as wide as he was tall. A distinctly Roman nose dominated his face. Deep black eyes peered from beneath a wiry tangle of salt and pepper brows. Crooked lips and missing teeth were souvenirs from a past life of street fighting. Mama plunked the glass onto the table as Papa kissed me.

"You tell that big husband of yours that Papa sends his congratulations," he said, tears filling his eyes.

"I will, Papa. Thanks."

Mama hadn't asked us what we wanted to eat. She appeared a few moments later with a huge Italian sandwich for James and a salad, baked chicken, and Italian green beans for me. She patted my cheek. "You must eat healthy lunches now. For the bambino, si?" she said in explanation, then left us to enjoy the meal.

James took a big bite of the sandwich. I looked longingly at the crusty bread filled with salami, ham, pepperoni, cheese, tomatoes, onions and olive relish. James opened the sandwich and added more oil and vinegar from the cruets on the table. "Mmm, this is great. Too bad you can't have one of these," he said with a twinkle in his eyes. "It was clear that Mama wasn't going to serve you one."

"Yeah, too bad. I love those things, but I'd probably have heartburn for a week. I guess the chicken is better for me."

"And don't forget your milk," he said with glee. He knew how much I hated the stuff.

"Humph," I responded as I took a big swig of the nasty white liquid.

We ate in silence for a while.

"Something wrong, babe?"

James's brown eyes weren't smiling now. His brow wrinkled with concern and he pressed his lips into a thin line. He was my best friend, and I was used to sharing my feelings with him. But things were different since I'd married Buck. I shared my thoughts and dreams with my husband now. What I was feeling would be better shared with another woman, but I didn't have a female confidante.

"I'm scared, James," I began in a quiet voice.

"Is something wrong between you and Buck?"

"Oh, no. Things couldn't be better."

"Is McDuffie bothering you?"

"No. I can handle Ike."

"Did that jerk Danny Dean do something?"

"No."

"Well, what is it?"

"If you give me a chance to talk, I'll tell you!" I snapped. "Let me finish before you butt in, OK?"

James performed a pantomime of zipping his lips shut, leaned his elbows on the table, crossed his arms, and looked at me.

"I've always been one of the guys," I started. "You know that. I'm good at arm wrestling, target shooting, football playing, beer drinking, and even cursing. I don't know anything about girl things like having babies and raising kids. I've never been around a bunch of women while they were talking about such things. My mom is dead. Buck's mom is dead. My godmother is dead. I don't have anyone I can ask. I'm out of my element and don't know what to do."

He laughed. "Is that all?"

"Damn it, James. I'm being serious, and you're making fun of me!"

"Simmer down, babe," he said as he reached across the table and took my hands in his. "You can find out most of what you need to know from the nurses in your doctor's office or maybe from the doctor himself."

"They act like I should already know this stuff—like I was born with the knowledge or something."

"You're a warm, caring person. As long as you love that baby, you can't go wrong," James reassured me. Then his eyes wandered from my face to my ample chest. A twinkle of mischief flashed in his eyes. "The kid'll never be hungry," he said with a chuckle.

"You're a huge help. C'mon. Let's go. Your turn to buy."

**

Back at the office, I plowed back into the stack of paperwork on my desk, but my mind kept wandering, so I picked up the phone and dialed Buck's private number.

When I got no answer, I tried the switchboard and spoke to his secretary. She informed me that he was in a captains' meeting, so I left a message that I was just checking in and all was well. I couldn't tell her I just wanted to hear his voice.

After finishing the paperwork, I walked to the conference room at 2:45 p.m. The television news reporters were still setting up their cameras and microphones. Ike and Tom stood in the corner conversing, but they stopped talking and approached me as I entered the room. Most of the press corps already had gathered. I smiled and nodded greetings to everyone and noticed several looks of surprise on the faces in the crowd.

At 3:00 p.m. sharp, I stood at the podium with Ike at my side. I introduced Ike, outlined the facts we could release about the Dean case, and asked for questions.

"I bet you're the first pregnant sheriff in the state, Bernie. When are you due?" asked a female radio news reporter.

"Since I'm the first female sheriff in the state, I imagine you're right, Bonnie. Delivery time is about seven months from now."

"You said Danny Dean posted bail. Did he use his own money?" asked a beat reporter from the newspaper.

"Commissioners Ruskin and Torrino posted the money."

"They paid cash?"

"Yes."

One of the TV anchors stood and I acknowledged him. "I heard Danny Dean would only talk to you, Sheriff."

"That's correct, Melvin."

"Why?"

"He said he trusts me."

"Is that because you and he were…How should I put it? An 'item' a while back?" asked a sleazy reporter from a small weekly paper. He had not bothered to stand up to ask his question, but slouched in his chair while resting his feet on a chair in front of him.

I knew it was better to get this issue over with today. "County Administrator Dean and I have never been an 'item,' Casey. He simply wants to speak to me because he trusts me."

"Was Sally Keith his girlfriend?", he continued.

"Yes, he said she was."

"Why did he kill her?"

"Mr. Dean said he did *not* kill her."

“Was the gun his?” Casey asked.

“It was.”

“And wasn’t he holding it when your deputies arrived?” he asked while stifling a yawn.

“Yes.”

“Looks like that pretty much puts the murder in his hands, doesn’t it, Sheriff?”

“That’ll be for a jury to decide, won’t it? That’s all for today, ladies and gentlemen. Thank you for attending.”

I exited the room, and Ike followed. We left Tom to hand out printed statements. Then we made our way to the detective division office and sat at Ike’s desk.

“I’d like to talk to the condo security guard tonight,” I told him. “Were you able to contact any of the residents by phone?”

“I reached two of them, but they both said they didn’t see anything.”

“We’ll knock on some doors tonight then. If we have time, we might also see who walks the beach at night. Someone had to have seen or heard something. I need to use your phone.” I picked up the handset and dialed Buck’s private number again.

He answered on the second ring. “Sheriff Buck Davis.”

“Hi, this is Sheriff Bernie Davis,” I said with a smile in my voice.

“Hi, honey. I’m glad you called.”

“I’ve got to work on this case tonight, Buck. I may not be home until the wee hours. If it’s really late, I may get a hotel room in town and come home in the morning.”

Buck was silent for a few seconds. “OK, honey. Call me during the evening so I can hear your voice.” I heard his disappointment. We both knew sometimes we’d be apart at night. Our jobs weren’t exactly nine-to-fives, so it was bound to happen. Slowly I put the handset into the phone cradle then heaved a deep sigh.

“You hungry yet, McDuffie? C’mon. I’ll buy you dinner.”

Chapter 10

Wednesday Evening

Ike and I feasted on buckets of steamed shrimp at the Phillippi Creek Oyster Bar on the South Trail. The place was packed with people eating the early-bird special, so we didn't leave until after 6:00 p.m.

Mark Ritter, a tall Arian blond with an angular face, was on duty at the Phoenix Sun Condominiums when we arrived. He was dressed in black slacks; a crisp white shirt with a patch above the pocket that read, SECURITY; and polished black shoes. He had stepped out of the guard shack to check the IDs of a group of people in a car with Canadian plates. Then he opened the gate to allow them to enter the condo complex before he greeted us.

Ike and I introduced ourselves and showed him our badges.

"Well, this is indeed an honor, Sheriff Davis," he said with a singsong accent that identified him as a likely transplant from Minnesota.

"My detective and I have a few questions for you, Mr. Ritter."

"Sure thing, Sheriff," he said. Though his lips smiled, he looked at me with cold, hard blue eyes.

"Did you know the deceased, Sally Keith?" I asked him.

"I'd seen her many times, but I didn't know her." Though attempting to keep his manner calm and cool, Ritter's neck twitched at the mention of Sally Keith's name.

"What made you go over to her house Monday night?"

"I didn't *go* over there," he said. "I heard a noise like a shot come from that direction and called nine-one-one."

"Wasn't it storming that night?" Ike asked.

"Yeah. It rained a lot."

"I'll bet the wind out here was something fierce," Ike continued.

"Yeah, you betcha. It was almost enough to knock you over," Ritter said with a little snort.

"Must have been a mighty loud shot for you to hear it over the sound of the wind and surf," Ike said.

"The wind probably helped carry the sound up here," he replied with a scowl. His neck twitched again and he crossed his arms across his chest.

I kept my gaze fixed on his. "You aren't a local, Mr. Ritter. Where did you live before you moved here?"

"I'm from Upstate New York. Born and bred in the hills near Binghamton," he said, although his accent belied that.

"What did you do up there?" I asked him. I walked a few paces down the drive and then back. Ritter stopped talking when I moved. "Go ahead. Don't stop. I'm still listening."

"Security at the Ansco manufacturing plant. I've worked security most of my life." Ritter made an effort to relax by resting his hands on his hips.

"Did you know the man who was arrested for Sally Keith's murder?"

"Naw," Ritter said with another neck twitch. "I've seen him plenty of times, though. He's on the news occasionally He spent a lot of time at that beach house."

"How do you know how much time he spent there?" I asked.

"He had to pass by here to get to the house and again to get back to town. Like I said, he was a regular over there. One of my hobbies is keeping logs of things." He pulled out a well-worn composition notebook. "I keep track of cars that pass by. See? I write down the date, time, make of car, tag number, and direction traveled, either north or south."

"Can we borrow your book, Mr. Ritter? We'll return it when the case is over." I held out my hand to emphasize my demand for the book. He clearly had little choice but to give it to me.

"I guess it would be OK. I have a new one I can use. Don't want to miss any, you know." His neck twitched and he lifted and lowered his shoulders before passing the notebook to me.

"What hours do you work?" I probed.

"On at six and off at two."

"Does someone else come on at two?"

Ritter shook his head. "Nope. The day guy works ten a.m. to six p.m. No one here from two a.m. to ten a.m. We can't afford a third shift. Not much happens out here in the middle of the night. Checkout for rental condos is at noon, and check-in is at four p.m., so our busiest times are then. I give lots of directions for dinner and let everyone in and out of the complex for that. The full-time residents come and go with pass cards. The temporary residents can use the keypad, but most of them just let me open the gate for them."

"I noticed you wear a weapon. Not many guards at the condos around here are armed," I commented.

Ritter smiled proudly and stood more erect. "Most of the guards are old farts who don't want to go to the trouble to get a permit. I like being armed."

"Did you see the defendant pass by here on the night of the murder?"

"Yeah, you betcha."

"Did you see Ms. Keith pass by?"

"No," he said. "I'd stepped away for a moment to use the facilities."

"When did you hear the shot?" I asked him.

"A few minutes after Dean passed by."

"And when did you call nine-one-one?"

"Right away. The deputies arrived within five minutes."

"Anything else you saw or did?"

"Naw," he said. "That's it."

"Thanks for your time."

"Yeah, you betcha."

Ike and I walked through the lobby and took the elevator to the fifth floor.

"There's something not quite right about that guy," I remarked. "We'll need to check the exact time of the nine-one-one call. We'll also need to time how long it takes to drive from the Tiki Bar to Keith's house. Something isn't ringing true."

"I presume you noticed his accent," said Ike.

"Yeah, you betcha. He'd be an obvious outsider in Upstate New York. Wonder why he lied? Better do a background check on him. See if the condo keeps any personnel records too. Maybe he listed some previous employers."

The condo opposite the elevator was unit 511. There was no doorbell, so I knocked on the door. After several minutes I knocked again.

"Looks like no one's home," Ike said as we headed for the next door in the hall.

"Hello," a voice sounded from the door of unit 511.

A tiny crack had appeared. "Hello," I echoed.

"What?" A raspy female voice with a strong Brooklyn accent threw the word at us.

A pair of dark-brown eyes peered out from the tiny slit in the door. I moved closer to the slit and put my eyes in line with the woman's. "I'm Sheriff Bernie Davis, ma'am. We'd like to ask you some questions if you don't mind. May we come in?"

"Show some ID," she barked.

I removed the photo ID from my lapel and placed it near the slit. Her eyes scanned the card. "Just a minute."

Ike and I heard the sound of a deadbolt turning. A second bolt turned, a chain rattled, and the knob turned slowly. The door opened to reveal the bent form of an elderly woman. Her hair was dyed a flat black, and cherry-red lipstick outlined a set of thin lips. Electric-blue eye shadow accentuated her deep-brown eyes. Osteoporosis had affected her neck and spine to the point that she walked almost bent in half. A walker supported her frame as she slowly backed away from the door to allow us to enter.

"What do you want?" she asked bluntly.

"There was a murder in the house next door. Did you know that?" I asked.

"There was a murder every night when I lived in Brooklyn," she croaked. "Who got it?"

"The woman who lived in the house to the north of this building was the victim."

"Oh, the bimbo. I'm not surprised."

I raised an eyebrow. "Did you know Sally Keith?"

"You've got to be kidding me! I don't associate with her kind."

"What do you mean, Mrs…?"

"Sommerstein, Mildred Sommerstein. I'm from Brooklyn. Did I tell you that? Come sit down. I can't look up at you from here. Damn osteoporosis." She edged the walker into the living room and sat down in an electric lift chair. Then she pressed a lever. The motor slowly lowered the seat of the chair to a position where she could look at our faces. "Sit, sit," she commanded.

Ike and I carefully lowered ourselves onto an ancient Oriental settee, richly upholstered in brocaded silk. I was grateful it was able to support our combined weight. A rosewood Chinese console stood against the wall behind the settee. Upon it were displayed a varied collection of ornately glazed ceramic parrots. Hand-painted silk screens defined the living room space. Framed calligraphy adorned the deep red walls. The only item in the room that was not of Asian style was the electric lift chair. It's size and bulk spoiled the harmony of the elegant setting.

"What do you know about Ms. Keith?" I asked as the motor sound of the chair subsided.

"She loved the men. Cars went in and out of there at all hours of the day and night. I don't get out much and don't sleep well, so I sit on the balcony a lot. There's nothing to do out there but watch. Apart from the parties, there were three men over there regularly. One guy drove a white car with a yellow tag. He's probably a government worker. The big one drove a blue sedan. I don't know cars, so I don't know the make or model. Never needed a car in Brooklyn. The sneaky one acted like a peeping tom. He must have parked on the street because I never saw his car."

Mrs. Sommerstein reached for a package of Camel cigarettes resting on a ceramic Chinese garden stool near her chair. She placed one in her lips, lighted it with a Zippo lighter, and inhaled deeply. "This is my one last vice," she explained. "Gave up smoking when I was in my thirties, but I started up again on my seventieth birthday. Just couldn't stand waking up each morning wanting one."

"Did you see anyone over there the night before last?"

"The sneaky one was hovering around. I didn't stay outside that night because of the rain. I figured something had happened when I saw the flashing lights, but I didn't go out to see what it was. I can't see well in the dark anyway." She took another long draw on the cigarette. "Don't ever get old, my dear," she said to me. Everything goes to hell."

"What more can you tell us about the three men? Did you recognize any of them?" I asked her.

"I mostly saw the tops of their heads. The sneaky one always wore a black baseball cap and black clothes. He often stood looking through the windows when one of the other two was there."

"You're kidding!" Ike broke in. "He was watching them?" Mrs. Sommerstein stopped speaking and looked hard at him. Her eyes chastised him silently for interrupting. "Sorry," Ike apologized.

"Where was I? Oh, yes. The sneaky one watched through the windows. The government worker usually visited around midnight and stayed only a few hours each time. They spent lots of time in bed."

"How do you know that?" I interrupted, at the risk of incurring her steely gaze.

"She always kept all the lights on. You could see everything she did. The big guy is new. He's only been coming around for a couple of months. He spent a lot of time in bed with her too."

"Can you describe these men to our sketch artist?"

"Sorry. I don't think so. I never saw their faces up close."

"What else did you see from up here?" I asked as I wandered over to the glass doors that led to the balcony.

She gave me a puzzled look. "Do you mean the witches?"

"Tell me about the witches, Mrs. Sommerstein."

This was the second time someone had mentioned these so-called witches during the course of this investigation.

"They come out here for a ceremony to worship the moon. I see them gather out there on the jetty every month," she said with a gesture toward the water, "but I don't know exactly what they do. They pass through the bimbo's yard to get out there. You should ask the witch next door about it."

"She's really a witch? Where does the lady live?" Ike asked.

"Right next door in five-thirteen."

"We'll ask her about it," I told her. "Thank you. We may come back if we have more questions."

We let ourselves out and knocked at the door of unit 513. A meek little gray-haired man with cataract glasses greeted us. Upon entering, we found ourselves in a scene from 1960s Greenwich Village. The room was decorated in bright colors of orange, hot pink and lime. Overstuffed pillows were arranged on the couches and dotted the floor. Framed posters from the hippie era covered the walls. Strings of glass beads in the doorways and lava lamps on the tables completed the look. Patchouli incense smoke curled from brass receptacles, and the scent permeated the air. Eerie music provided a soft background sound. I recognized the unique string melody of a zither as well as a gong, a fife, and the punctuating rattle of a tambourine.

Sitting on the couch in the living room, Ike and I saw a woman who might well have been the world's oldest living flower child. Her long, dark hair was streaked with gray. Wide brown eyes peered through rose-colored John Lennon–style glasses. Her skin was milky white, and she was dressed in a soft, loose-fitting caftan. Long ropes of chains and beads adorned her neck; bangle bracelets clustered on her wrists; and a black onyx scarab ring dominated her right hand.

"I'm Lenore," she said as a matter of introduction. Her deep, throaty voice directed the little man, "Rudy, extinguish the incense. This child is practically green from the aroma."

The dutiful man pinched the ends of the sticks and opened the sliding glass doors to allow fresh air to circulate. I smiled my thanks to him.

"Please be seated," he offered, as he took his place on the couch next to Lenore. Ike settled into a beanbag chair, but I perched on a small hassock.

"I know who you are," she said before I could introduce myself. She pointed a long, bony finger at Ike. "You're familiar to me. We've met before."

Ike looked surprised but said nothing.

"I suppose you know why we're here?" I asked.

"Of course, dear," her voice purred.

"You have a pretty good view of the house next door from here. Did you see anything the night before last?"

"No, we usually retire early, except on the nights of the new moon and the full moon. I sleep like a log." Lenore casually picked up a small amethyst crystal from the coffee table and rolled it between the fingertips of her right hand. "Rudy takes his hearing aids out to sleep so he hears nothing after that. I felt Sally's death before we read about it in the papers."

"Really?" I asked skeptically.

She nodded serenely. "Oh, yes, dear. One can feel the rift when a spirit is so violently released." A soft sigh escaped her lips and her head bowed in sympathy.

"How about you, sir?" I directed the question to Rudy. "Is there anything you can tell us about Ms. Keith?"

"I sometimes walk on the beach in the early morning." The old gent's dentures clacked as he continued, "she was often walking out there at the same time. We never had a conversation, but she always smiled and said hello. Such a pretty thing. Too bad someone took her life. I was asleep early Monday night and didn't see or hear anything."

"Did you see anyone at her house during the day?" Ike asked.

"No, I saw no one," Rudy said. "She has several regular visitors, but none of them were there on Monday, as far as I know."

"Can you describe these visitors?" I asked him.

"One is much older than Sally. The other is tall and muscular, like a football player. There is a man dressed in black, but he always visits after dark, so I can't describe him. He'd come up on the deck to look in the windows. I presumed he was an old lover."

"You never called the sheriff's office to check on this mysterious man?"

"No. He wasn't our concern. He didn't seem to do any harm."

I turned back to Lenore. "What do you do on the nights of the new moon or the full moon?"

"I go to the ceremony, of course. Our coven meets on the jetty to honor the new moon and her sister, the full moon. It's right out there." She placed the crystal back on the coffee table and pointed in the direction of the gulf.

"Your coven?"

"Never fear, my dear. We're good witches," she said to reassure us.

"What exactly do good witches do?" I asked matter-of-factly.

"We cast love and protection spells, mix healing potions, dance and sing for joy, honor the moon, and love earth's creatures." She rose from the sofa, made several graceful dance movements, then settled back on the sofa with her hands crossed in her lap.

"Sounds harmless enough," I said. "Do you have organized coven meetings on a regular basis?"

"Well, of course, dear. They're scheduled the week before each ceremony. Would you like to join us?" she asked with a note of excitement.

Ike began to cough violently.

"Rudy, get this boy some water," she directed.

Ike followed Rudy into the kitchen and returned a few moments later with a relieved expression. "Sorry, ma'am," he said.

I stood to leave, thanked them for their time, and followed as Rudy led us out. Once we were in the hall, Ike quivered, and his eyes were watering. The next instant he burst into uncontrollable laughter. "I just couldn't hold it in anymore," he explained.

"They *are* sort of interesting, aren't they?" I responded with a smirk.

The third condo unit on the fifth floor was 515. We knocked and were immediately greeted by a dapper gentleman with a long white handlebar mustache. Wiry white eyebrows overshadowed sparkling black eyes. "*Buonasera*," he said in a thick Italian accent.

Ike and I introduced ourselves and presented our ID badges.

"Tomaso Marconi, at your service, he said with a little bow. I was just going out to the beach to walk Pugsly." He gestured to the brown-and-white bulldog next to him.

"Do you often walk on the beach at night?" I asked hopefully.

"*Sì, sì*, every night we go."

"Do you have a few minutes to talk to us?" I said. "It's about the girl who lived in the house next door."

"Pugsly cannot wait too much. Come. We all walk together," he said as he led the way to the elevator.

Once outside, the dog ran to the grassy area surrounding the pool and visited the nearest tree. Then we all traveled down a set of lighted stairs to the beach, and the man unfastened the leash. The animal ran ahead of us, barking and charging at the waves. We walked in silence for a few moments enjoying the peaceful beauty of the scene.

The night sky was dotted with stars. I could identify the constellations Orion, the Seven Sisters and the Big Dipper at a glance. The surf gently lapped at the white sand. Fiddler crabs scurried to their burrows to avoid our footsteps. Threads of dried seaweed, caught by the breeze, rolled silently past us. From time to time the pop of a seashell breaking under the weight of our feet broke the silence.

We stopped in the sand.

"Can you tell us if you saw anything different or odd on the beach night before last?" I asked.

"That would have been Monday night," Ike added for clarification.

"It was the same as always, but only a few people were walking in the stormy weather. Pugsly and I came out once but were turned back by the wind. We came out again after the news, when the rain had stopped and the wind was less."

"So you were out here at eleven thirty or thereabouts?" I asked.

"*Sì*, after the news."

"What time did you come back in?"

"Around midnight, I believe."

"Please think carefully, Mr. Marconi. Did you hear anyone or anything as you made your way back?"

The old man placed his fingers against his forehead and was silent for several moments. "I remember one thing was different," he began. "We come to the gate. Pugsly starts to growl. I open the gate, but he go to the patio and growls to the fence."

"What fence?" Ike and I asked in unison.

"Come, come. I show." The old man walked up the steps from the beach to the edge of the patio. He waved us toward the lot line between the condo property and Sally Keith's land. Thick stands of oleander ran the length of the condo property, and behind them stood a wooden privacy fence. We thanked Mr. Marconi and made our way down an incline to the sandy land near the fence. Scrub undergrowth covered most of the ground on Sally Keith's property. Between that undergrowth and the condo fence was a well-used path. Ike and I walked the entire length of the fence, which ended at the street.

"Let's walk back again," I told him.

I pulled a small flashlight from my purse and shined it on the fence boards as we walked. Approximately ten feet from the beach end of the fence, I saw grooves cut in a semicircular pattern on the wooden slats. When I pushed lightly against the wood a group of boards swung back and forth. Nails had made the marks. The action of the loose boards scraping against the fence had worn the grooves. Someone could come and go between the properties without being seen; the dense foliage would hide an individual on either side. Judging by the depth of the rub marks, someone had used this opening frequently.

As we headed to Ike's car, I pondered the significance of the passageway. I could see that someone on Ms. Keith's land might want to get onto the condo property to use the pool or health club. Or perhaps someone wanted to enter the condo discreetly for a clandestine romance. Drug deals might explain the need for a secret passage. Burglary was also a possibility, provided the items stolen were small, such as jewelry or cash. Maybe the "man in black" was simply a cat burglar who enjoyed a little peep show every now and then. Could he have been a condo resident who wanted to sneak over to Ms. Keith's house for a little romance? If so, why not just walk up from the beach? Why sneak through the fence? The sneaking part was what concerned me.

"Sheriff," Ike said, interrupting my train of thought, "do you still want to go to the Tiki Bar tonight? If you don't mind my saying so, you look worn out."

"Yes, let's go there. We need to time how long it takes to get there from here. It's ten fifteen now. Log your odometer reading while you're at it."

Ike wrote the time in his notepad and jotted down the numbers from the dashboard. We entered the bar at ten forty-five. We had traveled twenty-four miles. If Danny Dean and Sally Keith had left the Tiki at eleven thirty Monday night, that would place them at her house around midnight, precisely the time Mark Ritter, the guard, had said he'd heard the shot. Danny said he had stopped to purchase gas. How long had he stayed at the station? Long enough to put him outside the window of opportunity?

The door of the Tiki Bar was guarded by a set of crossed flaming torches. Lighting inside was dim. A U-shaped carved mahogany bar had openings on each side for service staff to pick up orders. A dozen rattan barstools surrounded it. Small booths, with roofs of palm-tree thatch, lined the walls and two-set tables occupied all the floor space. Carved wooden tiki dolls, with candles burning on the tops of their heads, adorned each table. There were few patrons in attendance, but I figured it would fill up after the hospital's shift change.

We identified ourselves to the bartender. Lawrence wore a loud Hawaiian print shirt and cheap plastic lei. He was a heavy man with long black hair pulled back in a ponytail and tied with a leather band adorned with puka shells. The shape of his eyes and skin color were Asian, but his Deep South language patterns belied his heritage.

"I understand Sally Keith was somewhat of a regular here?" I asked, as Ike and I took seats at the bar.

"Oh, sure. Sally loved to have fun. Sorry to hear about her death."

"Was County Administrator Dean a regular too?"

"He met Sally here often," the man said. The door opened and Lawrence called out a welcome to the entering guests.

"Did she meet anyone else here?" I continued.

"No one regular. Sometimes she had a quick drink with one of the hospital crowd, but she was usually with Dean." He stopped to open two bottles of beer, placed the bottles and two frosted mugs on a barmaid's tray, and rang the sale on the cash register.

"Were they here the night of her murder?" Ike asked.

"Yeah. She came in about ten minutes after eleven. Dean had been here about an hour by then. They had one drink and left."

"What time was that?"

“About eleven thirty.”

“Do you remember what she drank?” I asked.

“A virgin screwdriver—just orange juice. I remember because she really liked booze. I was surprised she didn’t want any that night.”

“What did they do?” I probed. “How were they acting?”

“They sat in that corner booth where it’s rather dark. That’s their usual spot.” He pointed to the booth. “I keep trying to remember to fix the bulb back there, but I think they liked it that way.”

Ike walked toward the booth Lawrence had indicated as Danny and Sally’s favorite and looked up at the light fixture. He reached up, twisted the bulb, and light streamed down on the table.

“Hey, man, thanks,” said Lawrence. “Can’t believe that’s all it needed.”

“You were describing Ms. Keith and Mr. Dean’s actions,” I said to get him back on the subject.

“They were agitated—you know, talking a lot and using lots of hand gestures and movements.” Lawrence excused himself and filled another drink order for the barmaid.

"I sure would like one of those beers," said Ike. "I know. I know," he continued when he saw my sideways glance. "I don't drink on duty, so don't worry."

The bartender finished his order and rejoined our conversation.

"Were they fighting about something?" Ike asked.

"No. I don't think it was a fight, but they seemed distressed. I can tell from facial expressions even if I can't hear the words."

"I take it you couldn't hear any of the conversation?" I asked.

"No. Too far away. Sorry. They were only here a short time."

"Thanks. If you think of anything else, please call us." I added as we turned to leave.

"That was a big zero." I complained to Ike.

"At least we know Danny Dean told the truth about coming here. Timeline fits with his story too."

"That's something, I guess. The timeline also fits perfectly with the time of Sally's murder. Check Dean's personal items and his county car. See if there's a credit card slip or receipt for gas in there. We need to pin down how much time he spent at that station."

"Sheriff," Ike said with a bit of irritation, "we've been at this since eight a.m. It's after eleven now. It's time to quit for today."

I heaved a small sigh. "You're right. Can you take me back to my car?"

"Are you sure you're able to drive home? I could take you to a hotel and pick you up in the morning."

"I'm fine. We'll start at nine a.m. tomorrow. That'll give us an extra hour of sleep."

**

My drive home was an ordeal. I fought sleep and many times found myself blinking feverishly to stay awake. It was a bad decision on my part to insist on going home. Staying at a hotel in town would have been smarter, but I missed Buck and wanted to see him. Talking on the phone wasn't the same as snuggling with him.

The night was very dark. Clouds had built since we walked on the beach, and the stars were no longer visible. The only light came from my headlights. Eddies of fog swirled across the road that skirted the state park, so I slowed my speed from fifty-five miles an hour to forty-five. The fog intensified as I drove over a short bridge near the park entrance. The moisture was so dense that it covered the windshield as if it were raining. I switched on the wipers and further slowed my speed as I exited the bridge. It felt as if I were creeping along, but the speedometer read forty miles an hour.

I cursed as something crashed into the side of my car. The impact on the damp pavement pushed me into a skid, but I recovered easily. I knew there had been nothing in front of me, but I definitely hadn't dreamed that noise or the blow. I pulled to the shoulder, grabbed my flashlight and gun, and cautiously opened the door. The side-view mirror was gone, and I noticed a huge dent in the driver's-side door. Something was screaming in the darkness. I followed the sound until the light from my flashlight reflected from two glowing eyes. I breathed a sigh of relief when I saw that it was a small deer. I hadn't wished to encounter any dangerous wildlife while alone in the dark.

Cautiously I approached the suffering animal. A wounded buck could still do harm with his hooves and antlers. I paused, aimed my weapon at its head, and put the animal out of his misery. I felt bad about shooting the animal, but I could hardly leave it in pain on the side of the road. The number of deer had increased dramatically in the past few years. Fewer people hunted for sustenance or recreation. Most of the deer's natural predators had been run off by civilization, so there was nothing to stem the population increase. I'd call the state park if I saw the animal was still there on the shoulder in the morning. In the dense underbrush near the park entrance, I heard the sounds of foliage being trampled by something large. I hurried back to my car and got inside. The movement stopped, and the sound retreated gradually until all was quiet again. I started the engine and eased slowly back onto the road.

I couldn't keep my mind off the animal I'd killed and what had chased it onto the highway. The Myakka River State Park encompassed fifty-seven acres along the Myakka River and had existed for as long as I could remember. Mom, Dad and I had visited it many times. Sometimes we planned a group event with other families, but it was usually just the three of us. A trip to Myakka was an event that required much advance planning. When I was a child, the area had very few facilities, so we had to bring everything we needed with us. We'd pack the station wagon full of food, a charcoal grill, ice chests, fishing poles, and folding chairs and leave home early in the morning so we'd arrive as soon as the park opened. We'd set up our camp near a path that provided easy access down the steep bank of the river. Then we'd dig up worms, and fish until the alligators gathered in hopes of getting a free meal. My dad always threw our fish to the gators, but Mom scolded him for doing it because she said the gators were becoming too comfortable with people. She didn't want them climbing the bank up to the campsite.

The river's current moved slowly in this area. The water hyacinths had clogged much of the waterway over the years, but the state recently had introduced manatees into the river system to eat the rapidly growing foliage. The giant mammals often could be spotted drifting among the kelly-green leaves and soft-purple flowers of the hyacinths. They seemed to cohabitate peacefully with the gators, probably because they didn't compete with one another for food.

Dad was the one who cooked when the grill was involved. We ate hot dogs and hamburgers, accompanied by Mom's macaroni salad and coleslaw. For dessert we always roasted marshmallows. After we'd cleaned the dishes and doused the fire with river water, Dad would lie down for a nap, and Mom would pull out one of her crossword-puzzle books. They wanted to relax, but I wanted to explore the park. The rangers had cut trails through the underbrush, so I always started off by walking along one of them. My mother had warned me about snakes, raccoons, opossums, wild pigs, spiders, ants, wasps, and the redbugs that lived in the Spanish moss that hung from the oak trees, but she allowed me to venture out on my own after I promised to be careful. I found out later that she made my dad follow me the first few times I walked down the trails. After he was sure I wasn't going to get lost, he allowed me to go alone.

In the 1950s and 1960s, very few structures existed in the park. The ranger station, bathroom building, and one or two covered picnic areas were all that had been built, or so I'd thought until one special day. I was about ten years old, and had wandered farther away from the camp than I'd ever gone before. I followed one of the trails, as I always did, but when I came to a less dense portion of palmetto scrub, I ventured off the trail and found myself at the edge of a huge meadow. Multi-colored wildflowers poked their heads up among grass that was drying in the early-autumn sun. Butterflies clung to every flower sipping nectar. The entire meadow rippled in the breeze and looked as if it were alive. As I walked slowly through the grass, I disturbed the butterflies and they rose into the sky in a huge swarm of vibrant yellow. It was so beautiful!

Carefully I made my way across the meadow until I reached a shaded hammock of oaks on the western edge. Nestled among the massive oaks was a small barn. I saw stalls along one side as well as hay bales through an open window on the second floor. I assumed this was where the rangers kept their horses, but it wasn't occupied at the moment. Of course I had to see whether the door was locked. It wasn't, so I slowly opened it and peered inside. Fresh hay was strewn on the floor and in the empty stalls. A row of wooden shelves lined one wall, and I cautiously entered and made my way toward them. A variety of jars filled the shelves. All were labeled with strips of paper affixed to the glass with cellophane tape. Inside the jars were specimens of wildlife in various stages of development: snakes, frogs, gators, piglets, opossums, and birds. All had been preserved in some kind of clear liquid. It was both fascinating and gruesome.

Turning to my right, I spotted a ladder that led to the hayloft, so I made my way up the rungs. The view from the loft window was spectacular. I saw to the edge of the meadow and into the swampy land beyond it. Oak trees surrounded the entire meadow, and egrets roosted in them. After carefully descending the ladder, I wandered toward a small room in the corner. The door was locked, so I turned again to see if anything lay beyond the main room. My heart jumped into my throat when I came face-to-face with the biggest wild boar I'd ever seen. The wild pigs my parents and I often saw in the park were usually two or three feet long and stood a couple of feet high. The beast in front of me was as long as my Dad's Ford Anglia, and its eyes were at the same level as my own. The deep-yellow orbs stared at me. The sharp tusks extending from its lower jaw were at least six inches long. I made an effort to run, but my feet were frozen to the ground. The beast didn't charge. In fact it didn't make any movement at all. I breathed a deep sigh when I suddenly realized it was a stuffed boar; I felt foolish for having been scared.

I'd been gone quite a while and knew my parents would be worried, so I made my way across the barn to the outside door. I pushed the door open and ran directly into one of the rangers. He was tall and thin with a kind, boyish face.

"Well, what do we have here?" he asked with a smile.

"My name's Bernie," I said in a quiet voice, as I stuffed my hands into my pockets. I was embarrassed that he'd found me trespassing in his barn.

"I'm Ranger Simmons. Did you see Old Tusker back there?"

"Yes, sir. He's huge. Did you shoot him?"

"I did. He was the biggest boar we'd ever seen, so we took him to the taxidermist and brought him back here. He was charging the horses and creating quite a problem—we had no choice but to kill him. He might have endangered or killed some of our guests. He's a beautiful animal, though, isn't he?"

"Yes, he is. Did you gather all those animals in the jars?"

"I've been collecting these since I've been stationed here," the ranger said. "We wanted to make a little museum, but it'll take more than just this to start it. I imagine we'll have enough things collected in the next ten years or so."

I shifted my feet nervously. "I didn't see a sign that said I couldn't come in. I hope you don't mind."

"No, Bernie. I'm glad you enjoyed seeing my work. Come back any time."

"I'd better get back to my parents before they worry."

"Good idea. Nice meeting you, young lady."

My parents had been worried about me. I usually was gone no more than an hour, but visiting the barn had added an additional hour to my trip. They were relieved to see me walk into the camp after my adventure and glad I'd found such an interesting place.

I smiled at my memories of the park. Thinking of them kept me awake for the rest of my drive home.

I had to use my flashlight to see the numbers on the combination lock that fastened the chain on the gate to the ranch. The incident with the deer had disturbed me and my hands were still trembling. I had to try the combination twice before I could open the lock. The drive from the gate to the house seemed to take forever. I drove slowly in an effort to keep the noise down.

It was dark in the foyer. I pushed the heavy door closed and locked it behind me. I did my best to be quiet, but every move I made seemed to echo through the massive rooms. I pulled off my shoes and tiptoed across the bedroom floor. I stripped off my clothes, dropped them in a heap by the bed, and crawled under the covers.

"You're mighty late," Buck whispered.

I jumped at the sound. I'd thought he was asleep. "I'm sorry I woke you. I was trying to be quiet."

"You and the elephant herd," he said with a chuckle.

I exhaled a deep sigh, and Buck's chuckle escalated into a laugh. The habit of sighing loudly when I was perturbed was one I'd picked up as a child and couldn't seem to lose. Buck pulled me toward him and wrapped me gently in his arms.

"You're trembling," he said. "What's wrong?"

"I hit a deer out by the park, or I should say he hit me. He tore off the side mirror and put a pretty good dent in the door."

"Are you OK?"

"It shook me a little, but I'm fine. I had to shoot it. It was in such pain."

"I'm sorry, honey. I'm just glad you weren't hurt."

"Something must have scared him to make him bolt across the road like that. I figured it was a panther. If I'd hit him head on, he would've damaged the engine. Guess I should be grateful for that."

"Time for sleep, sweetheart," he whispered.

I drifted off before his sentence ended.

Chapter 11

Thursday Morning

Morning dawned much too soon. Six hours of sleep wasn't nearly enough for me, and I had to drag myself out of bed. I wrapped myself in my warm robe and joined Buck in the kitchen. He was dressed and ready to go out the door, but he stopped when I entered the room.

"Hey, why don't you go back to bed for a while?"

"I told Ike I'd meet him at nine," I said with a yawn.

"So he doesn't have a phone? He's probably just as tired as you are, you know."

"He probably is, but we have a lot to do, and starting late won't help. I already pushed our day back an hour."

Buck walked me to the breakfast bar and gently pushed me into a seat. He took off his jacket and hung it on the back of another chair. Then he placed a glass of milk and another filled with orange juice on the counter in front of me and started breakfast. I smiled at the sight of my broad-shouldered, six-foot-six husband wearing a shoulder holster and one of my ruffled aprons. He placed the plate of eggs, bacon, and toast on the counter, kissed the top of my head, and grabbed his jacket.

"Gotta run. Captains' meeting at eight today."

"They'll love the new uniform," I said as my eyes fell on the apron.

"Yeah," Buck said with a snort as he tossed the apron onto the counter and kissed me again. "Maybe you can knock off early today? I miss you."

"I'll try," I promised.

**

Ike arrived early again, and I smiled my approval.

"We need to locate Ms. Keith's mother," I said. "Will you go to forensics and get her address book and the letter from her mother while I work on this pile of stuff in my in basket?"

Ike went on his mission, and Dottie knocked on my doorframe a few seconds later. "The state's attorney has called several times. He said he'd be in and out of court today, so he'll try to catch you later."

"I don't have much to tell him that he can't read in the reports. We don't have any evidence to refute the charge of murder. Sally Keith was Danny Dean's mistress or girlfriend, and it appears everyone knew it. Hmm…I wonder if his wife knew it."

Dottie smirked a little. "Wouldn't that be his ex-wife?"

"Yes, you're right. I wonder if she knew."

Ike appeared with the book and letter, and Dottie headed back to her desk.

"After I call to try to find the mother, I want to go see Danny Dean's ex-wife," I told him. "Can you find out where she lives? I'll meet you in the detective division after I finish these calls."

"Sure thing," Ike said with a slight salute.

I pulled the letter from the evidence bag, squinted to read the city name in the faint ink of the postmark, and dialed the operator to find the number for the police in the town of St. Peter, Minnesota. I was put through to Chief Paul Cleverdon.

"Chief, I'm Sheriff Bernie Davis of Sarasota County, Florida."

"What can I do for you, Sheriff?" he responded in a friendly tone.

"I hope you can help me locate the closest relative of a woman named Sally Keith. I believe her mother may live in your town."

"What's Sally done now?" he asked with a little laugh.

"You know Sally Keith?"

"Sure. Her mother, Alice, is my secretary. You spoke with her on the phone before she transferred you to me."

"I'm afraid I have bad news. I'm glad you're there to relay this to her. We have Sally Keith's body in our morgue."

A few seconds elapsed before the man spoke again. His voice sounded sad, and he spoke softly. "What happened? Car accident?"

"No, sir. I'm sorry to say she was murdered."

Several more seconds passed before he resumed speaking. "There's no possibility of a mistake, is there?"

"I'm afraid not. I got the name of your town from the postmark on a letter in Sally's purse. The letter was signed, 'Mother.'"

"Sally lived on the beach somewhere in your area," Chief Cleverdon said. "She was an ER nurse. Is that the girl you have in the morgue?"

"Yes, I'm sorry, but I believe it is. She was an attractive blonde, about five foot four, twenty-five years old, and in good shape. I'd fax a photo, but I'm not sure it would be of any help with identifying her. She's no longer a pretty sight. Can you verify Sally's address and phone number? That way we can be sure."

"I'll ask Alice to verify that information before I tell her. Give me the address and phone number you have for her and your phone number too. I'll call you right back."

My phone rang ten minutes later. "It's her," Chief Cleverdon said. "Alice is coming down there."

"You have my private number," I told him. "I'll also give you the number for my office manager, Dottie. She can always locate me. I can have a deputy meet Mrs. Keith at the airport if she'd like that. I'll just need the flight information. If she'd rather not do that, please ask her to call when she's settled, and we'll arrange a time to meet at the medical examiner's office."

"OK," he said quietly then broke the connection.

Chapter 12

Thursday Morning

Ike and I knocked on the door of a large suburban home in a well-to-do neighborhood on the South Tamiami Trail. A petite, middle-aged redhead with angular features and overdone makeup opened the door. She wore a tight pair of red slacks, red leather boots, a white turtleneck sweater, and a necklace of emeralds and pearls fashioned to look like mistletoe. Her expression transformed from curious to angry when we identified ourselves.

"What do *you* want?" she spat as she directed her angry green eyes at me.

"I want to know where you were two nights ago."

"I was at home, taking care of my children," she retorted.

"May we come in, ma'am?" Ike asked. He had stepped slightly in front of me and donned his most charming smile. Kelly Dean stared at him, glared again at me, and stepped aside to allow us to enter the house. We followed her to an ornately decorated formal living room. A massive Christmas tree filled one corner. The tree decorations matched the colors of the room – white, hunter green and burgundy. A white baby grand piano faced a wall of sliding glass doors. Beyond the glass doors, steam rose from a heated swimming pool. Mrs. Dean sat on one end of an L-shaped sectional sofa. We sat at the other end.

Ike picked up the questioning. "Can you give us information about your whereabouts on the night Sally Keith was killed?"

"What for? Am I a suspect?"

"We have to rule out anyone associated with the victim," he explained. "Until we're able to do that, you'll remain a suspect."

"Associated with her? Are you kidding? I wouldn't kill the little tramp. She's not worth killing. Besides, I have my children to look after. It wouldn't do me any good to go to prison for murder." Kelly Dean reached toward a thick glass coffee table and picked up a mug made in the shape of a Santa face. She took a long sip and the scent of bourbon wafted across the room.

"Was there anyone else here on Tuesday night?" Ike asked.

"No, just me and the kids." She pushed a few stray red hairs away from her face. "The oldest one goes to bed at ten on school nights. I'm usually in bed shortly after that."

Ike paused for a few moments while he jotted some notes. "Can anyone verify that you were at home that night?"

"My mother can. She called about ten thirty and we talked for around an hour. You can check the phone records or call her."

"We'll do that," he said. "Thanks."

"Did you ever meet Ms. Keith? Did you know where she lived?" I asked.

Kelly Dean's demeanor changed as she turned to answer the question. Her lips formed a hard line, and daggers of hatred shot from her eyes. "Yes, I knew her," she said coldly. All that venom could mean only one thing.

"So your husband was having an affair, and you knew about it?" I asked.

"Of course I knew," she admitted. "We moved here from Minnesota to get away from her, but somehow she ended up in the same town, and they started up all over again."

"I thought you had moved from the Midwest, Chicago or Milwaukee, or somewhere in that vicinity. I had no idea you were from Minnesota," I said.

"Yea, you betcha," Mrs. Dean said using the strong accent so prevalent in the land of ten thousand lakes. "Danny worked in Chicago and Milwaukee, but we were both born and raised in Minnesota."

"Is that why you got divorced…because of his affair with Ms. Keith?"

"Yes, Danny couldn't stay away from her. He just loved women. You ought to know that, Sheriff."

"What do you mean, Mrs. Dean?"

"What do I mean? What do I mean?" she screamed at me.

"Calm down, ma'am," Ike said.

"I will *not* calm down! The ink wasn't even dry on the divorce papers before this one was in the sack with him," she shouted, and pointed angrily at me.

"Mrs. Dean, that's not true," I said quietly. Anger was building inside me, but this wasn't the place for a confrontation.

The hatred in her eyes warned me away from further comment. She wasn't thinking rationally. Nothing I could say or do would dampen her anger right now.

Ike made no further attempts to question her. "We'll come back another time, ma'am," he said. "Please don't leave town. We'll show ourselves out." We left Kelly Dean seething on her sofa.

"Sorry that was so unpleasant, Sheriff," Ike said once we were in the car. "If we need to question her again, I'll come back alone."

"Thanks, Ike. But don't allow yourself to be alone with her. Bring a female deputy with you. With another female there, she would be able to make any sexual assault claims. I don't want her to damage the entire department just to play out her revenge against me."

"Ma'am, I have to ask you something," Ike said. His cheeks were pink with embarrassment, so I anticipated his question.

"No, Detective, I didn't have a sexual relationship with Danny Dean."

"That's not what I was going to ask. Are you able to account for your whereabouts two nights ago?"

"What?"

"We need to eliminate you as a suspect, ma'am. Do you have an alibi?"

"I was at our ranch with my husband," I answered stiffly. I knew Ike was doing the right thing. In a murder case, no one should be above suspicion, not even the Sheriff, but I didn't have to like being questioned.

"Can Sheriff Davis—I mean your husband—swear to that, ma'am?"

"Yes, he can. It's absolutely the truth, but you should ask him yourself."

"I had planned to do that, ma'am. Sorry."

"That's OK. You're just doing your job."

We sat in the car in silence for a few moments before he spoke again. "I forgot my wallet and my star. Can our next stop be my apartment?"

"Sure. OK if I use your bathroom? I didn't want to ask Mrs. Dean if I could use hers."

Ike snickered as he turned onto the highway.

Chapter 13

Thursday Afternoon

Ike's apartment was a ten-minute drive away. Each of us was lost in thought, so we spoke little during the trip. Ike pushed the door open to allow me to enter first. A large orange tabby meowed loudly and rubbed against our legs in greeting.

"Meet Skitzo," he said. "He probably won't warm up to you right away. I got him from the rescue shelter and he doesn't trust many people. Have a seat, ma'am. I'm a bachelor, and I need to clean up the bathroom a little before you go in there."

"OK," I said, hoping he'd hurry. Ike's apartment was a wreck. Clutter covered every level surface of the kitchen, dining area, and entry alcove. One entire wall of the living room was dominated by a sturdy entertainment center. Its shelves contained a collection of stereo equipment and a giant projection television set. Stacks of vinyl albums and cassette tapes teetered perilously amongst a tangle of headphones and cables. Speakers and a subwoofer were positioned for optimum listening enjoyment with obvious disregard for appearance. A small molded plastic kiddie pool, filled to capacity with empty beer cans and bottles, had been pushed into one corner of the room. "Beer spatter" was visible on the walls near the pool, presumably the result of bad aim. The only other piece of furniture in the room was a black leather couch, so I sat there. Skitzo jumped into my lap immediately and kneaded my chest. I petted him softly, and he purred with happiness.

"Looks like he's taken to you. That's high praise, ma'am."

I gently moved the animal aside and rose from the couch. Clouds of orange fur covered my lap and jacket.

"Sorry," Ike said. "He sheds like crazy. I'll get a lint roller for you. I keep them all over the place. Everything I own has fur on it."

The mess in the bathroom wasn't as bad as I'd expected. Ike had thrown dirty towels and clothing into the tub, so the floor was clear. I smelled cleaning solution, so I imagined he had cleaned the toilet and sink. He had neglected to put any soap by the sink, so I opened the medicine cabinet to look for some. There was no soap, but I noticed a bottle of Aramis cologne. He must not have worn it very often because he never carried the scent. The cabinet also housed aspirin, toothbrush and paste, manicure tools, a razor, shaving cream, and a box of condoms, which I wished I hadn't seen.

When I returned to the living room, Ike offered me a lint roller. After I removed as much of the cat hair as I could, we returned to his car.

"Do you know where Mr. Dean lives, ma'am? I couldn't find him in any of the directories. The personnel office still lists his address as the house we just left. He gave us that address on the arrest report too. We need to see him again, and I really don't want to go back to ask his ex-wife for his address."

"He lives in one of those new apartments on Lockwood Ridge Road," I said. "I don't remember the unit number, but we can figure it out."

**

I rang the doorbell, but Danny Dean didn't answer. Ike knocked on the door, and when there was still no answer, he knocked more forcefully.

"He's here," I said. "I saw his county car in the parking lot."

Ike was about to pound even harder when the door opened. A bleary-eyed Danny stood there in an old terry-cloth robe.

"Bernie, this is too early for a call," he slurred.

"It's past noon, Danny. Can we come in?"

He opened the door wider, and we entered a room that was so dark that it took a few seconds for my eyes to adjust. The place looked and smelled like a garbage dump. Newspapers littered the chairs and floor; fast-food containers were scattered across tables and countertops; and empty liquor bottles lay on an ornate wooden bar. He'd only been out on bond for about twenty-four hours. It would take longer than that to make such a mess.

"What's going on, Danny?" I asked.

"What the hell do you think is going on?" he shouted. "I've been arrested and charged with murder!" Danny stopped in front of a full-length mirror hanging on the wall of the living room, to check his appearance. He combed his fingers through his hair in an attempt to neaten it, then rearranged the front of the robe and adjusted the belt.

"How does this help?" I said as I gestured around the room.

I cleared a place on a custom-made sofa and Ike and I sat down. Danny was still standing near the mirror.

"It helps dull the pain," he said quietly, then leaned his forehead against the wall and began to cry.

I waited for his sobs to subside before I spoke again. "We have some more questions to ask," I began. "I understand you were seeing Ms. Keith when you lived in Minnesota."

"Who told you that?" Danny, suddenly dry-eyed, snapped his head in my direction.

"It doesn't matter," I said flatly. "Is it true?"

"Yes," he said as he walked into the living room and sat in a leather recliner.

"Is there anything more about your relationship with Sally Keith that you didn't bother to tell me?"

He closed his eyes for a moment, leaned his head against the back of the recliner, and sighed deeply. "I don't know."

"This is important, Danny. You asked me to find out who killed Sally, but right now all the evidence points to you, and I haven't heard anything to the contrary."

"I didn't do it," Danny said as he rubbed the palms of his hands over his face.

"You keep saying that, but there's no proof of your innocence."

"She had a new boyfriend." He looked defeated as he said it. "Maybe he did it."

"Do you know who he is?" I asked.

"No. She wouldn't tell me."

"Did you ever see him?"

"No."

"What did you and Ms. Keith argue about in the bar Monday night?"

He looked down at the floor for a moment. "We didn't argue."

"OK. What did you discuss?"

Danny was silent for a few long seconds.

"The truth, Danny," I prodded.

"All right," he began but then went silent again. "All right. I told her I was going to remarry my wife."

"Really?" The surprise in my voice was genuine. Kelly Dean had made no mention of this new development. Was Danny telling the truth?

"Yes, really." Danny rose from the chair and began to pace across the living room carpet. "I can't live like this. I miss my wife, my kids, being at home, and having stability. I spent Thanksgiving alone. My wife and kids went to the annual family get-together in Minnesota. I wasn't invited. Sally went to be with her mother. Everyone in town had family to visit except me." Danny stopped the pacing and stood directly in front of me. "I even called you, Bernie, but your phone was disconnected. Then I remembered you'd gotten married and didn't live there any longer.

"I can't spend Christmas that way, so I went back to Kelly and asked her to marry me. I even took her roses and got down on one knee like I did the first time." Danny knelt down in front of me to illustrate his proposal to his wife, then straightened and began to pace again. "Oh, she had her list of conditions. Kelly wouldn't be Kelly without conditions, but she said yes. The first item on her list was getting rid of Sally. That's what I was trying to do the night she was killed. She was really upset when I told her in the bar, so I followed her home. I wanted us to part as friends and this was the last time I would be seeing her, so I had to make this work. If I hadn't stopped to get gas, I might have prevented her murder, or at least I might have seen who did it."

Danny suddenly grew quiet, then returned to his place in the recliner. He slowly wiped away the tears trickled down his cheeks. "I really loved Sally," he continued. "Back in Minnesota I was having a midlife crisis, and being with a pretty young girl helped me get through that. When I found out she was living here, I was so happy. I guess it wasn't fair to Kelly, though. She gets so jealous and has such a temper..." His voice trailed off, and a look of horror crossed his face for a moment. He abruptly changed the subject. "Anything else you need to know? I guess I'd better clean up this place."

"One more question," I said. "Why did two county commissioners post bond for you?"

"We're friends. They just wanted to help," he answered smugly.

"That's bullshit, Danny. Torrino and Ruskin don't have friends. No one is civil to them unless they want something. Those two would sell their mothers for a couple of case quarters, so why would they help you?"

Danny was silent again. He clearly was trying to think of a quick lie, but nothing came to his mind. "That's it for now," I said. "We'll be back if we have more questions."

It was after two when we left Danny Dean's apartment. "I know we hoped to be at the hospital at three," I told Ike, "but I *must* eat something, even if we drive through a fast-food place."

"How about a hot dog from the Hob Nob? That'll be quick."

"That's where high school kids go on dates."

"So pretend we're sixteen and on a date," he said with a shy smile. "Their chili dogs are great. Hey, what's a case quarter? You said the county commissioners would sell their mothers for a couple of case quarters."

"You've never heard that expression? It's twenty-five cents in one coin, rather than a combination of pennies, nickels, and dimes. It's a piece of money you can put into a soft drink case."

Ike shook his head. "Where do you get this stuff?"

After the quickest lunch in history, we arrived at the hospital administrator's office at two forty-five. We advised him that we needed to interview everyone who worked the three-to-eleven shift in the ER. He gave us the name of the shift supervisor. Carolyn Harrison was the picture of efficiency. A starched white cap sat upon wavy steel-gray hair. I recognized the maroon stripe of ribbon on the edge of the cap as a sign that she had graduated from the school of nursing at Florida State University, which meant she was a degreed nurse with a much more extensive education that most of her coworkers. Her trim, matronly figure was housed in a crisp white uniform, and her demeanor was confident. She smiled as we entered her office.

"How can I help you, Sheriff?" she began, after introductions had been made. She gestured to chairs opposite her desk, and continued after we were seated, "I'll do anything to help bring Sally's murderer to justice."

"Did she seem upset about anything the night she was killed?"

Carolyn thought for a moment before replying. "No, she acted normally. She was a good nurse, very efficient, kind to the patients and their family members, and she could charm even the grumpiest doctor. She was an asset here."

"Was she close to any of her coworkers?"

"She made friends with everyone—you know, the life-of-the-party type—but she was closest to Terry."

"May we speak with her?"

"In this case it's not a her—it's a him. Terry is a male nurse. I'll get him. You can talk with him here in my office."

Terry Clarke was a short thin man in his forties with effeminate mannerisms. His voice was high, and he batted his eyelashes as he talked. "I can't begin to tell you how broken up I am about Sally's death," he said with tears in his eyes. "She was a lovely creature, full of life and vitality. She was my best friend."

"Was she upset about anything or anyone recently?"

"Not particularly. She was a little concerned about the baby. You know she was pregnant, right? She hadn't told the father about the child yet."

"She told you before she told the father?" Ike asked with a raised eyebrow.

"We girls tell each other secrets," he said with a giggle. "I've told her plenty of mine."

"Did she tell you who the father was?" Ike continued.

"No, I just assumed it was Mr. Dean's, but I never asked." The little man smiled at Ike, who backed his chair farther into the corner of the room.

"Did she tell you anything about her other boyfriend?" I continued.

"Not much. I know he was a big hunk with lots of stamina, if you know what I mean," he said with a wink and another glance at Ike, who pushed himself as far away as the close quarters of the little room would allow. "I know he worked during the day, so they couldn't get together as often as Sally would have liked. She was sweet on him, maybe even falling in love with him. I don't imagine Mr. Dean would have liked that too much."

"Why do you say that?" I asked.

"Well, after all the years they spent together, I don't think he'd appreciate the competition, especially from someone younger than him."

Another nail in Danny's coffin, I thought as I thanked Terry for his help. We spoke with two more nurses, two lab techs, and three doctors but got no more useful information.

"Let's call it a day, Ike," I said as we drove away from the hospital.

Chapter 14

Thursday Evening

I usually enjoyed the daily hour-long drive home. After working in the city, I traveled down peaceful two-lane roads through farmland, pastures, groves, and virgin woods. There weren't many people living out this far from town, so I encountered few vehicles. This was the time I usually spent reviewing the events of the day and making mental checklists of things to do the following day.

Sally Keith's mother hadn't made contact with me yet, though there could be a message at my office. I supposed she'd be coming to the morgue the next day, though I couldn't be sure. She might know if Sally had been having trouble with anyone, who the second boyfriend was, or who had fathered Sally's child. Alternatively she may have known nothing about her daughter's life. Young women often move to Florida to get away from family members they don't get along with or to start new lives away from any baggage from their pasts. I was reasonably sure Sally's mother would be a mental wreck.

Gathering further information might have to wait until another day.

The forensic team hadn't sent me any reports yet. They were trying to identify fingerprints and evaluate the hair samples from Sally Keith's car, as well as analyze all the photos taken at the scene in hope of finding clues. I knew they'd revisit the scene more than once before making any final conclusions. They'd also perform ballistics tests with Danny's pistol. We had to wait for lab analysis from FDLE on the residue swabs taken from Danny's hands. Since he had picked up the weapon, there most certainly would be powder residue on them regardless of whether he had fired the shot. How much residue was present might indicate innocence or guilt. Tests were not totally conclusive.

Ike and I had a lot of footwork to do still. We needed to find out more about Sally Keith, and from that we might discover who killed her. We'd probably split up to gather data. We'd try to talk to anyone she knew—doctors, dentists, pharmacists, grocers, hairdressers, dry cleaners, paperboys, delivery persons, gardeners, mechanics, gas station attendants, and perhaps more local shopkeepers. We needed to check her bank records, phone records, and credit card data. Did she belong to a gym or a tennis or golf club? Who were her friends other than her coworkers? Did she keep in touch with anyone in her old hometown? Who was her newest boyfriend?

A more delicate inquiry needed to be made into the relationship between Danny Dean and the county commissioners who had posted his bond. All their financial records needed to be checked. If they discovered we were investigating them, however, they'd try to stonewall our efforts. They were wealthy, powerful men with friends in every walk of life, so Ike and I would have to be careful.

Kelly Dean's phone records had to be examined, and we needed to visit the gas station where Danny said he had stopped the night of Sally's murder. We'd also canvas more condo units. Someone must have seen or heard something that night.

If someone analyzed what I was doing, it might seem I wasn't doing a very good job with this case. That was what the state's attorney was going to think. A man had been arrested at the scene. Shouldn't I be trying to firm up the evidence to prosecute him instead of trying to find another suspect? Even though I felt it in my gut that Danny was innocent, everything we'd discovered so far pointed toward him as being the killer.

Before I knew it, I was at the main entrance to the ranch. I unlocked the chain, moved through the gate, and snapped the lock back in place behind me. Then I parked in the barn and walked down the path to the house. As I placed my key in the lock, I saw Buck's car enter the barn. He followed the same path I'd just taken. He hugged and kissed me on the doorstep.

"I'm so glad you're home," he said as he opened the door.

"It's great to see you too. This has been a long couple of days."

We removed our jackets and shoulder holsters and tossed them onto a chair in the living room. Then we made our way to one of the sofas and collapsed into the soft leather. I propped my feet on the coffee table. My ankles were swollen.

"Oh, I wish I could have a drink," I lamented.

Buck grinned. "I'll get you a glass of milk."

"Yuck. That's not what I had in mind."

"Hey, what's all over your slacks? Do you have a new red-headed boyfriend?"

"It's cat hair. Ike has an orange tabby. We went by his apartment for a minute, and the cat sat in my lap. I couldn't get all of it off." I sat up suddenly. "Hey, can you grab an empty evidence bag from the trunk of my car?"

"Sure. Back in a second."

When Buck returned, I placed several hairs in the bag and sealed it.

"What is it, Bernie? I can almost hear the wheels turning in your head."

"Will you go with me to the crime scene on the key tonight?

He was silent for a moment. I knew he wanted to spend a quiet, romantic evening at home, rather than running off to do more work.

"Sure, honey, but can't this wait until tomorrow?"

"Actually, it can't, and I need to go there without Ike. We could have dinner somewhere then go to the scene. I only need a few minutes."

"OK. Let's go," he reluctantly agreed.

The drive to Siesta Key took an hour and a half. We ate dinner by candlelight in an intimate restaurant on the water. Our conversation began as two lovers enjoying each other's company, but it eventually gravitated back to the case. In our marriage we shared everything and often used each other as sounding boards for new ideas as well as problems we needed solved.

It was very quiet at Sally Keith's beach house. I moved the crime scene tape aside to unlock the door. I flicked on the light switch, and Buck and I made our way to Sally's bedroom. I opened the door to the closet, withdrew a large man's jacket, and placed it on the bed. Several short, orange hairs clung to the fabric. I pulled them off and placed them in an evidence bag.

Buck picked up the jacket from the bed where I had laid it. Out of habit he searched the pockets. From the inside breast pocket, he pulled a small wad of pink paper. It was a crumpled phone message slip that obviously had been in the pocket for a long time and probably had been through a wash cycle. He smoothed the paper, read it, scowled a bit, and handed it to me. My face fell as I read the note. It went into another evidence bag.

The ride home was quiet; I was lost in thought. Buck knew I needed time to digest what we had found. The evidence we'd gathered had dampened the happy mood of the evening.

"C'mon, honey. Let's take a little walk before bed," he suggested when we arrived at the ranch.

We headed down a dirt path alongside the nearest pasture. The night was peaceful and quiet, and Buck held my hand as we walked. I enjoyed his touch. After half an hour, we stopped. He held me in his arms and tenderly kissed my lips. I felt the heat of his passion building.

"Let's go back to the house," he whispered.

Chapter 15

Early Friday Morning

At six the next morning, I arrived at the forensics lab. I told the tech on duty that I wanted the prints on the condom boxes and the bottle of Aramis analyzed immediately and that results had to be ready in thirty minutes. I handed him a fingerprint card for comparison and stood in the lab while he worked. The prints found on one box, the bottle, and the card all matched. Next I gave him the two bags that contained orange hair samples—the one from my clothing and the one from the man's jacket in Sally Keith's closet. Though a definite match couldn't be made without chemical testing, the length and color patterns were identical. I asked the tech to compare the samples with the hairs found in Sally Keith's car, but I already had the evidence I needed.

At 8:00 a.m. I walked into Captain Jackson Stone's office, closed the door, and plunked the bags containing the cologne, condoms, pink message slip, and cat hair on his desk.

"We have a problem, Jack." I outlined the results of the fingerprint comparison and the cat-hair analysis and showed him the pink message slip that read, "Sheriff's Office" across the top. Jack's face fell.

"What do you want me to do, Bernie?"

"Get him in here."

**

Ike was surprised to see me in Jack's office. His eyes darted to the bags of evidence I'd placed on Jack's desk, and his entire body slumped.

"Why didn't you tell me, Ike?" I asked quietly.

"I wanted to find her killer. I wanted to be there when we had enough proof to convict him."

"Do you realize the suspect list now includes you?" I asked him. "You're the big guy. You're her *second* boyfriend. In addition you've compromised the integrity of this office by allowing me to place you on the investigating team. Whatever we do now will be even more closely scrutinized than before."

"I know, and I'm sorry. I just loved her so much that I couldn't help it. I didn't kill her."

"You'll be on paid leave until I find undeniable proof that you did *not* do this." I paused and exchanged glances with Jack. "Was the baby yours?" I asked Ike.

"I'm pretty sure it wasn't." His eyes drifted to the box of condoms on Jack's desk. "We always were very careful."

"For crying out loud, Ike," I said as I tossed the bag containing the pink message slip in front of him. "Why didn't you just write it on the wall—'Sarasota County Sheriff's Office Detective Involved in Murder'?"

Jack tapped his desk with his index finger. "Star and piece on the desk. Now."

Ike placed the objects on the desk then turned to face me. "I'm really sorry, Bernie. I used poor judgment. I certainly never meant to hurt you...or the office."

I was too angry to respond, so he got up and left the room.

"Damn, damn, damn," I swore and pounded my fist on Jack's desk. "Get Tom in here."

As Tom stepped into the room, his expression was one of apprehension. I knew my eyes were still shooting lightning bolts. He hesitated as he crossed the threshold then eased into the chair. I outlined what had happened.

"Is there any way we can put a positive spin on this, Tom? I don't want the headlines to read 'Sheriff Appoints Killer to Investigate His Own Crime.'" I placed my thumb and forefinger on the bridge of my nose and pressed. I could feel a headache building.

"It's probably worse than that, ma'am," he responded.

"What could possibly be worse than that?" I shouted.

Both Tom and Jack winced at the volume and intensity of my words.

I closed my eyes for a moment wishing that I had been able to control the outburst. "I'm sorry, Tom," I said calmly. "You did nothing wrong. I apologize for being so vocal."

"No offense taken, ma'am. What I meant was that there's more to worry about."

"Great! What?"

Tom squirmed in his seat. He opened his mouth to speak then closed it without saying anything. He thought for a moment, and then dropped a bombshell of words. "Ike's been in love with you for years."

"What? What did you say?" I felt the blood drain from my face as I began to comprehend the severity of the situation.

"He has a puppy-dog crush on you," Tom said. "It's been like that for years. I know you've never noticed, but most everyone else has."

I exhaled deeply and sat back in my chair. "No, I never noticed." I allowed a little smile to touch my lips. "I had a crush on him in junior high, but he never noticed me. If we don't keep this from getting out of hand, the press will have Ike and me as lovers planning the murder together. Any ideas?

Jack, can you think of any graceful way to get us out of this?"

Jack's face was grave. His lips were drawn into a straight line; his jaw was clenched; and his normally smiling brown eyes were cold and dark. "No, there's nothing good about this situation," he said grimly. It won't be easy to extract ourselves without some dirt rubbing off on all of us."

"We should do another printed press release with limited information," Tom suggested. "I'll write one for you to review. Do we have any new details I can give them, other than this one?"

"Until this morning all the evidence pointed to Danny Dean. He had motive and opportunity, and he was caught at the scene. We had nothing to dispute that until the identity of her second boyfriend became evident. My gut tells me Danny didn't do it. I don't see Ike as a killer, but he hasn't exactly been forthcoming with us. I know nothing new other than his entry as suspect number two."

"I'll do one of those 'Investigation Continues' boilerplate releases. If the evidence leads to Dean, let's leave it at that for now." Tom rose from the chair, excused himself, and left the room.

"Sally Keith's mother will be here in the next couple of days," I said to Jack. "I hope the morning's newspaper doesn't print any headlines that'll make her visit worse than it has to be."

"Do you want someone to replace Ike?" he asked.

"No. If someone else comes in, it'll draw attention to the fact that he's been replaced. I'll work the case by myself for a while."

Chapter 16

Friday Afternoon

I returned to my office, closed the door, and drew the drapes across the large window that overlooked the business office. I needed to think. The bottom drawer of my desk made a great footrest, so I pulled it out, placed my feet on the edge, and leaned back in the high-backed leather chair. Dottie had placed a stack of pink message slips on my desk, and I rifled through them. Amid the callback requests from the newspaper office and television stations were messages from Alice Keith and Doc. Both informed me that they had arranged for the identification of Sally Keith's body at two today. I glanced at my watch. I had a little more than three hours until that meeting. I needed to organize the information I hoped to obtain from Mrs. Keith. I was a list maker. Compiling things into lists helped me think and organize, so I pulled out a yellow legal pad and jotted down information.

Who might have killed Sally Keith? So far there were three possible suspects: Danny Dean, Kelly Dean, and Isaac "Ike" McDuffie.

Who had the opportunity? Danny had been found with the murder weapon in his hand. Had he fired it a moment before in a fit of anger? Kelly said she had been at home on the phone. Phone records would verify that, but she still would have had time to get to the Sally's house to pull the trigger. I'd been so angry with Ike that I hadn't bothered to ask whether he had an alibi. If he did, I hoped it was ironclad.

What was the motive? Both Danny and Ike had proclaimed their love for Sally. Many a murder had been committed because of love triangles. Kelly Dean hated Sally, but was her hate strong enough to make her kill? Danny Dean had his fingers in lots of things. Had he done something to someone powerful who wanted him out of the way? But why would that someone kill Sally? If anyone wanted Danny out of the way, why not just kill Danny?

Too much was missing. I needed to learn more about Sally Keith's life and her past. Perhaps her mother could shed some light on these things. Maybe she knew of a problem in her daughter's life that could have resulted in her murder. I planned to ask her after she identified her daughter's body today. It was unkind to question her at this time, but I had to do it.

I sat up and glanced at the blotter-style calendar that covered half my desk. Then I circled the day Sally Keith had been killed: early Tuesday morning. I marked a little X on Wednesday and Thursday and placed the pencil on Friday—today. Printed next to the day and date was a thin crescent-shaped icon. Tonight was the night of the new moon! This would be the perfect opportunity to see what had happened on Sally Keith's property during the ceremony Lenore had mentioned. I shouldn't go out there alone, and I no longer had a partner on this case, but I did have a husband who was a law enforcement officer.

He answered his private line on the second ring. The sound of his deep, resonant voice always gave me butterflies inside. I found myself smiling.

"Hello, my love," I said. "Are you doing anything tonight?"

"Not particularly. I was hoping my wife might be available to go shopping for our Christmas tree."

"Uh-oh. I know we need to do that, but I was wondering if you'd go on another working date with me tonight."

"What's going on, Bernie?"

I told Buck about shelving Ike and about the new moon ceremony.

"Witches?" he asked.

"Good witches supposedly," I said with a laugh. "There's only one new moon each month, so I only have one opportunity to go out there. I need to see if any of these people could have had anything to do with Sally Keith's murder."

"I'll go with you, honey. I don't want you going out there alone. Pick you up at seven."

"We may be outside for several hours, so I'm going to wear my jumpsuit and boots."

"Good idea. Bring your night-vision binoculars too. That rock jetty extends into the water. Do you know when the moon rises tonight?"

"No, but I can find out. Can we have a dinner date before we get down to business?"

I pictured the smile on Buck's face. "Sure, darlin'. See you tonight."

I made a call to the television weather office. Moonrise was at 10:47 tonight, so Buck and I would have to be in place before then. I heard a knock at my door as I hung up the phone. I looked up to see James's face in the glass and motioned for him to come in.

"Time for lunch, babe."

"Not now, James. I have things to do."

"I have a bit of news that might interest you."

"I only need good news right now," I said with a sigh.

"Oh, this is good, but I'll only tell you over lunch," he said with a broad grin.

**

James and I squeezed into a tiny booth at Yoder's Lunch Counter. The Yoder family had relocated to Sarasota from Ohio years ago. They were well known as farmers, and had expanded the family business to include a restaurant. Yoder's featured home-style foods, pies and baked goods. They used fresh ingredients, not restaurant service packaged items. The vegetables were grown on the Yoder farm; the cooks and bakers were wives of the Yoder men; and servers were Yoder children, grandchildren, nieces and nephews.

"Give, James," I said as the young waitress left to place our orders with the cook. We had both ordered the blue plate special – pork chops smothered in onion gravy, mashed potatoes, and steamed broccoli. The pie of the day was baked peach, so we ordered that too.

"I heard about Ike," he began.

"You must be slipping. That news is more than four hours old, and you just heard about it?"

"No, I just wanted to get you to eat lunch."

I exhaled deeply and leaned back in the booth. "You don't have any news, do you?" I felt totally deflated.

"Oh, ye of little faith," he said then laughed one of his deep, evil-sounding laughs. He was going to make me wait for whatever tidbit he planned to divulge.

The server brought our meals and we ate hungrily. I was still waiting for James to continue, but he was purposely silent.

I rolled my eyes. "Are you enjoying this?"

"Oh, yes, I am. Here it is: Ike can't be the murderer."

I sat up quickly and leaned forward to look him directly in the eyes. Our faces were inches apart in the narrow space. "How can you be sure?"

"Because he was in Tampa."

"Don't stretch this out sentence by sentence, James. Just tell me."

"You know Larry, the day shift patrol supervisor, is getting married next weekend, right?" I nodded. "Well, a bunch of us crammed into Eddie's van Monday evening, kidnapped Larry, and drove along Dale Mabry Highway to hit the titty bars."

"Always a classy group."

"Yeah, well, Ike went with us. We didn't get home until after two in the morning, so he couldn't have been there at midnight to kill that girl."

"Thank God," I murmured.

"Are you going to reinstate him?"

"He still needs some kind of reprimand for not having told me about it. What he did could have damaged us all."

James patted his lips with the napkin. "Put him on a desk for a week. Those guys hate that."

"OK. Maybe. I need to meet the victim's mother at the morgue at two. After that will you go with me to Ike's apartment? I don't want to go there alone."

"Sure. In fact I'll take you to the morgue. We'll go there after lunch."

James and I arrived at the health department building with little time to spare. I expected Sally Keith's mother, Alice, to be a voluptuous blonde, like her daughter, but was surprised to find a petite, fifty-year-old woman with short, curly, brown hair waiting outside the ME's office. Make up was absent from her pale, tear-stained face. She was dressed in traditional mourning clothing: black suit, tailored white blouse, and simple black pumps. She wore no jewelry except for an unadorned wedding band. I introduced James and myself and offered our sympathies for her loss. She swallowed hard before attempting to speak. Her voice shook with emotion as she thanked me.

At precisely 2:00 p.m., Doc's door opened, and he emerged with several other staff members. The group made its way to the hall, and Doc stopped in front of Mrs. Keith and offered his sympathy. The four of us—Doc, Mrs. Keith, James, and I—rode the elevator to the bottom floor, where our nostrils were assaulted by the foul smell that forever lingered there. I immediately regretted eating lunch beforehand and desperately fought back a wave of nausea.

"Sheriff," said Doc, "you need to go back upstairs. Lieutenant Kenwood can represent your office. We'll be back up in a few moments." He saw my hesitation, so he gently held my elbow and escorted me back into the elevator. "Please do this," he continued. He smiled fondly, and I nodded my consent.

True to Doc's word, the trio was back in his office in ten minutes. Mrs. Keith was visibly shaken. James disappeared for a moment and returned with a cup of water and a canned cola, which he placed on the conference room table in front of her. She smiled her gratitude and sipped the water.

"Mrs. Keith," I began, "I realize you've endured a horrible ordeal. I can't imagine how awful you must feel right now. If there were a way to avoid asking you these questions, I'd do it, but the longer we wait, the colder the trail will get. We all want to find out who murdered your daughter. Is there anything you know that might help us? Can you tell us about Sally?"

Mrs. Keith was silent for a moment. Then she heaved a sigh and spoke in a quiet voice. "Sally always had a knack for finding trouble wherever she went. This was true even when she was little. In grade school she picked fights with the other children; in junior high she hung around with the shadier kids. By the time she reached high school, she was entrenched in the drug scene – from marijuana to LSD. She did it all. When she entered nursing school, I was thrilled. It seemed she was finally turning her life around. She moved here, found a job, and bought a house. Everything seemed to be going in the right direction. Now I suspect this new normalcy was simply a ruse. Her career choice may have been made to further her advancement in the drug culture. A nurse has access to drugs, and there's always someone who will buy them. Her move to Florida may just have been a step up the ladder."

The woman stopped speaking and collected her thoughts. A small smile appeared on her lips, and her grey eyes had a faraway look. "I remember the day we got Sally. She was only a couple of weeks old. My husband, Sam, and I adopted her through Catholic Social Services. She was so tiny and fragile. Sam made a little joke that day. It was funny then but not so funny now. He said, 'It's hard to believe, but even criminals start out like this.' He would have been horrified by some of the things Sally did."

I looked across the table at Doc and James. Both were engrossed in Mrs. Keith's story.

Mrs. Keith stopped speaking again, and her eyes welled with tears. She pulled a tissue from her purse and dabbed them away. "Sam was chief of police in our town when we were married. After a couple of years, it was obvious we weren't going to have any children, so we adopted Sally, as I told you. He adored her, and as she grew, she became very attached to him. She followed him around wherever he went. He was a big man. He soon became aware that he shouldn't stop so suddenly when he was moving around the house, because his little shadow would run into him and fall down."

A smile covered Doc's freckled face. I imagine he was thinking of a similar memory about one of his own children.

The poor woman laughed at the memory, and then she continued. "Today is the anniversary of his death," she said. "It's been twenty years now. Sally was in first grade and doing well in school. She was such a happy little girl then. Sam had gone to the bank, as he often did in the mornings. His high school buddy was the bank manager, and they went out for coffee a couple of times each week. My husband had no idea the bank was being robbed when he walked through the door. The thugs gunned him down on the spot. That was our worst Christmas ever."

And now her daughter dies at Christmastime, I thought. *Everyone else is enjoying the holiday, but all she has to remember is tragedy.*

"Things were tough for us after that," she said. "I had to go to work and leave Sally with a sitter each afternoon after school. Sally was devastated and was silent for more than a month after Sam's death. She retreated into herself and emerged as an angry child and became an even angrier teen. After moving here she seemed happier. It was as if she could finally leave all those bad memories behind." The woman's body shook with emotion, and sobs racked her small frame.

I got up from my chair and did something I knew was very unprofessional. I knelt in front of Mrs. Keith's chair and wrapped my arms around her. She laid her head on my shoulder and cried.

After several minutes, she finally lifted her head. "I'm sorry, Sheriff," she said. "I'm not handling this very well."

"Mrs. Keith, is there anyone who can stay with you today?" I asked her, still kneeling.

"No. I don't know anyone in town."

I turned to Doc. "Is there a bereavement counselor who can help Mrs. Keith today?"

"Let me make a call," he said.

After a few minutes, we heard a knock at the door. A kind-looking woman entered. She smiled at all of us, nodded to Doc, and introduced herself to Mrs. Keith. The two left Doc's office, and James and I stood up to leave.

"Doc, did you get the blood toxin report yet?" I asked.

"It came back this morning. I'll send a copy to you for the file."

"Any drugs present?"

"Not a thing. She was clean."

I knit my brows in concentration. "I wonder whether she really had turned her life around. If so, that in itself could be a motive for murder."

Chapter 17

Friday Afternoon

James and I were silent as we rode to Ike's apartment. He parked the cruiser in a guest slot and turned off the engine.

"It's a bit unsettling, isn't it?" I said.

"Always is," he responded.

"I'm going to give McDuffie some work to do on the case," I said as we made our way across the parking lot toward Ike's apartment building.

"Are you sure that's wise?" James cautioned.

"If he loved her as much as he said he did, he'll certainly put forth his best effort. I'll make sure he does all his investigation from a desk, though."

Ike looked terrible. His face appeared drawn, and his skin was pale. He was silent as he opened the door to let us in.

"McDuffie, you're back on the case," I said. His face brightened a bit, but he still said nothing. "Lieutenant Kenwood told me about the foray to Tampa on Monday night, so we've eliminated you as a suspect. But you'll do all your investigating from your desk—no street work. Understand? You'll start Monday morning."

"I can start right now, ma'am."

"It's late Friday afternoon. Most of the things I'm going to ask you to do would best be accomplished during normal business hours, but if you want to start now, that's fine with me. Take some notes."

Ike grabbed a notebook and pencil, and we all sat down in the living room. Skitzo jumped into my lap, settled himself, and fell asleep.

"First, we need to investigate Sally's finances," I told him. "Check her bank records and wage records. Find out how much she paid for her house, the payment arrangements, and who the seller was. See if she owned anything else of value and how she paid for it. Second, do background checks on everyone in the ER on the three-to-eleven shift, including the doctors. Contact the hospital administrator for the personnel files, but don't rely on everything you find there. Do your own investigation."

Ike was making a simple checklist on the notepad. He was having difficulty writing as fast as I spoke, so I paused for a moment. I contemplated telling him about a possible drug connection in the ER, but thought better of it. If there were such a thing, he would find it.

"Third, make a photocopy of that book of tag numbers the security guard kept."

"What book is that?" James asked.

"The security guard at the condo to the south of Sally Keith's house logged the tag numbers of vehicles passing by the guard shack," I explained.

"Is that something the condo management asked him to do?" asked James with a puzzled look on his face.

"No," said Ike. "The guy is weird and that is one of his hobbies."

James raised his eyebrows, shrugged, and settled back on the couch.

I continued with instructions to Ike. "Find out the tag numbers for every vehicle Kelly and Danny Dean owned and the tag number of his county car. Highlight those on the pages from the book. Then highlight the tag numbers for the vehicles you drive, including the department cars. Finally, highlight any tag number that appears regularly on that list and find out who owns the vehicle."

I was on quite a roll; I took a deep breath and continued. "Fourth, check the Deans' finances, both together and separately. Find everything they own—property, stocks, bonds, vehicles, boats, time-shares, everything. Fifth, find out whether Danny Dean had any business with the two commissioners who posted his bond. Something's shady there. The best under-the-table money is available from developers, so my guess is that some kind of land deal was hushed up. Maybe they were meeting outside the parameters of the Sunshine Law and he knows about it."

"OK, got it," said Ike. "I won't let you down, Bernie."

"Hey," warned James.

"I won't let you down, Sheriff," he corrected.

Back in the car I said, "James, check into Ike's finances. You know the routine. Check his phone records too. Discreetly, of course."

"Is he still a suspect?"

"He couldn't have killed her, but wouldn't I be derelict in my duty if I didn't investigate his involvement just the same?"

Chapter 18

Friday Evening

Buck appeared at my office door at seven o'clock. He was dressed, as was I, in navy coveralls, black military boots, a hip holster, and a navy cap with a sheriff insignia. He ducked his head automatically as he entered the room. At six foot six, he had learned about nonstandard door heights. I rose as he entered and fell into his arms in an instant. He held me close as we kissed in greeting. I grabbed my purse and jacket, slid a flashlight into my belt, and locked the door behind us.

Buck raised an eyebrow. "Where's your vest, Bernie?"

"In my locker."

"We need to go back for it."

"I can barely breathe with that thing on. I've… outgrown it."

"I can't believe that you are going to violate your own policy. I know you require that your line officers wear them."

I sighed. Buck was right. I was acting foolishly. I had made the rule for a reason. I retrieved the vest, pulled its Velcro straps tightly across my torso, and we left the building.

We ate a quick meal at Happyland, one of the oldest restaurants on Siesta Key. The eatery opened in the late 1950s and held the distinction of having the first salad bar in Sarasota. A modern version of the bar spanned an entire wall of the main dining room. My mother always had enjoyed the excellent variety of pickled vegetables, and I navigated toward the same items. Happyland's delicious fried seafood followed the salads. I felt drowsy after the big meal. *Sure hope I don't fall asleep during the surveillance,* I thought. *Buck never would let me hear the end of it.*

We secreted Buck's car on the opposite side of the street from Sally's house in the shadows of a stand of Australian pines. When the security guard was occupied, we moved across the condo driveway to the fence. I showed Buck the secret opening before we moved to the westernmost section of the fence where the bushes were thick enough to conceal us. It wasn't long before we heard the raspy scrape of wood against wood. I smelled her before I saw her; Lenore tiptoed along the path with a trail of Patchouli incense following her. She stopped abruptly to look back over her shoulder and remained glued to the spot. Her head tilted this way and that, as if she were listening to something. *She can't possibly hear our hearts beating, can she?* I wondered. After this moment's hesitation, she grinned and continued toward the gulf to the rock jetty that extended from the beach. A breeze caught her gauzy costume. It billowed gracefully as she stood on a high point looking over the water.

Quiet whispers in the dark alerted us to the appearance of more people. A small cluster of women moved briskly past us and joined Lenore on the rocks. The group grew gradually in size until thirty-some souls stood talking and laughing on the rocks. Eerie strains of music began quietly and grew louder as time passed; I identified a violin, a flute, and a small drum. Figures moved in unison in a circle, and a high-pitched voice sang in a language I didn't recognize. Buck took out a pair of night-vision binoculars from the case that hung around his neck. When he trained his view to the jetty, a small whistle of air escaped between his teeth.

"Those women are all naked out there," he said. "It's *not* a very pretty sight. Oh, wait a minute…wow!

"What?" I whispered as I fitted my binoculars to my eyes. Three shapely, young, buxom women had moved to the center of the group. The others sat down on the rocks, and the three danced sensually to the eerie music. As the new moon appeared in the night sky, the pace of the music and dancing intensified. More voices rose in song. The featured dancers became more animated, and their bodies jiggled and bounced to the beat of the drum.

"I hope you aren't enjoying this too much," I said to Buck.

"You know I only have eyes for you, darlin'," he said with a snicker, but he didn't lower the glasses from his eyes.

My ear caught the slight raspy sound again. A male figure made his way noiselessly down the path, across the yard, and up to the deck of Sally Keith's house. He was dressed all in black. He settled himself in the shadows of the eaves, and I saw a flash of light reflecting on glass. The man was watching the ceremony with night-vision glasses, just as we were.

Tiny pinpricks of light appeared one by one on the rocks. Someone was lighting candles. It looked as if stars had fallen from the heavens onto the dark rocks of the jetty. A breeze from the gulf carried the scent of lighter fluid to my nostrils, and a whisk of flame appeared in the center of the circle of women. They had made a fire on the rocks. Combustible material was gradually added. Soon a roaring inferno reached skyward amid the dancers. It seemed as if they were setting the stage for something. From time to time, someone tossed objects into the fire, causing the flames to spark. I yawned and shook my head in an effort to throw off the drowsiness I felt after eating a big meal. I was about to suggest that we pack it in for the night, but Buck was still watching the scene intently.

"There are exactly thirty-six people out there, Bernie," he whispered. "I've counted over and over, which is no easy task with them bouncing around like that. I've heard that thirteen is a magic number in witchcraft. Thirty-nine is a multiple of thirteen. So I believe three people are missing. Maybe the group is waiting for the last three to arrive before they finish the ceremony. It's eleven forty-five. Let's stay until midnight to see what happens. I imagine midnight is a magic time for them."

"How do you know that?"

"Just guessing."

As Buck predicted, at eleven fifty-five, three more figures appeared on the beach. They seemed to materialize out of nowhere. Suddenly I saw movement on the deck of the house. The man in black had seen the figures too. The three newcomers were male and also nude; they joined the young women near the fire. Members of the outer circle placed their hands on the six central figures. When they stepped away, the six shimmered in the firelight as if coated in gold. The outer circle settled down again as the six danced to an eerie tune. After the touching and caressing by the women, the three males were fully aroused. At the stroke of midnight, the music stopped abruptly, and the three couples dropped to the ground. It was obvious what they were doing.

"I daresay this is the climax," I said with a snicker. "Let's get back to the car so we can see where they go after this."

"Hey, where's the peeper?" Buck asked.

I turned around to see that the man in black was gone. He had been there moments before, but now the deck was empty.

"We'll have to pick a group to follow. They arrived a few at a time, so they must have used multiple vehicles," I said as we made our way back to the street. The guard wasn't in his shack, so Buck and I crossed the street and got into our car.

"That was the weirdest thing I've ever seen," said Buck. "Do they do this every month?"

"I have no idea. Rituals are usually repeated on some schedule, so I suppose they do it every month. They do something for the full moon too. I bet that's a doozy. Hold on. Here they come."

The witches appeared happy as they loaded into a collection of cars and vans. Then they sped away in a caravan toward town.

"I wonder if they're all going to the same place."

"Could be," Buck said. "Look. The guard just entered the shack. Think he could be the peeper?"

"Maybe. There's something odd about him. He lied about his background, which makes anything he says suspect. I don't trust him. It would be easy to operate as a cat burglar under the guise of being a security guard. He seems sleazy enough to be doing something shady."

Buck and I followed the little procession through town to a small apartment complex. The entire group parked in the lot. Lights were ablaze in all the windows of the building except one on the bottom floor. The lively crowd returned to their apartments but reappeared moments later to make their ways to a separate building near the pool. We left the car and headed for what was probably the rec room. A large sign, lettered in black and silver, announced the night's activity: HIVE MEETING TONIGHT.

"What's a hive?" I whispered.

"Don't know," said Buck. "It might be a good idea to call for backup. Lots of people are in there. They seem harmless, but we have no idea what they're doing."

"You're right. Give me your keys. I'll call in. Then I'll see why one apartment is dark over there."

After using Buck's radio to call for a patrol car, I eased my way along the apartment wall up to the dark window. The sudden appearance of a face at the glass made me jump back with a start. Seconds later a door opened, and a tiny old woman ventured out. Her pale skin was so thin it appeared to be transparent. Permed white hair surrounded her frail face. She wore a thin robe over her full-length nightgown.

"Are you here to arrest them?" she asked.

"Why should I do that, ma'am?"

"They do scary things. Something must be illegal."

I remembered something I'd heard the day I'd first gone to Sally Keith's house to begin the investigation. "Are you Mable?"

She shrank back in fear. "How did you know that?" she asked in a quivering voice. "Are you one of them?"

"No, I'm a sheriff, and your friend Rose Ermine at Phoenix Sun Condominiums mentioned your name. She said you lived in a place full of witches."

"Oh, thank goodness," she said, as relief swept over her delicate features. "That's what they are—witches. There are three covens here. A coven is thirteen witches, you know. Each coven has a high priest and priestess. Thirty-eight witches live here. One lives in that condo you mentioned. I'm the only one here who isn't a witch. The hive meeting is tonight."

"What's a hive?"

"A group of covens. In this case there are three."

"You know a lot about them."

"I ought to. I've lived here five years, and I've been scared every day. One time I found a dead chicken hanging in my kitchen. Another time someone released dozens of crickets in my bathroom. Sometimes voices come through my air-conditioning vents."

"Did you call the sheriff's office?"

"No, since I can't prove anything, it would only make things worse."

"Why don't you move out?"

She shrugged. "I don't have the money. You need all kinds of deposits to start in a new place." She stopped speaking as Buck joined us. The little lady's eyes looked up his tall frame. "My goodness, you're a big fellow. Handsome too. My husband, Morris, was handsome like you. I miss him so."

"Thank you, ma'am," Buck said with a smile. "Backup is here. They'll cover the rear and side doors if we need them."

After Mable retreated into her apartment, Buck and I quietly headed back to the rec room. Buck knocked on the door. "Sheriff's office. Open the door, please."

The door opened slowly to reveal a man dressed in a black cloak. "May I help you?" he asked in a tone that reminded me of Bela Lugosi in the old Dracula movies.

We identified ourselves. "We need to ask some questions regarding a murder that took place early Tuesday morning," I began.

"Who was murdered?"

"A young woman named Sally Keith. May we come in?"

The man moved aside as he gestured for us to enter. Lighting was subdued inside the rec room. Tables were arranged as if for a party. A buffet table against one wall held dishes of food, plates and cutlery. In the center was a round black cauldron from which steam was rising. Punch cups were arranged around its base. Some people were seated at the tables, but most were milling about or conversing in groups of two or three. All eyes fell upon us, and the room grew silent. Then a soft voice broke the quiet.

"Sheriff, I'm so glad you could come to our meeting," said Lenore. The frail lady moved so smoothly across the floor that it seemed she was floating above its surface. She lifted my hand and shook it gently.

I heard a note of surprise in the cloaked man's voice. "Did you invite her here, Lenore?"

"Yes, Damien. She was invited to attend this meeting. I asked her to join our group as well." When she placed her palm on my midsection, I took a step back. "This beauty would bring new life to a coven."

"We're here to ask questions tonight. Did anyone know the blond woman who owned the land you traverse on the way to the jetty?"

My eyes roamed the faces of the assembly. No one acknowledged knowing Sally Keith; in fact no one spoke at all. I spotted a knowing smirk on the face of a man in the back of the room, but he said nothing.

"Do you have a membership roster?" I asked.

"Of course, dear." A small blue-haired lady stepped forward and handed me a piece of yellowed parchment hand-lettered in black ink. "I'm the secretary," she said proudly. "Our membership list is always up to date."

"Who are the coven leaders?"

Six people raised their hands.

"Can you give me your names?"

As each spoke a name in turn, I checked it off the list. The smirking man in the back of the hall was Marcus Sherlock, and his wife, the high priestess, was named Rowena. They would be the subjects of surveillance tomorrow, and they would be at the top of the list for background checks. I wondered if the names on the membership roster were real. Many of them looked like they were lifted from the pages of a movie script. If they were aliases, it would make our work more difficult.

I made a mental note to check the condo guard's notebook to see whether any vehicle tag numbers belonging to the Sherlocks, or whatever their names were, appeared on nights other than those of the moon ceremonies.

**

I dozed a little on the drive home but woke fully when we turned off the paved highway.

"Did you see the guy in the back?" asked Buck.

"Yes. I figured you probably noticed him too."

"He knows something about Sally Keith. He may not have anything to do with her murder, but he didn't own up to knowing her. He might bear some watching. I could say he gave me a funny feeling, but the whole pack of them did that."

"Yeah, me too. I'll revisit this group in the next few days."

"Please don't go over there alone, Bernie. These people aren't right."

I smiled slightly. "I'll assign a couple of detectives to watch them for a while." I felt my smile grow into a grin. "You might want to follow up with old Mable. She was warm for your form, in case you hadn't noticed. Should I be jealous?"

"Humph," Buck snorted, but he had no retort.

Chapter 19

Saturday Morning

The next morning Buck drove me to my office since we'd left my car in town after our midnight adventure. In the detective division, I assigned a team to watch Mr. and Mrs. Sherlock. I gave Ike the hive membership list and asked him to check everyone for aliases and priors. I also asked him to obtain tag numbers for comparison against the guard's list. Most of Ike's work had to be done on weekdays, but he could start on the background checks today.

I called the phone number of the hotel where Sally Keith's mother was staying, only to find she had checked out. I supposed she had no reason to stay. Sarasota is a beautiful place, but she wasn't likely to see it as such.

There were two key items on my agenda. First, I wanted to revisit the crime scene alone. Second, I'd call some of the people in Sally Keith's address book. Since today was Saturday, I hoped to find a few of them at home. I decided to go to the beach first and make the calls later.

Traffic on theTrail was heavy. Winter visitors puttered down the highway at thirty miles per hour. Frustrated residents were forced to join the mass of vehicles. Two bridges led across the bay to Siesta Key. The most commonly traveled was the Stickney Point Road Bridge, the newer and larger one. The older bridge was accessed via Siesta Drive. I chose the older two-lane structure in hopes that it would be less traveled today, but cars were bumper to bumper across the entire span. Once in line I had little choice but to creep along with the rest of them.

As I sat in the traffic, my mind wandered to my childhood years. My family had gone on beach outings almost every Sunday. We always packed a picnic lunch of sandwiches, hard-boiled eggs, chips, Kool-Aid for me, and beer for my parents. We'd leave early in the morning after returning home from 6:15 a.m. Mass. We drove across a rickety wooden bridge that had spanned the water before the concrete structure replaced it. We parked in the shade provided by huge Australian pines at Beach Access Number Three. My mother always brought an old sheet to place on the sand in the sun and an old quilt or blanket to place on the ground under the trees. The trees dropped little spine-covered seedpods that were uncomfortable to lie on. The blanket offered some protection from the prickly pods.

As soon as my dad turned off the engine, I'd jump out and run to the water. "Be sure to shuffle your feet for the rays and look for sharks," my mother would say as I ran across the sand.

Stingrays often gather under the sand in the shallow water. They're skittish creatures that avoid human contact unless they're scared, surprised, or trod upon. When entering the water from an uninhabited beach, we always shuffled our feet in the sandy shallows to scare away the rays. I knew to do this, but my mother reminded me to do it every time. Everyone also knew sharks cruised off the edge of the sandbar. They usually didn't cross the bar into shallow water, but on rare occasions we'd see them. Before swimming I always scanned the waters, looking for the tips of their fins.

Each Sunday many families were regular visitors to Beach Access Number Three. Those who arrived early could park in the shade of the trees. Others had to park in the blazing sun in the residential area across the street. Several of our friends would arrive early, as we did, secure a primo shady space, and set up for the day. Most of our friends went to the same church as we did, and the children of those families attended St. Martha's Parochial School, where I went to school as well. We frolicked in the sparkling waters of the Gulf of Mexico, built sandcastles, searched for seashells, and walked for miles along the shore. I remember our friend Vivian who walked down the beach on her hands instead of her feet. I always wished I could do that.

I was still smiling at the memory as I pulled into Sally Keith's driveway. To my surprise, a cream colored Ford was parked near the house. The tag indicated it was a rental. I stopped some distance from the car and called in my location, as well as the vehicle tag number, to dispatch. I approached the house cautiously, but as I drew near, I saw Alice Keith leaning against one of the pilings on the gulf side of the house. She was staring out at the water and hadn't heard me approach. I didn't want to startle her, so I quietly spoke her name. Her head snapped toward the sound of my voice. A look of relief crossed her face when she recognized me. I walked across the sandy yard and joined her.

"I figured I wouldn't be breaking any laws by standing here, Sheriff."

"As long as you just stand here, there's no problem. You know you can't cross the crime scene tape, don't you?"

"I know," she said sadly. "I just wanted to see the place before I left town."

"We'll remove the tape soon, and then you'll be able to go inside. I assume the property will be yours now."

"I have no idea, Sheriff. I don't know if Sally had a will. She never mentioned it to me. We hadn't been very close for many years."

"So she didn't confide in you about any friends or lovers?"

"I'm afraid not. Sally did come home for Thanksgiving. I hoped we might warm to each other, but I think the rift between us was too wide to be mended. It seems I know very little about my daughter." A tear slowly made its way down Mrs. Keith's drawn face, but she made no move to wipe it away. "I need to make my way to the airport. With all this traffic on the roads, I'll barely make it on time. Find my daughter's murderer, Sheriff. She deserves that justice."

Without another word, she turned and headed to the car and down the drive. As I watched Mrs. Keith's rental car disappear among the tall Australian pines that lined the driveway, I became aware of a familiar scent wafting on the breeze. I turned around sharply to find Lenore standing behind me.

"Sheriff Davis, how good to see you again," she said in a husky whisper. The soft lines of her gauzy caftan and flowing hair gave her an ethereal aura. If not for the scent, I might have thought she was a figment of my imagination.

"Not a great idea to sneak up on a law enforcement officer, Lenore."

"I mean no harm, Sheriff," she whispered again.

"You realize, of course, that this is a crime scene. You shouldn't be wandering around here."

"I'm not wandering aimlessly. I saw your car in the driveway, and I came over to see you."

"Did you remember something you wanted to tell me?" I asked her.

"Oh, no, dear. I told you everything I know. I came for another purpose."

"And what's that?"

"I wanted to give you this amulet I made for you." Lenore offered me a black, silken, cord necklace. Attached to the end was a small burgundy chiffon bag that was tied with a tiny piece of pink satin ribbon. "Please take it," she implored.

"What's in here?"

"A few talismans for protection. They'll help should you find yourself in harm's way."

"What *exactly* is in the bag?" I asked again.

"Bits of this and that—the dried leaf of the althea plant, a nip of ague root, toad flax, a bud of the balm of Gilead, some dark-red bloodroot, bark of cinchona, a peony seed, and dried resin of a dragon's blood palm."

"Why do you want to give this to me?"

"In case you need it, my dear," she said sweetly. She smiled wistfully, but her eyes pleaded with me to take the packet.

In college I had studied a little about herbs and plants. Many plants are toxic, and some are thought to have healing properties. The Gypsies I had known since childhood had made me aware of the powers of potions and spells. The items in the amulet were things I'd heard of but never had seen. I often could sense danger from people, but I had no bad feeling about this woman. I took the amulet, placed it around my neck, and tucked it into my blouse.

Lenore looked relieved. "You'll be grateful for its protection," she whispered.

"How so, Lenore?"

"On your travels, my dear," she whispered as a soft smile crossed her face. With that she turned and made her way across the sand to the fence. She disappeared into the bushes, and I heard the rasp of the fence board.

Chapter 20

Saturday Afternoon

I didn't know what I would find in Sally Keith's house. The forensics team already had searched the place and gathered evidence. They'd been very thorough, and I had no reason to follow up on their work. I just had a feeling I'd find something. My hunches paid off sometimes.

I walked out to the beach then turned back to look at the house. It made me sad to see this little structure dwarfed by the huge concrete-and-glass monstrosities that towered above it. It probably wouldn't be here much longer; it would give way to progress and become a parking lot. I stepped lightly up the stairs to the deck and examined the benches built against the walls of the house. The peeper probably had been sitting on one of these during the new moon ceremony. I saw nothing of interest, so I crossed the crime scene tape and unlocked the front door. I stood still for a few minutes, looked around, then closed my eyes and tried to imagine what Sally had done each day when she walked through this door.

A small rattan table stood against the wall on the left. A mirror decorated with bits of beach glass and seashells hung on the wall above it. She probably put her mail in the basket that sat on this table. There was a single drawer in the table. My mind's eye saw her put credit card receipts inside it.

I tried to put myself in Sally's shoes. What would she have done that night if she had made it through the door alive? She would have turned on all the lights. Danny said she was afraid of the dark. I wondered whether she always had been afraid of the dark. If this was a new fear, something in this house may have caused it. Had she known about the peeper? Had she seen him? Did she *know* him? The thought struck me like a bolt of lightning. The killer knew Sally turned on the lights as soon as she got home. That was why he or she had murdered her outside! If the killer had entered the house, he or she would have been visible in the light. Danny knew that. The people living in fifth-floor condos knew it. Who else knew it?

Sally was dressed in her white uniform and shoes. She probably would have changed clothes right away. I walked through the living room and into the bedroom, where the dust of fingerprint powder clung to every surface. I wondered whether anyone ever would clean it or whether the house would remain vacant and untouched. I pulled a pair gloves from my purse, pushed my hands into them, and tossed my purse onto the bed. Then I searched the room. I opened every dresser drawer and examined underneath them, inside the dresser frame, and behind it.

I did the same with the nightstands. I took each picture off the walls and checked them inside and out. I looked under the rugs, under the bed, and behind the headboard. In the closet I touched every inch of shelf space, looked in each shoebox, and rifled through the articles of clothing. I pushed on every board in the closet walls and floor.

The bathroom also showed signs that the forensics team had been there. Fingerprint dust lingered on the counter, mirror, sink, toilet and tub. I searched in the linen closet, in the medicine cabinet, under the sink, and behind the toilet. The kitchen was next. Old-fashioned cabinets with glass fronts housed dinnerware and glassware. Cookware was stored in lower cabinets. Drawers held cutlery, kitchen utensils, tools, and table linens. I saw no step stool, so I hoisted myself onto the countertop and stood to check the highest shelves. Neither Buck nor my doctor would have approved of this activity, so I didn't plan to tell them about it.

The pantry was a simple set of built-in shelves with a soft aqua curtain that served as a door covering. Sally's spice collection was generous. I opened all the jars and sniffed each to verify the contents. Then I touched every can and box in the panty. Nothing was hidden among the spices; nothing was glued to the cans or tucked behind them. Sally's cookbooks filled two complete shelves of the glass cabinets. I thumbed through each one and found only a few recipe cards among the pages. I examined the inside and outside of the refrigerator as well as behind it. Someone needed to discard the food before it rotted. The dust behind the refrigerator made me sneeze, so I grabbed a paper towel from the roll by the sink. In my haste I knocked over a little African violet plant on the windowsill. I righted the plant but realized the watering well was now dry. I looked under the sink again to see if there was any violet fertilizer fluid. Finding none, I added tap water to the well. I mopped up the spilled blue liquid from the shelf with another paper towel but noticed that most of the liquid had leaked through a crack in the sill. Closer examination revealed two small screws on either end of the crack. I gently pulled up on the two screws. Bingo! The sill lifted completely out of the window. I hoisted myself up on the countertop again and peered into the void. I saw the handle of a metal box and pulled it from the cavity.

The file box was secured with a locking latch. I touched the closure, and it moved slightly. It wasn't locked, but the moist, salty air had caused rust to accumulate around the button. It was stiff but finally gave way to my prodding. I carefully lifted the contents one by one. The box contained three journals dated 1980, 1981, and 1982; a small spiral photograph book; several envelopes with the return address of a local law firm; a wristband from a hospital visit; and a couple of jewelry boxes. Maybe the peeper was a burglar looking for the jewelry. I replaced the sill into position and set the plant on top.

As the living room was the final room for my search, I quickly finished the task, closed and locked the door, put the metal box in the trunk, and left the premises. I'd spent more time at the scene than I'd intended, so I headed home instead of the office. I called dispatch to report that I'd left Sally Keith's house and could be reached at home, if necessary. I knew better than to get my hopes up, but I had every reason to believe the documents in the box would give me some insight into Sally Keith's life…and perhaps her death.

Chapter 21

Saturday Evening

I reached the ranch at dusk. I parked the car in the barn, grabbed the metal file box, and headed for the house. Suddenly I heard the sound of hoof beats behind me and turned to see Buck rein in his huge black stallion, Thunder. I smiled at the image of my husband, the quintessential rancher. Dressed in jeans, boots, chaps, and denim jacket, he exuded masculinity. He alighted from the horse and led the animal into the barn. I retraced my steps and followed him to Thunder's stall.

"Hi, handsome."

"Thunder appreciates the compliment," he said with a grin. "Did you just get here?"

"Just pulled in. I still have more work to do, but I wanted to be home."

"Glad you're here," he said. "What's in the box?"

"Papers, journals, photos, and some jewelry. I found it in a secret compartment in Sally Keith's kitchen."

"That sounds promising."

"Sure hope so. We need something. At this point all the evidence leads to Danny Dean. I hope these things will either provide absolute proof of his guilt or innocence or add another suspect to the list."

"I still have to feed, water, and curry Thunder before I can come inside. Would you start a fire in the hearth? I cleaned it this morning and laid new wood. All you have to do is light it. Maybe we'll have time for some cuddling by the fire before you dig into that box."

"Sure will," I agreed. I stood on my tiptoes and kissed him on the cheek.

"We can do better than that," said Buck as he pulled me into an embrace. His kiss was warm and passionate. "That's just a starter," he said with a wink.

**

The fire was burning brightly by the time Buck entered the living room. He had removed his jacket, chaps, and shirt. As he walked toward the couch where I was sitting, the light from the fire reflected off the curly dark hair on his chest. My gaze wandered across his broad shoulders; flat abdomen; and lean, muscular legs; and my insides did a little flip. He bent down and planted a quick kiss on top of my head.

"I need a shower, honey. Back in a minute," he said with a little grin. I blushed as I realized my feelings were so transparent that Buck had seen my desire for him.

I was snuggled up in the bedcovers by the time he finished his shower. He slid in beside me.

"I miss you," he said, as he laid his warm hands on my body.

"Then let's make up for lost time," I said as I pressed my lips against his.

**

It was cozy and warm in the bed, but I knew I should get up to prepare dinner. Buck had been doing more than his share of the meal preparations lately. It was most certainly my turn to cook. I also was itching to look into Sally Keith's file box. Buck had pulled me close to him and had his arm wrapped around me in a vice grip. There was no way I could wriggle out without waking him, so I softly whispered his name. He opened his eyes and pulled me even closer.

"Hey, I need to get out of bed," I said.

"I know you can't wait to get into that box. I'm grateful for the time we spend together. Can't help it if

I want more." He pulled the covers off me, slapped me on the rump as I left the bed, and chuckled at my look of indignation. "I'll get something going for dinner. You go out by the fire and look at that box."

I smiled my gratitude, grabbed my robe, and headed for the living room. I threw a couple more pieces of split oak onto the coals, watched the flames grow, and curled up in a blanket. I'd left the box sitting on the table in front of the fireplace. Buck walked into the room from the kitchen carrying latex gloves, tongs, and tweezers. "Those items haven't been dusted, have they?"

"No, and neither has the outside of the box. I probably can't look at most of this stuff tonight. I'll take it to the lab tomorrow. Let me have those tongs for a moment." I put on the gloves, fished inside the box with the tongs, and pulled out the hospital wristband. At least I could read it without actually holding it in my fingers. I moved closer to the fire to take a look.

"Buck, this band is from a mental institution. Sally Keith's name is on it. The band was cut in order to remove it, and the place where the material separated isn't new. See how the edges are curled and yellowed? I can't make out a date. Everything is faded. Maybe the lab guys can get more. I really want to examine these things, but I can't figure out how to open those envelopes and read these journals without disturbing any prints."

"Don't compromise the case to satisfy your curiosity," Buck voiced what I already knew. "Further examination can wait until tomorrow."

"I know," I responded automatically without really meaning it.

I lifted the little photo album with the tongs and rested it on the edge of the box. The edges of the book were yellowed. The salt air had caused the plastic pages of the album to stick together; they snapped when I pulled them apart. Faded Polaroid shots filled the book. Using the tweezers, I carefully turned the first page. A much younger Sally looked at me. In one photo she was alone in the doorway of a stark room in an obvious institutional setting. In another, people in hospital attire surrounded her. Others showed Sally in a recreation room, outside playing volleyball, and flying a homemade kite. In the back of the book was a pocket for placing negatives. Since there were no negatives for Polaroid pictures, the pocket seemed to be empty. I looked a little closer, however, and saw a small bump in the plastic. I pushed the tweezers into the pocket in an attempt to retrieve something wedged in there, but moisture had caused it to stick inside.

"Buck, can you bring me a short paring knife?" I called toward the kitchen. When he brought it to me, I asked, "Could you hold this pocket open with the knife while I try to pull something out with the tweezers?"

As Buck did as asked, I inserted the tweezers again and pulled. The object was a standard photograph that had been torn into tiny bits. I placed the little clump on the leather couch and allowed the album to drop back into the box. Using the tongs and tweezers, I pieced together the torn photo as one would piece together a jigsaw puzzle. I was speechless when I finished. As Buck looked over my shoulder, a low whistle escaped his lips.

A battered, naked Sally lay upon a metal framed hospital bed. Her hands were tied to the metal bars of the frame with padded hospital restraints. Her eyes were swollen and purple from bruising. Scratches and bruises covered her arms and legs. The bed linen was streaked with blood.

"What in the world happened in that place?" I asked, though I didn't expect an answer. I gathered the pieces of photo into a plastic bag and dropped it into the box for the lab techs to assemble again. I retrieved a cardboard carton from the hall closet and placed the metal box in it. I'd take the box to the lab tomorrow.

Buck had stopped cooking dinner and sat on the couch in front of the fire. I sat next to him and moved into his arms. He held me tightly as we sat silently absorbed in our thoughts. I jumped when a large piece of oak fell through the grate with an explosion of sparks. Buck moved me aside to tend to the fire. He added several split logs, and soon the flames roared and crackled again. He returned to the couch and placed his hand against my cheek. "I'd kill anyone who did that to you."

"You wouldn't have to," I whispered. "I'd kill him myself. I have to find where that place is and go there."

"Honey, it's almost Christmas. Can you get up there and back so we can spend our first Christmas together? I don't think I have a prayer of convincing you to put this off until after the holiday."

"There are too many unknowns for me to try to do this by phone, or I'd try that. I have to go to Minnesota. It shouldn't take more than a few days, and I can be back in plenty of time for us to celebrate Christmas. I don't want to miss spending the holiday with you." I snuggled closer into him. "First I have to find where this institution is located. I'm surprised Mrs. Keith didn't mention that Sally was institutionalized, but I'll begin my search by asking her about it."

"That woman was at her emotional limit when you spoke with her," said Buck. "I imagine there are many things she did not mention."

"You're right. I'm being unfair. The chief probably can help me with jurisdiction and obtaining any search warrants I might need. I'll need a copy of Sally's death certificate. They'll be more likely to release medical records if they know she's dead. I hope to speak to other people in town too. Her address book contains a few names in her hometown. Maybe a friend or an old teacher or clergyman can shed some light on her life."

"Your 'to do' list sounds like it will take more than a day or two to complete, my dear," Buck said as he stood up.

"Oh, I don't think so," I said optimistically.

"Let's hope not," Buck responded quietly.

"I wonder if anyone was aware that she had this photo. She kept it hidden for a reason. Sally appears to have had a good lifestyle on just a nurse's salary. I was thinking she was dealing drugs for additional income, but maybe she was blackmailing someone. That certainly could be a motive for murder."

"Do you want me to go with you?" Buck offered.

"I'd love to be with you, but I'm going to be doing basic interrogation and background work. I can do it alone."

"Are you taking McDuffie with you?" Buck asked as a dark shadow passed across his face.

"Hey, there. Don't be jealous," I said playfully. "No, he's a desk jockey now. I've got him doing research on financial information for Sally and the Deans, as well as background checks on her coworkers and the witch group. This close to Christmas, he'll have difficulty finding people in authority who have the information."

"You'll check in regularly, won't you?"

"Of course. What's wrong?"

"I just worry about you sometimes."

"Don't be silly. I'm a sheriff, just like you. And I know how to handle myself, just like you," I said with a bit of annoyance in my voice.

"Don't get your dander up. I worry about you as my wife, not the sheriff of Sarasota County."

Chapter 22

Sunday Morning

The only legible prints on the journals, photo album, jewelry boxes, and hospital wristband were Sally Keith's. The envelopes with return addresses of law firms contained a variety of smudges but nothing that could be identified. Attorneys, secretaries, and postal workers had handled the envelopes, so the smudges were chalked up as probably belonging to those people.

The lab made copies of everything for me, including the autopsy photos and death certificate. I had a long plane ride to Minnesota ahead of me. There would be plenty of time to read. Buck had insisted I buy a first-class ticket and pay the difference between coach and first class from our personal funds. I had adequate space in my seat and made good use of it.

I began reading the oldest journal first and found that Sally was logging her days at the direction of her psychiatrist. She began by writing a question across the top of the first page: "Why am I here?" Her answer:

"I'm here because my mother put me here. I hate her. I'm here because no one understands how sad I am. I'm here because I wish I was dead! I'm here because I take drugs." The book described how bad she believed the world to be, how unfair life was to her, and how she had no friends but the pills and capsules she ingested. The journal was filled with pages and pages of ranting narrative by a very disturbed, lonely young woman.

Volume two began with many of the same statements regarding Sally's dissatisfaction with the world around her but became lighter toward the end. It seemed she had discovered an area in which she could excel—volleyball. The institution apparently had gathered enough young women within its walls to form two teams, and competition was fierce. Sally enjoyed the physical exercise as well as the game, and soon she was orchestrating moves for her team to take advantage of each player's strengths. She became a true leader. For once in her life, it seemed she had a purpose.

The third notebook began with the daily routine of a happy Sally. She rose early, did her chores, exercised, and attended classes to get her GED. She also learned to sew and cook, balance her checkbook, and live within a budget. She helped new girls adjust to institutional life and led group discussions regarding how to survive. She mentioned that she had met an interesting man and that he told her nice things. He said she had a great body and promised he'd find out how great it was. She was excited about the prospect of doing something naughty, but then the journal entries stopped. Several pages had been torn from the notebook. The last page was blank, but the lab was able to lift words from impressions of the writing that had been placed on the previous page. It read, "Why did he do this to me?" And then there was nothing.

The photos in the album had been difficult to copy since they were Polaroids. The lab had photographed the shots again and provided me with copies of the new photos. There were many shots of inmates and staff, both male and female, and I hoped someone would be able to put names to those faces.

The legal documents consisted of a warranty deed to the beach house, an order of restoration of competency, and a will that left all of Sally's worldly goods to her mother; everything seemed to be in order in that regard. Photographs of the jewelry were included in my file. While they weren't the crown jewels, they looked like pieces of good quality. An appraisal certificate from Shrode's Jewelers on Main Street accompanied each item. All told, the jewelry was worth thirty thousand dollars. I'd left instructions for Ike to call the store to see whether anyone remembered the pieces and who had purchased them. It was highly unlikely that Sally had purchased them for herself, but stranger things had happened. It also seemed unlikely that Ike had that kind of money or that Kelly Dean wouldn't miss thirty thousand dollars of her husband's income. What about Mr. Sherlock? Had he been involved with Sally too? Did he have those kinds of funds?

By the time the plane touched down at the Minneapolis-St. Paul International Airport, I'd read all the documents in the file box. I rented a black mid-sized car and drove down Highway 169 to St. Peter, the town where Sally grew up and where her mother still lived. Once there, I checked into the Uplands Motel, the only motel in town. Then I called Buck to tell him I'd arrived safely and to give him the name, address, and phone number of the motel.

"Hi, honey. Good to hear from you," his deep, resonant voice said through the earpiece. I wished now that he had come up here with me. He had offered. It would have been so simple just to say yes. "I bought a Christmas tree today" Buck continued. "It looks great in the living room. Devereaux is going to help me decorate it, and we'll cut some fir branches for the mantles and doors this afternoon. We'll put candles around the room too. You'll love it."

A lump formed in my throat, but I managed to keep my voice upbeat. "I know it'll be beautiful. Thanks for doing all this."

"Can't wait 'til you get home to see it."

"Me too. See you soon. Love you."

I sat on the edge of the bed in the little motel in St. Peter, Minnesota. My body slumped from fatigue and guilt, and tears trickled down my face. I wished I were finished with this. I wanted to be home preparing for the first Christmas I'd spend with the man I loved. I just wanted to be with him. I was feeling sorry for myself. This was ridiculous. A woman was dead, and my job was to find out who had killed her, not to wallow in self-pity.

Chapter 23

Monday Morning

At 8:00 a.m. sharp, I walked up to Alice Keith's desk at the police station. She was positioned near a glass door painted with the chief's name. She was surprised to see me but welcomed me warmly.

"I need to see the chief, Mrs. Keith."

"Is there any news?"

"Not really. We've reached several dead ends, but I'm hoping to unearth something here that'll help."

The chief of police, Paul Cleverdon, walked in at that moment. His craggy face reminded me of the Native American minted on the faces of nickels. A prominent brow accented by bushy eyebrows guarded piercing black eyes. His dark hair was permanently dented as a result of wearing his hat in the same position every day. Though it was morning, and he probably had just shaved, a shadow of stubble had already darkened his chin. He warmly shook my hand. We exchanged introductions, and then we went into his office.

The heels of my shoes echoed loudly on the well-worn floor planks. The building was old and lacked a modern linoleum floor. The heavy wooden office door housed thick frosted glass. I heard the rumble of a furnace somewhere in the distance and was grateful that warm air was being vented into the room. We sat in serviceable government chairs covered in burgundy leather that was cracking at the edges.

"I expected you to come up here eventually, Sheriff."

"Why's that, Chief?"

"I don't know. Call it intuition. Sally had a shady past that was bound to catch up to her one way or another. How much do you know?"

"I know she was a troubled young woman and had been confined to a mental institution. I'm counting on you to help flesh out the story. Do you know who might have killed her? A man named Danny Dean is my primary suspect. I believe he also spent some time in this town."

"There's a lot I don't know. There's a lot her mother doesn't know too."

"Then let's talk about what you *do* know," I said. "I need all the help I can get to bring this girl's killer to justice. We all want that."

"Of course we want that. I'm in the same business as you, Sheriff. I work on a smaller scale perhaps, but we're both in the justice business."

Chief Cleverdon was silent for a while. Perhaps he was deciding how much to tell me. Perhaps he was reminiscing. He closed his eyes for a few moments. When he opened them, I could tell he had made a decision. He would tell me what I needed to know.

"As I said, Sheriff, there's a lot I don't know about what went on. But maybe I can give you enough to get to the bottom of Sally's story once and for all. You know she was adopted and her father was killed in the line of duty, right?" I nodded, and he continued. "He sat right here at this desk every day, just like I'm doing now. It was difficult for me to be here that first day. Sam was my friend, and I wasn't sure I could ever fill his shoes. Over the years I did everything I could to help Alice and Sally, but I could never do enough."

"Did you catch the men who robbed the bank and killed Chief Keith?" I asked.

He smiled a little. "Yeah, we got them. Lot of good that did," he said with sarcasm in his voice.

"I imagine it meant a lot to Mrs. Keith."

"Maybe so," he responded sadly. The man slumped in his chair. His thoughts were far away. After a lengthy silence he continued, "Sally took Sam's death hardest of all. You could say her life ended the day he died. She never really recovered from it. She withdrew inside herself and emerged as a changed child. I don't believe in possession by the devil, but if I did, I witnessed it in that little girl. How such a beautiful, freckle-faced, blond angel could be filled with such hatred is beyond me, but that was Sally.

"Her second-grade teacher was old Miss Corrigan. She was my second-grade teacher twenty-five years earlier. She was a good teacher and a good woman. She came here to the station one day after school to talk to me about Sally. The child picked fights with the other children, both boys and girls, and no amount of talk or threats of punishment could persuade her to stop. What brought Miss Corrigan to see me was worse than that, though. Sally was biting and pinching other children. She had bruised some and drawn blood on others. Parents were tolerant up to a point, but they drew the line when she drew blood from the bites."

The chief picked up a letter opener from his desk. It was a beautiful replica of a Medici dagger and certainly not Government Issue. He toyed with the piece for a moment and then continued, "No one wanted to harm Sam and Alice's little girl, but they had their own children to protect. Miss Corrigan knew I couldn't arrest a child, but she wanted to make me aware of the severity of Sally's actions and ask me to try to step in as a surrogate father. I'd just married and didn't have any children of my own yet, so I agreed to try.

"I ate dinner at the Keith house a couple of nights a week, helped Sally with her homework, and helped Alice get her off to bed. Then I'd go home. My new bride put up with all of this for a while, but when she became pregnant with our first child, she put her foot down, and my visits to the Keith home dwindled and eventually stopped."

He leaned back in his chair. His eyes were clouded with the fog of memory. Though he looked straight at me, he did not see me.

"Sally's reaction was to be even meaner to the kids at school. She had gotten older and wiser, though, and she waited until school was out to attack her victims. The school couldn't interfere with student behavior off campus, but this is a small community, and word spreads quickly. Again a teacher came to me for help. Sally began to see a child psychiatrist when she was nine years old. The man succeeded in calming her down for a while, but Alice couldn't afford the level of care she needed, so the sessions only served as a bandage on an open wound."

At that moment we heard a knock on the door. Mrs. Keith brought in a tray with two cups of coffee and a plate of doughnuts. "Cop food," was all she said as she deposited the tray on the desk and closed the door behind herself. I was grateful for the snack.

The chief picked up his story where he had left off. "When Sally reached her preteen years, drugs had begun to seep into our little town. It started with marijuana and expanded into pills and LSD. Sally slid right into that scene. It made her feel better, or so she said. God help me—I couldn't put that girl in jail for the rest of her life. I did my best to help her, but she got deeper and deeper into drugs."

"Was there any way to separate her from the kids who were influencing her?" I asked.

"No. Like I said, this is a small town. We don't have alternate school choices. Alice couldn't afford to move away. I'm not sure anything would have helped anyway."

"There are many children caught up in the same dilemma, Chief," I said hoping to negate the feelings of guilt that he harbored inside himself.

"I know, Sheriff, but I keep telling myself that there must have been something I could have done. Wait. It gets worse. One Saturday night, when Sally was fifteen, she and two friends dropped some acid. They'd gone out to the state park to be away from prying eyes. During their acid trip, they climbed to the top of the fire tower. The boy in the group attempted to fly. Some campers found his body the next morning. They were able to get the two girls down from the tower and held them until I arrived."

I remembered seeing people experiencing LSD trips while I was in college. Many did not take the drug purposely, but instead ingested it unknowingly by drinking from an open punch bowl at a party. They did crazy things and had no memory of them later. Some were forever haunted by the experience. Some died.

"Alice asked the judge to commit Sally to the state mental hospital, and he did. She was gone for almost three years. Then one day Alice got a call to come up to the hospital right away. She asked me to go with her, and I did. I couldn't believe what I saw."

Chief Cleverdon fell silent for a moment. His black eyes had hardened, and his face was drawn into a grimace. His voice cracked when he spoke again.

"Someone had beaten that girl to within an inch of her life. She'd been raped too. No one there knew who had done it, whether it was a staff member or another patient. Alice and I bundled her up, put her in the patrol car, and took her to County General. She recovered physically, but I imagine her mental state was forever scarred. She went to a rehab center after a week in the hospital, and she actually seemed to get better there. She befriended a little girl who was recuperating from surgery and warmed up to her family. Sally was nineteen by this time, and the girl's parents offered her a job as a nanny. She jumped at the chance and moved in with the Dean family. I imagine you can guess their first names. It wasn't long before Sally left the Deans' employ, moved to her own apartment, and enrolled in nursing school. Her mother was so happy. Sally's life was actually improving."

"Did the Dean family live here in St. Peter?" I asked.

"Yes, both Danny and Kelly were born here. They moved away for a couple years, but came back when Danny's job ended."

"Where was he working?"

"Chicago, I think. He had a temporary job there.

"Much later I found out that Sally was having an affair with Danny Dean. It started at their home and continued after she moved into the apartment he had rented for her. He was in his forties and having a midlife crisis. He liked having a cute young thing make a fuss over him. Kelly Dean found about the whole thing and gave him an ultimatum. He took the job as county administrator in your county, and they moved away. When Sally finished nursing school, she found a job in Florida. Looks like they picked up where they left off here, though I didn't know that until she was murdered.

"That's it in a nutshell, Sheriff," he said as he took a sip of coffee and leaned back in his chair. He looked tired. Dark circles had formed beneath his deep eyes and his skin color had paled. Relaying the sad story clearly had taken something out of him. I felt sorry for the man. This troubled girl and his inability to prevent her ultimate demise would haunt his mind forever.

"Did you ever find the man who had attacked her?" I asked.

"I went back, questioned everyone in the place, but got nowhere. The administrator has a brother-in-law high up in the state government. They didn't want a scandal that might cause a loss of federal funding, so they stonewalled me at every turn. Mind you, I don't think anyone really knew who did it, but I wasn't going to be allowed to do a thorough investigation no matter what. I know there's nothing I can say to keep you from going up there and poking around. But I would ask you to be careful. You'll be messing with some powerful folks."

"You sound like my husband," I said with a smile.

"Wise man. What does he do?"

"He's the elected sheriff in the county to the east of mine. He's also a rancher and an orange grower."

"Hmm. Busy man. Well, in this case, he's justified in his worry. As I said, you'll be messing with some powerful people."

"I'll be careful."

"Call here if you need help," he said with a slight smile. "I'll do my best."

"What will I need to access Sally's medical records? A court order?"

"Yup. Let me see if I can get one for you. The judge knew Sally. Give me a call later today."

"Thanks, Chief," I said as I held out my hand for a parting handshake. "Mind if I talk to Mrs. Keith for a little while?"

"Naw, we're not busy. It'll be OK." He opened the door for me to leave.

Alice Keith was on the phone when I approached her. She smiled at me, finished her conversation, and motioned me to a chair next to her desk. "Anything?" she asked hopefully.

"I'm sorry, but not yet. The chief elaborated on some of the events in Sally's life that you touched upon last week. You mentioned that Sally had been in trouble, but I didn't understand the extent."

Mrs. Keith was silent for a few moments, and as she began to speak, tears ran down her cheeks. "It's difficult to admit to anyone that the child you love was a druggie and a slut, Sheriff. But she was still my daughter, and I loved her. I suppose I feel guilty because I couldn't help her. I feel guilty..." Her voice cracked, and she fell silent again. "I feel guilty," she began again, "because I feel relief that it's finally over. There—I said it. Sally is at peace, and I'm glad." She bowed her head in shame.

The chief's office door opened again. We both turned our heads toward the sound.

"Alice, why don't you take our guest out for an early lunch? You can take the afternoon off if you need to."

"Thanks, Chief," I said. "Great idea."

We gathered our coats, scarves, and hats and bundled up to brave the bitter cold. The sun had been shining when I arrived at the police station, but now the sky was overcast and gray.

"Looks like we'll have snow tonight," said Mrs. Keith. "Have you ever driven in snow, Sheriff Davis?"

"No, I haven't. I don't expect to go anywhere tonight. The plows will clear the road first thing in the morning, right?"

"The plows keep the major roads clear, but I'll be happy to give you a short driving lesson, if you like. It can be a little tricky as first."

"Thanks, I may take you up on that."

We walked as we talked. At the next block, Mrs. Keith turned into a bright little diner named "The Moose Head Café". "Hi, Hank," she said to the man behind the counter.

"Hi, yourself. Eating early today, are you?" he chortled.

"Yeah, you betcha," she answered in true Minnesota style. "Say hello to Sheriff Bernie Davis, all the way from Florida."

"Hi to you too," said Hank. The little man was so thin that his horn-rimmed glasses over powered his face. He wore a blue and white checked shirt with the buttons fastened all the way up to his neck. The tip of a pipe protruded from his right shirt pocket and a collection of ballpoint pens lined the left pocket. His thinning brown hair was combed straight back from his face without a defining part. It curled behind a pair of the largest ears I had ever seen.

"Nice to meet you, Hank," I said as we seated ourselves in a booth.

"Special today is meatloaf. Want a couple of plates?"

"Is it any good?" Mrs. Keith said with a wink in my direction.

"Good? I didn't get here at four o'clock this morning to make it and have it not be good. If you don't like it, I'll take it back."

"It'll be wonderful, I'm sure," she said with a laugh.

Hank busied himself by arranging napkins, cutlery, and glasses of water on our table, and then stepped back to the kitchen. He reappeared moments later. Hank beamed as he placed the plates on the table. "You want a glass of milk, Sheriff? Seein' as how you're in a family way, you might need the milk."

I accepted his offer and drank as much as I could. When we entered the diner, there were no other customers, but as the noon hour approached more guests arrived. Mrs. Keith and I were left to eat in peace while Hank served the others.

"Could you tell me more about Sally?" I asked Mrs. Keith. "I don't want to distress you, but something you say might help. You told me you adopted her."

"Yes. That was a happy day for us. She was a beautiful baby."

"Do you know who the parents were?"

"No, that information is a closely guarded secret. As I said, we got her from Catholic Social Services, so my guess is that she came from an unwed Catholic girl, probably someone living in this vicinity."

We ate while we talked. The meatloaf was quite good, as were the mashed potatoes and buttered carrots.

"Did Sally know she was adopted?"

"We told her as soon as she was able to understand. This is a small town. We didn't want her to hear it from someone else."

"Did she try to find out who her parents were?" I asked.

"I don't think so." Mrs. Keith was silent for a moment. "No, I don't believe Sally bothered to find out anything about her biological parents."

“Sometimes when children get older, they want to discover their roots, so to speak.”

“Not my daughter”, she began. “Sally just cared about Sally.”

“Is there anyone she was close to—a teacher, friend, neighbor?”

“She was fond of old Miss Corrigan, her second-grade teacher. That woman tried so hard to help Sally. She’s still alive, you know.”

“I wonder if I could speak with her.”

“I’d be happy to call her to ask.”

I made a mental note to remind her to make the call when we were near a phone.

“Anyone else? Did she keep a diary as a girl or have a photo album of friends?”

“She wasn’t one to build lasting relationships. After lunch we can go to my house, and you can look in her old room, if you like. I kept it ready for her in case she visited. She didn’t do that very often—visit, I mean.”

“I’d love to see her room. Thanks.”

After we finished eating, I used the pay phone in the diner to call Buck, as I promised I would. I also called Ike to check his progress. "Find anything?" I asked him.

"Background checks on the hospital staff and the witches were all squeaky clean," he said. "None of them has any convictions. None has ever been arrested. There were no outstanding warrants. They didn't even have any traffic violations. When I was checking license tags, I found that two members of the witch group are real estate agents. Get this—they were the agents who handled the purchase of Danny Dean's home and Sally Keith's beach house. I discovered that down in the recording department in the clerk of circuit court's office when I was checking to find out which properties the Deans owned. The real estate companies all stamp their names on the documents they prepare. Maybe that's why they felt comfortable traveling through her yard for their celebrations. Oh, you'll love this—the slogan for Sherlock Realty is 'Let us work magic in all your real estate deals.' How corny!"

"Oh, brother. Mr. and Mrs. Sherlock are the priest and priestess for one of the witch covens."

"Yeah, I know that from the membership list. Another thing, Sheriff…I visited Sherlock Realty myself—"

"Damn it, McDuffie! You're supposed to work your hours at a desk. I gave you a direct order to that effect, if you remember."

"Yes, ma'am. I know. I did this on my own time. I've been thinking about buying a house, so I figured I could learn something by visiting that real estate office. It was really creepy in there. The entire building is decorated in purple and black. It felt like I walked into a cave when I went through the door. There are all these weird statutes and ancient weapons, like knives and battle-axes. The art on the walls looks like Satan painted it. There were big splashes of red and black paint and all the figures looked like they were being tortured in hell. The receptionist was dressed in all black. She even wore black lipstick and nail polish. She was a beautiful woman, but all that darkness made chills run down my spine. I felt as if she could look into my eyes and see all the way to my soul."

"You have a soul?" I asked in jest. "Were the Sherlocks there?"

"Ha. Yeah, I do have a soul. Mr. and Mrs. Sherlock were out of the office, so I couldn't see them. I made an appointment to talk to them next week.

"Wait 'til you hear about this. In the lobby I saw a scale model of a building—some kind of temple or something. On an easel, next to the model, was an artist's depiction of the building. It was situated between two high-rise condos, and there was water in the background. I think the land in that painting was Sally's. Lettered on the painting was a title or slogan or something. It read, 'The Way, the Truth, and the Dark.' Get it? They're making a play on words from the Bible."

"Yes, I get it. I hate to say this after you disobeyed my orders, but good work. Did you ask about the model?"

"I asked the lady in black what it was, you know, just to start a conversation, and she just said it was part of a dream the owners had. She wouldn't expand any more on it. I didn't want to actually interrogate her since I hadn't told her I was a detective. I figured that could wait until later. I was just fishing at that point."

"Was there anything in the public records to indicate Danny Dean had paid for Sally's house? Was he on the deed?"

"No," Ike said. "Only Sally's name was on the deed and mortgage. I was going to try to find out who made the mortgage payments, but I'm having difficulty finding anyone in authority working in the banks this close to Christmas."

"Any info on the Deans' finances?" I asked.

"Same problem there."

"I was afraid of that."

"How about the license tag book?"

"I had a little more success there," he said. "Marcus Sherlock, the real estate agent and witch-coven priest, made regular trips to Sally's house several months ago. Nothing recent, though. He'd go there after she got off work, so I don't imagine they were discussing land sales. The last time his tag was logged was five months ago. Whatever they had going probably ended, I guess."

"Sorry, Ike. I know how much you cared about her."

He paused for a long moment. "That's OK," he finally said. "What's done is done." One thing surprised me. The guard didn't log Danny Dean's car tag in his book the night Sally was murdered. He told us he'd seen Dean drive by, but he didn't write down the tag number."

"For someone as anal as he is, that's a significant pattern break."

"I thought so too, so I called out there to see if I could stop by and talk to him. I know I'm not allowed to go out there, but I figured someone else could go. Doesn't matter anyway. He's on vacation. The manager said he went up to Minnesota for the holidays."

"I thought he said he was from New York."

"Yeah, right. Well, you're in Minnesota. Maybe you'll see him. You can ask him about the book."

"It's a pretty big state, Ike."

"Yeah, you betcha."

Chapter 24

Monday Afternoon

I followed Alice Keith's faded green Chevrolet to her home. Though it was early afternoon, the sky was dark and filled with ominous clouds. It was so cold; I was grateful we had to drive just a few blocks. The Keith home was a sturdy brick structure with a high-pitched roof. We entered through a heated garage into a tidy kitchen and walked through to the living room that was decorated for Christmas. A large spruce tree, adorned with handmade ornaments, dominated the room. I felt a rush of emotion when I saw the tree. I thought of Buck and Devereaux planning for Christmas at the ranch without me. Tears stung my eyes, but I blinked them away before Mrs. Keith could notice them.

She showed me to Sally's room, which was tastefully decorated in shades of blue. A set of wooden shelves held childhood memorabilia. There were dolls dressed in their finest clothes, a few stuffed animals, bright jewelry boxes, and an old brush, comb, and mirror set.

Mrs. Keith opened the closet and removed several cardboard cartons from the top shelf. "I saved these old things Sally left behind when she moved south. She was never one to hang on to mementos. I guess there wasn't much she wanted to remember about her life here." Tears filled her eyes again. "It's sort of a sad commentary about her life and mine," she said in a voice that cracked with sadness and regret. "I'll leave you alone to look through these while I make us some hot cider. Come out to the living room when you're finished."

The first carton held a baby book. Its pages were marked with Sally's progression through infancy, toddlerhood, and into grade school. There were photos of her first smile, first haircut, first step, and first tooth. Data had been logged in the neat penmanship of a caring parent. The carton also held baby clothes, a christening gown wrapped in tissue, and envelopes filled with curls from haircuts as well as teeth that the tooth fairy had pilfered. A white gift box held a carefully folded veil from Sally's first Holy Communion ceremony. Another box contained a tarnished silver infant's hairbrush, a white rosary and prayer book set, a silver rattle engraved with Sally's initials, and a few chains with holy medals attached. These were pieces of memories that should have been good ones for a child. These were things I would have cherished and taken with me if I had moved to a different place. I had similar items in boxes at the ranch. There was no way I would have left them in the closet of my old house.

The second carton was filled with old toys, puzzles, and games. The third held a variety of children's books; the titles of the books were familiar to me. The fourth carton was full of children's drawings and schoolwork. I laid some of the drawings on the bed. Many of them depicted houses with sunshine and three stick people standing in the yard. Images of trees, with and without leaves, denoted changes of seasons. As I placed more drawings on the bed, I noticed a shift in design. Only two persons stood in the yard, and they wore frowns on their faces. The clouds were dark, and there was no sun. Sally had depicted her grief in her art.

I started to put the books back into the carton when I noticed a copy of a Nancy Drew mystery titled *The Secret of the Old Clock*. I owned the same book. I sat on the bed and began to read the simple text of the children's novel. As I turned the pages, a strip of old photos slipped out. These were the type of pictures one might take in a photo booth at the mall or fair. An adoring Sally embraced a rather embarrassed-looking Danny Dean. I'd hoped to find something to save Danny, but instead I'd hammered another nail into his coffin.

I pulled the rest of the books back out and rifled through the pages of each one. Inside Sally's copy of *The Secret Garden* were three Polaroid shots of her in various stages of undress. Her seductive expression led me to believe a man probably had pressed the button on the camera, but I couldn't be sure. Teenage girls sometimes take compromising photos of each other as a lark. Maybe Sally had a friend who was as daring as she was.

At the bottom of the box of books was a class yearbook. The date of the book would have been when Sally was in junior high school. There were very few signatures inside. One boy and two girls had written comments. I kept the book out and returned the box to the closet.

When I returned to the living room, I saw that Mrs. Keith had illuminated the lights on the tree and placed a record of soft Christmas hymns on the turntable of the stereo system. The Lettermen were singing "Silent Night." She sat on the couch with a knitted blanket wrapped around her legs, but she rose as I entered the room.

"I found a few photos and an old yearbook in the boxes. Can I borrow these?"

"Sure. They're of no use to her now."

"Mrs. Keith, did Sally have any close friends? I saw only three signatures in her junior-high yearbook."

"She was secretive about her friends," she said, "but the three whose names are in the book also were troublemakers in her class. I think they stuck together because of that. When Sally experimented with drugs, they did too. Chief Cleverdon probably told you about the boy who died in the state park. He was the boy who signed her book. One of the girls was with Sally that night, but the other girl didn't go with them."

"Do the girls still live in St. Peter?"

"One of them does."

"Do you know how I'd get in touch with her?" I asked.

"She lives a few blocks away. I can take you there, but let's warm up with some cider first."

Chapter 25

Monday Afternoon

The sky was as black as night. I'd thought we would walk to the girl's house, but Mrs. Keith insisted we drive. "It's too easy to slip and fall, especially since the wind is fierce today. Let's take your car. I'll give you some driving tips."

I was surprised how difficult it was to keep the car in its lane with the wind pushing it on the snowy, frozen street. Mrs. Keith helped with simple instructions about turning into a skid and how to negotiate in whiteout conditions. I noticed that the street signs and stop signs were positioned higher on the poles than they were in Florida. Even so, drifts of snow had almost obscured them.

Alice Keith chatted as we made our way up one street and down another; dodging snow drifts as we went. "Nadine lives in her grandparents' old house," she said. "They married late in life. Her grandmother was an ex-nun who left the order at age forty-five. Her grandfather was a confirmed bachelor until his marriage at age sixty-five. Neither expected to have children, but the Lord works in mysterious ways, and Nadine's mother, Margaret, was born a year after they married. Margaret was in my class at school, and to say she was weird is an understatement. She was happy and laughing one minute and sad and depressed the next."

Mrs. Keith inhaled quickly and pressed her foot against the floorboard as I barely missed hitting a street sign. I smiled a weak smile and slowed the car's speed to a crawl.

"I imagine Margaret was manic depressive," she picked up the conversation where she'd left off, "but I don't believe she was ever diagnosed or taken for any treatment. I'm not sure anyone had even documented that condition back then. Her father died when we were in grade school, and her mother died when we were sixteen. She inherited the house and a trust fund of adequate size to cover her living expenses. She really needed medical help for her mental illness, but there was no one responsible for her care. She didn't have much of a life. It was more of an existence."

We were traveling down a narrow street in a middle class neighborhood. Except for varying paint colors, the entire row of houses looked the same. All were two stories high; driveways were on the right sides; and front walks led to doors centered in the walls. Blankets of snow covered bushes and all other distinguishing characteristics. I would certainly be lost here if I found myself in a white out condition.

"Margaret was pretty in a Marilyn Monroe kind of way," Alice Keith continued. "She was blond, with a voluptuous, soft, curvy body that attracted men. Unfortunately she attracted the wrong kind of men. A drifter moved in with her and left a few years later, leaving her with two toddlers and no help to raise them. The boy was as mean as a snake. He tortured the neighbors' pets, frightened poor Nadine to tears, and was abusive to his mother. He ran away from home at age fifteen and only reappeared when he needed money. Nadine inherited the house and the trust fund when her mother died. Here, this is the house." She pointed, and I eased the car into the driveway.

We entered the mudroom and knocked on the front door of a tiny brown house with asbestos siding and casement windows. Storm windows had been added to the outside. Boots and snow shovels lined the wall of the mudroom, and an open bag of salt leaned against them. A young woman with stringy blond hair and dark circles under her eyes answered our knock. Her jeans were streaked with black, possibly ash from a fireplace. A heavy grey sweater, with sleeves that hung almost to her fingertips, dwarfed her petite frame. She showed little expression on her face but opened the door to admit us.

"Nadine, this is Sheriff Davis from Florida. She wants to talk to you about Sally," Mrs. Keith said. "Sheriff, this is Nadine." The young woman made no welcoming gesture or comment. She simply walked from the entry hall into the living room. Mrs. Keith raised her eyebrows. "Nadine, I'm going to wait in the kitchen while you talk to the sheriff." She walked farther down the hall toward the back of the house.

I entered the living room and found Nadine seated on a rundown brown sofa. A fire burned in a small fireplace, and the room was quite warm. I tossed my hat, coat, and scarf over the back of a gold-colored recliner and sat next to the girl on the sofa.

"You heard about Sally, didn't you?" I asked her.

Nadine's head made a very slight nod. Her eyes were glassy with unshed tears.

"Do you have any idea who would want to do that to her?"

She remained silent as she shook her head slowly from left to right.

"I need help finding out who killed Sally. Will you help me?"

Nadine took several deep breaths then opened her lips to speak, "Sh-sh-sh," she began. "Sh-sh-sh-she was my only friend," the girl stuttered. "Now I'm alone." The poor girl began to sob. I waited patiently for her to recover her composure.

"I'm sorry about your friend, Nadine. I'll do my best to find who did this and bring that person to justice. Can you help me?" I asked again.

Nadine nodded slowly but said nothing.

"Did Sally ever call you or write letters?"

She shook her head.

"Did you talk to her since she moved to Florida?"

"Sh-sh-she came here at Thanksgiving."

"Did she tell you what she was doing in Sarasota?" I asked.

"Sh-sh-she was a nurse."

"Did she talk about her house or her job or her friends?"

"Beach. House on the beach."

"Yes, she lived on the beach. Did she have friends there?"

"Two boyfriends. Lots of friends. I'm still her friend."

"Could I show you some pictures of Sally? Would you look at them and tell me if you've seen them before?"

Nadine nodded, and I took the pictures from my jacket pocket. She pointed to the picture of Danny Dean and said, "Boyfriend." She recoiled in terror when she saw the coquettish pictures of Sally.

“What scares you about these, Nadine?” I asked hopefully.

“N-n-no,” she whimpered.

“Why was Sally doing this?” I asked softly.

Nadine shook her head violently, left to right. “N-n-no,” she moaned.

“Please tell me, Nadine,” I asked again softly. “Sally wouldn’t mind if you helped me.”

The young woman had curled her legs up under herself on the couch. Her arms hugged her body as she rocked slightly forward and backward.

“I can’t,” she whispered.

“It would help me so much if you could tell me,” I prodded.

Without a word, Nadine rose from the couch and walked out of the room. I sat there for a few minutes. I was about to get up to put on my coat when she appeared again. She held something in her hand and stopped in front of me, clearly struggling with her decision to show me whatever she held.

“You can show me, Nadine.”

She offered a faded Polaroid. I made a sharp intake of breath when I looked at it. A naked Nadine was lying on a metal bed with her hands tied to the headboard with hospital restraints. She had been beaten on the face, arms, and legs, much in the same manner as Sally had been in the pieced-together photo I'd found. There was blood on the sheets but not as much as was visible in Sally's photo.

"Who did this to you and Sally?" I asked quietly.

Nadine shook in terror. "N-n-o," she stuttered. "Can't tell."

"Was it her boyfriend?"

She shook her head emphatically.

"Was it a neighbor?"

More head shaking.

"Someone at school?"

Again she shook her head.

"Someone at the hospital?"

Nadine stopped shaking her head, and her eyes widened in terror.

"Who, Nadine? Who at the hospital?" I tried again.

"N-n-no," she moaned again and collapsed on the couch.

I waited. I didn't know enough about the hospital personnel to ask another probing question or state a name. Nadine picked up a throw pillow from the couch and hugged it to her body. For several minutes she squeezed her eyes shut and rocked back and forth slowly. Then she abruptly stopped. Her eyes opened, and silently she studied me over the pillow. Then her eyes settled on my abdomen.

"Baby?" she asked.

"Yes, Nadine. I'm having a baby."

"S-s-sally's baby dead."

"What?"

Nadine sat up. "S-s-sally's baby dead," she said again.

Good God, I thought. Could it be that the excess blood in Sally's photo was a back-alley abortion? Did she miscarry as a result of the beatings she had endured? How could I possibly verify any of this with this simpleminded girl? Did she know Sally was pregnant when she died? Was that the baby she was referring to, or was there another?

"Where did Sally's baby die, Nadine?"

"In bed."

So it *was* another child. Sally had lost a baby earlier. Mrs. Keith might know something about this.

"Who killed Sally's baby?" I asked.

Looks of anguish, sadness, and terror crossed her face. "Him."

"Who is he? What's his name?"

"N-n-no," she moaned again.

She wasn't going to name her tormentor. He had done a very good job of terrorizing the girl, and since I didn't know any names of the hospital personnel, I couldn't offer any to gauge her reaction.

"OK, Nadine. You've been a big help. Thank you. May I keep your picture for a few days? I'll give it back."

The girl thought long and hard before nodding.

I picked up my hat, coat, and scarf and headed in the direction Mrs. Keith had taken to the back of the house. I found her in the kitchen, washing the fronts of the cabinets. The room smelled of pine disinfectant, and I saw freshly washed dishes in the drying rack.

"I need a couple more minutes, Sheriff. Just want to clean the rest of the cupboards. I come by here every once in a while to check on her. She can make her own meals—simple things like soup and sandwiches—but she's not good at cleaning. There," she said as she finished the last door. "I'll come back later to do the bedroom and bathroom."

"She doesn't have any family who could help? Perhaps an agency could assist?"

"Her good-for-nothing brother doesn't help her at all. Don't know where he's living right now. She also doesn't qualify for any assistance because of her trust fund. It's enough money for her to live on but too much for her to qualify for any benefits."

"Was she in the mental institution with Sally?"

"Yes," Mrs. Keith answered painfully.

"Who beat Sally, Mrs. Keith? Do you know? Do you even have a guess?"

"I wish I knew," she answered with a sigh.

I pulled the photo of Nadine from my pocket and showed it to her. The woman stared in horror at the scene depicted. Then she lifted her face to me.

"He did the same thing to Nadine?"

"It appears Sally and Nadine were both abused there. My guess is that someone who worked at the mental hospital did it. Nadine won't give me a name. She's still terrified of him. Is there anything more about this that you know?"

"I know Sally had been sexually abused, and the pregnancy that resulted ended when she was beaten. They told me that at the rehab hospital."

"Did you ask Sally about it? Did a therapist talk to her?"

"I could never talk to her about it. I just couldn't. She had many lengthy psychotherapy sessions in rehab. I don't know if they were ever able to get a name from her, but I suspect not. The chief couldn't get her to tell him either, even though he kept trying to convince her that he could catch whoever did it and keep him behind bars."

It would serve no purpose to show Sally's photo to her mother. It wouldn't help catch the man, and it wouldn't do any good for her to see it. Besides, if this man found out I knew about both photos, he might slip away, and then I'd never find him. He was an abuser, a sexual predator, and most likely had murdered Sally's first unborn child. The thought that kept nagging me was, *Did he also kill Sally and her second unborn child?*

Chapter 26

Monday Afternoon

Mrs. Keith had promised she would arrange for me to talk to Sally's second-grade teacher, Miss Corrigan. Though I knew Sally's mother probably had reached her emotional limit for the day, she offered to go with me to introduce me to the old lady. When we got to the house, a prim maid in a crisp white apron and black uniform dress ushered us into a tidy sitting room.

"Miss Corrigan will be right with you, ladies," she said with a smile. "She'll just love having visitors."

A thin woman appeared at the door of the sitting room. We both rose to greet her. Her back was ramrod straight; her gleaming white hair was perfectly coiffed; and her clothing looked expensive. If I had to select one word to describe her, it would be *elegant*.

"Miss Corrigan, this is Sheriff Bernie Davis from Florida. She's here about Sally."

"Poor Sally," murmured the old woman as she gracefully settled into a high-backed wing chair near the fireplace. "There was nothing you could have done, Alice, so don't blame yourself. Sally was spiraling downward even when she was in my room at school. We all tried—you, Chief Cleverdon, and me. All of us tried to help her. But none of us succeeded. It was in her blood."

"Why do you say that, Miss Corrigan? Why did you use those words?" I asked. I watched the old lady intently. She had a smart wit. I could see she was carefully considering the words she should use in response.

"Alice, I'd like to speak to the sheriff alone. Will you go out and ask my maid to fix us some coffee and cake? We have a very tasty Christmas fruitcake I'd like to share with you."

"Yes, I'd be happy to do that," Mrs. Keith responded.

The retired teacher waited until Alice Keith was out of earshot before she continued. "Alice has been through enough with that child. She doesn't need another burden to weigh her down at Christmas. Have you ever been to the dog pound to adopt a puppy, Sheriff?"

"No, ma'am. I've never adopted a pet," I responded.

"Well, when you get there, you see a lot of cute animals. Some are puppies. Some are fully grown. All are barking and lonely. Some have been starved or abused or abandoned. Some are products of inbreeding and are damaged inside. You can tell when you look at those puppies that something is wrong. It's something that can't be fixed with love and care and a good home. If the animal control people detect a dangerous genetic flaw in a dog, they'll put it to sleep, and that's the end of it."

She paused, looking me hard in the eyes before continuing. "We can't do that with people. We spend lifetimes trying to fix something that can't be fixed. Sally was one of those who couldn't be fixed. I can see by your face that you think I'm a mean old lady saying bad things about the dead, but if you knew who her real parents were, you'd see things differently."

"Who were her real parents?" I asked with hope in my voice.

Miss Corrigan opened her lips as if to answer but thought better of it and closed them. After a few moments, she spoke again. "I can't tell you that, Sheriff. I know who they were as surely as I know my own name, but I have no written proof. I really can't tell you. The only way you can get that proof is to open the adoption record, and I daresay you won't accomplish that on this visit."

"Can you tell me your suspicions?"

"That would be like repeating idle gossip, which could do more harm than good."

"A woman is dead," I said with some emotion. "You know who is charged with her murder, don't you?"

"Yes, I know," she whispered.

"Unless I find some proof of Danny Dean's innocence, he could be put to death for this murder. That's not idle gossip, ma'am. That's fact. Something happened in this community that ended in the death of a beautiful young woman and her unborn child. If you know something that could help me catch her killer, I need to know about it."

The old woman's gray eyes softened as I stared into them. "Sheriff, I'm not an evil monster. I can't tell you about Sally's parents, but I can give you some assistance. I know you'll visit that mental hospital eventually. Get into her file. It has the information you're attempting to extract from me. You'll just have to dig for it."

Chapter 27

Late Monday Afternoon

I dropped Mrs. Keith off at her house, thanked her for her help, and headed back to the Uplands Motel. I found the old lady's comments both depressing and frustrating. If she would just tell me what she knew, it would make my work so much easier, but I couldn't force her to tell me, and I certainly couldn't haul her into the police station for questioning. They'd think I was crazy. Slowly I drove down the two-lane road and almost missed the motel driveway due to the intensity of the snowfall.

The message light on my phone was blinking, so I deposited my hat, coat, scarf, and gloves in the closet; sat at the sterile Formica desk; and called the front office. The message was from Buck, who was just checking in. I longed to hear his voice, but it was 3:50 p.m. already, which meant that it was 4:50 p.m. in Sarasota. I had ten minutes to catch Ike at his desk, so I called him first. Ike didn't answer, so I quickly called Jackson Stone's desk. He answered on the second ring.

"Jack, it's me. Where's McDuffie?"

"Hi, Sheriff. He's taking a few personal days for Christmas. I figured you knew about it."

"Hell, no. I didn't know about it!" I exploded. "We're working a murder case. He can't just take off! I talked to him a few hours ago. He didn't say anything about needing time off."

"Sorry, Bernie. I never thought he'd go off without clearing it with you first."

"I'll call his apartment." I punched in the numbers to Ike's home phone, but after ten rings and no answer, I hung up. Where the hell was he?

Next I called Chief Cleverdon and asked about the court order for Sally's medical records. He told me I could pick it up in the morning.

I kicked off my shoes, pulled the phone from the desk to the bed, leaned back on the pillows, and called Buck's private number. After half a dozen rings and no response, I dialed our home phone. Buck's deep voice came through the earpiece, and the troubles of the day melted away.

"I can't tell you how good it is to hear your voice, my love."

"Hi, honey," he said. "I miss you so much. How are things going?"

I summarized the day's events. Buck was sympathetic with my frustration about the lack of evidence.

"I'm going to try to get up to the mental institution tomorrow," I told him, "but there's a heavy snowstorm outside now. It's expected to intensify overnight. I don't know how travel will be after that."

"I know I don't have to ask you to be careful on those snowy roads, do I?" he asked with a chuckle.

"I actually received some snow-driving lessons from Mrs. Keith this afternoon. I'll be fine. I won't take any chances. Don't worry."

"I can't wait for you to get home to see the Christmas decorations. The house looks good, but it won't be great until you're back here."

"I want to be home with you so much," I said. "Did you find any mistletoe in the oak trees?"

"We found a little, but I don't have anyone to kiss."

"Save all your kisses for me. I'll be home soon."

"Bye, honey. Keep safe."

Chapter 28

Tuesday Morning

Two words described the scene outside the Uplands Motel the next morning: *freezing* and *white*. Several feet of snow had fallen, and the fierce wind had blown huge drifts against the buildings. Tree limbs were heavy with the weight of the snow; some had even broken from the strain. Although plows had cleared the main road in front of the motel, a crew was still clearing the driveways and walkways. I asked the desk clerk about the status of the roads leading to the mental hospital. She assured me they would have been plowed already. The mental facility employed many people from St. Peter, and those people needed to be able to get to work. She handed me a scraper and a hand broom to clear the snow from my car and asked that I return them to her when I checked out.

In no time at all, I reached the police station, pulled up to the curb, and made my way to the office of Chief Cleverdon, who handed me the court order. I thanked him for his help and carefully retraced my steps back to the rental car.

I was grateful to see that traffic on the highway was moving swiftly. The Minnesota State Hospital was situated on the outskirts of St. Peter, and I had no difficulty reaching it. I stopped at the guard shack at the main entrance to what appeared to be a rather large campus. A wall of fencing surrounded the entire facility. I showed the guard my photo ID, badge, and court order and was admitted to the grounds.

The starkness of the facility was enhanced by the dreariness of the winter sky. Huge drifts covered portions of the fence. The roofs of the buildings were heavy with the white stuff. After dodging mounds of blown snow, I parked in a visitor slot and made my way into a massive building made of tan stone. My footsteps echoed loudly on the marble floor of the deserted entrance hall. The inside of the aged building had probably been elegant once, but no amount of cleaning could wipe away the shabbiness of age. Floors were cracked, ceilings were stained, and paint was peeling. Over-sized framed portraits of previous facility directors and board members lined the walls. I noticed that none of them had smiled when their pictures were taken. From the looks of things, there was nothing here to make one smile.

I had visited the mental institution in Chattahoochee during college. It housed the most dangerous of Florida's criminally insane, as well as other tragic souls. I had hoped never to find myself in such a depressing place again, but here I was.

I had expected to see patients milling about, but they apparently were not allowed in this area. There was no visitor center, no information desk, and no people anywhere. I felt the hairs on the back of my neck rise in apprehension. I was uncomfortably alone here. Directional signs pointed to the right for the offices, so I walked down the long, musty corridor and entered a door lettered with the words, HOSPITAL ADMINISTRATOR. A perky, young, blonde greeted me and offered Christmas wishes. She introduced herself as Suzie Paulson. Ms. Paulson was obviously caught up in the spirit of the season, decked out in a bright red-and-green plaid wool skirt, a red sweater, and a red Santa hat. Her bright face and colorful attire was a sharp contrast to the dingy atmosphere of the halls. Within minutes she ushered me into a large formal office. Behind an enormous antique mahogany desk sat a thin man with grizzled eyebrows and untidy gray hair. When he smiled, a mouthful of very large teeth dominated his face.

"I'm Dr. Hiram L. Waters," he said as he rose to his feet.

"Sheriff Bernie Davis."

"Please be seated," he said and gestured to a comfortable overstuffed chair opposite the desk. "You're not from around here, Sheriff."

"No, I came from Sarasota, Florida, to investigate the murder of one of your former patients."

"And who might that be?" His smile disappeared from his face, replaced with a look of caution and concern.

"Sally Keith. She was a patient here several years ago."

"I remember Sally," the man said with sadness in his voice. "Her stay here ended poorly."

"I daresay that's an understatement, Doctor. Do you have any idea who beat her?"

Dr. Waters was silent for a while, clearly planning his response carefully. "At first I thought he was a member of my staff, but I found that wasn't true."

"How do you know that?"

"I conducted my own investigation. I verified the whereabouts of every single person who was working that night. Each one had an ironclad alibi verified by more than one person. I find it hard to believe that what was done to Sally was the act of an entire group of hospital employees. That's highly unlikely and almost impossible. A group of people never could keep their mouths shut or keep all the stories straight."

The doctor pushed his thick glasses up the bridge of his nose and continued. "I also verified the activities of all the patients. Most of the people in this facility are treated with medications, and most require some sort of sleep aid. It's very quiet here at night."

"What about criminally insane patients?" I asked. "Do you have any of those here?"

"Yes, we have a secured area. It houses people who have serious mental issues and are considered dangers to society. They are confined via court order. Each lives alone in a single cell. Double steel doors that lock independently with state-of-the-art electronic access protect the entire ward. No one gets in or out unless he or she is supposed to be doing so."

"Are any psychopaths housed here?"

"Yes," Dr. Waters said. "We have two."

"May I see their files?"

"That's highly irregular, Sheriff. Do you have a court order?"

"My court order is for access to Sally Keith's medical records."

Without further words, I opened my briefcase, removed two items, and placed them on the desk in front of Dr. Waters. The first was a copy of the torn photo of Sally tied to the metal hospital bed. The second was the photo Nadine had given me of herself tied in the same manner.

"My God," the doctor said as he picked up one photo and then the other.

"Do you have a patient in residence here who might do something like that?"

"I don't know what to say, Sheriff. I don't believe anyone could escape from our secure area to do this. I will, however, give you access to the files and allow you to interview some of the patients if you like." The man appeared sincerely distressed and shaken.

I then pulled the copies of the photos from Sally's album and placed those on his desk. "Are any of the people in these photos still working here?"

He examined each photo in turn. "This woman works in the kitchen. Her name is Olga. These two orderlies, Lawrence Nelson and Ramon Flores, are still here. The rest are gone. This is a high-stress job for most people, and turnover is high. The younger persons in these photos were patients. They're all gone. Except for the criminal ward, patients are usually treated here for a couple of years."

"May I speak with the three people who worked here at the time when Sally was here?" I asked.

"Of course. I'll arrange it."

"Doctor, did you keep any notes from your internal investigation into Sally Keith's abuse?"

He nodded grimly. "I added those to her file. You'll see them there."

"Did you investigate Nadine Barnard's abuse too?"

"Nadine wasn't abused here."

"What?"

"Her mother took her out of this institution after the incident involving Sally, but she hadn't been harmed. Nothing like that happened to her while she was here."

"Are you sure?"

"Of course." He leveled his gaze at me and watched me for several moments. "Sheriff, I'm pretty sure you checked with Chief Cleverdon upon your arrival in our little community. He most likely told you that I got this position because my brother-in-law is the lieutenant governor. Well, that's true. I got here because of political clout, but I *stay* here because I'm a damn good doctor and hospital administrator. People in this facility are cared for and treated well. What happened to Sally Keith was a blemish on my professional record, but it's also a permanent scar on my soul. I'm absolutely positive Nadine Barnard wasn't abused while she was a patient at this facility."

We sat in silence, lost in our thoughts. The man seemed to be sincere. He was definitely distraught about Sally's abuse, but was he distraught because of Sally or because of the possible repercussions that might affect his career?

Dr. Waters pressed a button on his intercom and called his secretary. The perky blonde in the Santa hat bounced into the room. "Ms. Paulson, Sheriff Davis will need a place to review some files. Perhaps she can use Dr. Lewis's office since he's on vacation. Please escort her there. Then pull these files from the archive room." He handed her a slip of paper. "She also needs to speak to Olga, Lawrence, and Ramon. If you would, please arrange for each of them to speak to her in turn."

"Yes, Doctor," she replied sweetly.

"Sheriff, I'll escort you personally into the secure area to view the two patients you wish to see. When you're finished with everything else, please let me know."

"Thank you for your time and assistance, Doctor," I replied.

The man stood and made a slight bow. I took that as the signal to leave, so I followed Ms. Paulson from the room. She led me to an office across the hall and excused herself to retrieve the files. She returned shortly, pushing a small card laden with a stack of file folders, a tray of sandwiches, a plate of Christmas cookies, and a glass of milk.

"I bet your mind works better when you have something to nibble on," she said with a smile. "I'll leave you to your task. Please come get me when you want to interview the staff members. By the way, the bathroom is down this hall on your left."

"Thanks for everything. I appreciate your kindness."

"No trouble at all," she said as she left the room.

Raymond Albertson's file was on top of the stack, so I began by opening it. Albertson, a patient in the criminally insane ward, had killed two people in his office. He had been a tax auditor for the state of Minnesota and was known for having an explosive temper when things didn't go his way, according to testimony from other members of the auditing staff. He was good at his job and often had unearthed discrepancies by "buddying up" to those he was auditing.

Rodney Jessup's file was next. He had worked as a night watchman at a balloon manufacturing plant in

Minneapolis. Jessup had beaten two people to death when they had left a gate open after sneaking out to smoke in the parking lot. He apparently took his job very seriously and tolerated no variance from the rules.

I mentally reviewed some of the material I'd studied in college in criminal psychology classes. Psychopaths love official jobs and uniforms. They have explosive tempers, are overly solicitous, and often are considered to be "too nice." They're cruel to animals and like to show their dominance over things or people that are weaker than they are. It looked like Albertson and Jessup fit the mold. Could one of them have had contact with Sally and Nadine?

Sally Keith's file was the last one in this stack. Much of what I read was familiar to me, as I'd heard accounts of her life from her mother and the chief. Sally was an unhappy, angry young woman who sought comfort in drugs. According to the notes in the file, somewhere along the way, Sally began to change for the better. She had attended regular group therapy sessions as well as individual sessions. Someone or something had gotten through to her. This was evident not only from the notes in the file but also from her journals and her actions after her release from the institution. She had attended college, performed well in her chosen career, and stayed drug free.

The papers in the file were in reverse-date order, with new entries placed on top of the older ones. The last and oldest item in Sally's file was an envelope that had been sealed with red wax and imprinted with the seal of the court. The court order I had in my possession allowed me access to the entire file, so I broke the wax seal and removed a yellowed copy of a court order that had been typed on onionskin paper. In the days before the widespread use of photographic copy machines, orders were hand typed with layers of carbon paper and onionskin sheets behind the original documents. These pages were now brittle with age. I carefully separated the sheets and began to read them.

Sally had been born out of wedlock to a pair of minors. The girl was fifteen years old; the boy was sixteen. Neither wished to keep the child; Sam and Alice Keith adopted Sally. The biological parents relinquished all rights to the child, as evidenced by their original signatures, which appeared on the copy of the court order. As I read the names of the two parents, I remembered what Miss Corrigan had said about Sally's flawed parentage. I slipped the copy of the order into my purse, closed the case file, picked up a sandwich, and leaned back in the chair to think. My thoughts swirled. The information in the adoption order had come as a complete surprise and definitely had a big impact on my investigation.

I quickly read through the personnel files of the three staff members then asked Ms. Paulson to arrange for them to visit me in the office. Lawrence Nelson was the first to arrive. His greying straight blonde hair was long and touched the tops of his shoulders. His pointed nose, square chin, and piercing blue eyes reminded me of a Viking. I could picture him dressed in furs, standing on the bow of a long boat holding a battle-axe. He was a senior orderly now but had been a new hire when Sally had been in residence. He had been responsible for the care of patients when they were in the common room. Female staff cared for the female patients in the residence wings, but males were stationed in the common areas because disturbances were more likely when the patients were all together in one place. Nelson's imposing size and bulk were helpful when the institution faced a violent disturbance. He remembered Sally only because he thought she was as beautiful as a movie star.

"Were you attracted to Ms. Keith?" I asked him.

"One couldn't help find her attractive, Sheriff, but I wasn't sexually attracted to her, if that's what you mean. She was a patient. I'm a caretaker. She was pretty. I'm a man who appreciates pretty women. You're very pretty. I'm not sexually attracted to you, but I certainly notice how nice you look."

"Thank you, Mr. Nelson. I appreciate your frankness."

"I didn't do anything to Sally Keith. I never touched her, much less abused her."

"Do you have any idea who'd do such a thing?

"No, but I wish I did. Someone like that deserves to be locked up here."

"Did you know Sally was murdered?"

"Yes, I heard. Things like that can't be kept quiet in a small town like this."

"Do you remember anything about Sally that could help me find her murderer?"

"I wish I did, ma'am," he said sadly. "I really wish I did."

The second orderly was assigned to the meal hall. Ramon Flores had moved from New York to Minnesota to look for work. He was hired for his size and strength. He remembered Sally as "*la senorita bonita*" but had no idea who had beaten or killed her.

Olga Swenson worked in the kitchen and meal hall. She was a pretty, matronly woman who had aged gracefully. She had kind blue eyes and a beautiful smile. She was obviously of Swedish descent, and her words were heavily accented.

"Yaw, I remember my little Sally. She was so lovely. Everyone noticed my little *kara barn*, my precious child, but very few could see how good she was inside."

"How could you see her inner beauty, Mrs. Swenson?" I prodded.

"She'd talk to me while she helped clean up after meals. That was one of her assigned chores. She talked about getting out of here, moving away, and starting her own family."

"Did she tell you any details, or did she just speak in generalities? Many teenage girls talk about getting married and having children."

"Oh, no. Sally had definite plans. She had a boyfriend, you know."

"Did she say who he was?" I asked hopefully.

She shook her head. "No, no, she never said his name. She asked me to help her to stay on a diet so she wouldn't get fat. Her young man had told her what a beautiful body she had, and she didn't want to gain weight by eating the starchy foods we serve here. I'd keep her mashed potatoes and give her an extra helping of vegetables. She always skipped the bread and dessert. I never forced her to eat anything she didn't want to eat."

"Did she say where her young man lived?"

"He was close by," she said, "but I don't know where. She was very secretive about that."

"Thank you, Mrs. Swenson. You've been a big help."

The woman offered another dazzling smile and left the room.

Chapter 29

Tuesday Afternoon

Dr. Waters escorted me through an elaborate electronic-door system into the top-security ward. Two sets of heavy steel sliding doors separated the criminally insane from the rest of the institution population.

"All patients in this ward are heavily sedated," Dr. Waters explained. "Out of an abundance of caution, we will also have a guard with us at all times."

"Of course," I said.

The cell rooms were small, and the doors were made of steel. Small windows in the doors were reinforced with steel mesh. Narrow horizontal open slits allowed the transfer of food trays. It would be very difficult to get out of these rooms without assistance. A jailer/orderly unlocked Jessup's cell and remained on guard in the doorway after the doctor and I entered.

The room was completely bare of decoration. Walls were painted a soft, moss green and the floor was tiled in dark green linoleum. Windows on the outside wall were narrow and placed near the ceiling. A neat metal framed bed, a stainless steel toilet and sink, a small desk and a straight-backed chair were the only items in the room.

Rodney Jessup stood at attention when we entered his room and remained so until Dr. Waters insisted that he sit on the edge of his bed. His back was ramrod straight and he refused to relax. He had a kindly face with soft brown eyes and a small button nose. His sideburns were beginning to gray, but the rest of his hair was deep chestnut brown. As first glance, it was difficult to believe he was a psychopathic murder, but Dr. Waters and I stood some distance away from him during the interview.

"Sheriff Davis has some questions to ask you, Jessup."

"Boy, things sure have changed on the outside when they have sheriffs that look like you, ma'am," he said with a sly smile. Moments ago, his face had been soft and peaceful. Now he glared at me with hatred in his eyes.

Ignoring his attitude, I asked, "Did you ever meet a young lady named Sally Keith, Mr. Jessup?"

"Not that I recall, Sheriff. Where would I have met her?"

"Here, Mr. Jessup, in this facility.

"Is she the blonde?"

"Yes, she was blond. Did you meet her?"

"Naw. I used to hear the guards talk about a hot blond patient named Sally, but I don't get out much. I never saw her or met her. You said she *was* blond. Does that mean she isn't blond anymore or she isn't *alive* anymore?"

"She's not alive anymore, Mr. Jessup."

"Can't pin this one on me, Sheriff. Never met the lady." With that he lay down on the bed and turned his back to us. The interview clearly was over.

The guard locked the door behind us and we made our way toward our next interview. Raymond Jessup began to laugh. His howling cackle could be heard for many feet down the hall.

Raymond Albertson didn't rise when we entered his cell. He sat on the edge of his bed with his feet flat on the floor. The man looked like a mild-mannered accountant. Gold wire-rimmed glasses sat on the bridge of his pointed nose. Thin lips curled into a quirky smile. Wrinkles surrounded dark eyes that shined with intelligence. I half expected to see a pencil parked above his ear.

"Whatever it is, I didn't do it," he huffed.

"No one said you did anything, Albertson," said Dr. Waters. "Sheriff Davis needs to ask you some questions."

“I heard you talking to Jessup. Not much insulation in the walls here, Doc.”

“Did any of the other patients ever make their way into the secure area, Mr. Albertson?” I asked.

“Not since I’ve been here. They’d have to be crazy to want to come in here. Oh, wait a minute. They *are* crazy! But none of them wants to come in here. Security is pretty tight.”

“Have you heard anyone talk about a girl named Sally Keith?” I asked, though I was pretty sure this was a dead end.

“I think one of the guards was hot on the trail of a blonde a few years back,” he said with a chuckle, “but all they ever talk about is women and hockey, so it’s hard to keep all the women straight in my head. That’s all I know.”

Chapter 30

Late Tuesday Afternoon

It was snowing again. I gingerly made my way across the parking lot and got into the rental car. My teeth were chattering. I wished the heating unit would push out more hot air. The sky was dark with snow clouds, and the wind whipped the flakes as they pelted the windshield. I breathed a sigh when I saw that traffic was moving steadily on the highway. I merged carefully and steered the car into the ruts made by the other vehicles. After an agonizing hour, I saw the sign marking the road that led to my motel, and I turned off the main highway. No cars were ahead of me on this secondary road. I drove even more slowly to make sure I stayed on the pavement. "I'm never moving up here," I muttered.

Out of nowhere a pair of headlights appeared behind me and quickly closed the gap between us. The driver was riding my tail, but I couldn't move out of the way to let him or her pass because I didn't know where the pavement ended. The engine roared as if to pass by me, but to my shock and horror, the vehicle slammed into the back of my car. I controlled the rental car with some difficulty. Then I heard another roar and felt an even stronger impact, which made my car spin. I made a vain attempt to straighten it, but the momentum slammed me into a stand of pine trees along the road. Before I could restart the engine, something smashed through the driver's-side window. Then I saw an arm reach into my car. Before I could do anything about it, a cloth covered my nose and mouth. I smelled chloroform for a few seconds before I succumbed to the fumes.

**

Freezing. My entire body was shaking. I wiggled my hands and feet in an effort to stimulate circulation, but my arms and legs were stiff and heavy from the cold. Terror at the thought of freezing to death made my heart beat so hard that I felt it in my head and heard it in my ears. The same terror had infiltrated my subconscious last week, but I had paid the warning no heed. After I slowly opened my eyes, a hollow feeling engulfed the pit of my stomach as I viewed my surroundings. The room was drab and windowless. I saw one exit door and one louvered door, which I assumed was a closet. The walls were completely barren. Plastic light panels in the drop ceiling illuminated the room. I was lying on a narrow bed. My arms were bound to the metal headboard with hospital restraints. Sally and Nadine's nightmares had become mine.

My head throbbed, and one of my eyes was almost swollen shut. As I ran my tongue across my bottom lip,

I felt a tear in the skin. The metallic taste of blood filled my mouth. I lowered my gaze and saw I was completely naked. An ugly bruise was forming on my left breast and another on my left hipbone. An angry red mark, made by the seatbelt, stretched across my midsection. These were all reminders of the collision of my car against the pines.

My bladder was full, and it was only a matter of time before nature would empty it. Then I would be cold *and* wet. The room was chilled but by no means as cold as the temperature outside, so I knew there was a heat source nearby. I saw no ducts or vents in the ceiling or floor, but I heard the low drone of a furnace. I said a prayer of thanks that I was trapped inside instead of out in the blizzard. Then I said a prayer to St. Bernadette, my patron saint, asking her to help guide me through what I knew would be an unpleasant ordeal. I pushed the feeling of panic aside and allowed hope to spread through my body. I thought of Buck and his baby inside me. I swore to myself that I would come out of this alive, no matter what it took.

My resolve wasn't shaken when I heard the click of the door handle and watched my captor step into the room. I stared at the face of Mark Ritter, the security guard from the Phoenix Sun Condominiums, the man who had made the nine-one-one call the night Sally Keith was murdered.

The crisp black and white uniform he had worn when Ike and I interviewed him was gone. Instead, his tall frame was clothed in a pair of faded blue jeans and a well-worn grey sweatshirt. Lips were drawn into a sneer. His blue eyes were as hard and as cold as those of a shark before it makes its attack.

"Howdy, Sheriff," he greeted me. "You aren't so imposing without your badge and your clothes, are you? You look like all the rest of us. Actually you look a whole lot better than most. I promised myself I'd get a little piece of your action before I killed you."

He folded his arms across his chest and glared down at me with steely eyes. "I wish you hadn't come up here. Sally was a two-bit whore. Nobody cares if she's gone. When I saw you here in town, I knew it wouldn't be long before you found out I used to live here, and then you'd piece everything together. Sally and I were close a long time ago, but she called me a psycho. Can you imagine that? Nobody calls me a psycho and lives to tell about it."

His laugh was haunting; it took all my willpower to push the terror to the back of my mind. I realized no one had the slightest idea where I was right now. There would be no knight in shining armor to rescue me. I'd have to get out of this myself somehow. I *was* going to stay alive, and so was my baby.

My eyes fell on the amulet that Lenore had placed around my neck. It was supposed to offer some protection against evil. I guess she didn't get that spell completely right.

"What's that thing hanging around your neck?" he said, noticing that I'd glanced at it. "I was afraid to touch it. I saw that witch put it there, and I didn't want to have a hex on me for taking it off."

"You were wise not to remove it, Mr. Ritter. Lenore is a powerful witch who wouldn't take kindly to anyone interfering with her spells."

A scowl of displeasure appeared on the young man's face.

"You've watched their ceremonies on the jetties, haven't you, Mr. Ritter? You must enjoy creeping around in the dark, dressed in your black clothing, spying on people."

"So what if I have?"

"Then you know how much influence they have with the spirits, don't you?" He was silent, but I could tell he was afraid of Lenore and didn't wish to displease her. "You've already displeased her by bringing me here. Didn't you think of that?"

"You shut up!" he roared as he slapped me across the face. "Shut your mouth," he screamed as he struck me again. I saw stars and shook my head to clear it. Hitting me in my vulnerable position obviously bolstered his courage. The smug look he had worn on his face reappeared. "You think you're smart, don't you?" He grabbed my breasts and squeezed them so hard that I gasped in pain. "Ooh, look at you. Does little Miss Rough-and-Tough like her sex rough? Well, I'm your man for that!" He unfastened his belt and unzipped his pants. He was on top of me in an instant and penetrated with cruel harshness.

"You're very good, Sheriff. There's more where that came from. We can do this again later. You'd like that, wouldn't—" He stopped in midsentence as a loud thud came from somewhere above us. "What's that stupid bitch doing now?"

He ran from the room, leaving the door ajar. His sneakers had made no sound on the linoleum floor. I heard the raspy squeak of a door hinge and slow, careful footfalls from the darkness beyond the door. A moment later a face appeared at the door. I couldn't believe it. It was Ike McDuffie.

"Sheriff—Bernie, oh, God! What has he done?"

A sharp report of gunfire halted Ike's conversation. Blood colored the sleeve of his jacket. He stumbled, and I saw two more muzzle blasts in the darkness beyond the door. The rounds hit Ike in the back, the impact of the shots propelling him forward. After he fell facedown on the floor, Ritter sauntered into the room with a smoking pistol hanging from his right hand. A crazed look covered his face. This was the ultimate high for him.

I couldn't see Ike's entire body, but blood seeped onto the floor near his torso. He lay motionless, and I couldn't tell whether he was breathing. Ritter reached down, picked up Ike's pistol, and stuck it into the waistband of his pants. "What do you want to bet he's not alone? I bet that stupid chief is up there somewhere." He stood quietly, listening for other signs of movement above us. "I'll be right back, Sheriff. Don't go anywhere. *Ha*!" After he disappeared into the darkness, he cursed quietly as his footsteps caused a board to squeak. He was going up a set of stairs.

"Ike," I said. "McDuffie, are you OK?" No sound. Tears filled my eyes as I realized he probably was dead. A slight movement drew my attention to the door again. A small hand reached around the doorjamb. Then a face appeared.

"Nadine," I whispered. "My goodness, I'm so glad to see you."

"Sh-sh-sheriff?"

"Yes, Nadine. Can you unfasten these belt restraints?" She shook her head violently. "Please, Nadine. Do it before he hurts my baby."

That did it. That was the trigger to get her to act. She tiptoed into the room, stepped over Ike's body, and untied my right hand. My fingers were stiff and cold, so I couldn't unfasten the buckle on my left hand by myself. I worked my fingers back and forth and shook my hand and arm to increase the circulation. Nadine was painfully slow, but she eventually unfastened my left hand. I rolled from the bed and collapsed on the floor next to Ike. My legs wouldn't support me, but I was able to kneel on the icy tile. I stretched my arm to his neck and felt for a pulse. He was alive. I moved across his body toward his feet and found what I knew would be there.

"Well, well," a voice sounded from the doorway.

In one fluid motion, I turned and fired Ike's backup pistol. The little 9mm round entered Ritter's forehead right between his eyebrows. I knew Ike's weapon was loaded with hollow points, so I wasn't surprised to see the back of Ritter's head separate from his body and splatter across the wall. The last thing I remembered was lowering my arm and dropping the weapon.

Chapter 31

Day Unknown

Hushed voices. Low whispers reached my ears. What was that smell? A gagging medicinal odor filled my nostrils. I thought I must be in the morgue. Was I dead? I struggled to think, but a swirling fog engulfed my brain. Sounds pounded in my ears. I couldn't open my eyes. I couldn't move my body! Was I tied up again? My heart pounded in my chest, but as I realized my arms were lying flat beside my body and not tied to the headboard, my panic subsided. I seemed to drift around the room, looking down on its occupants. I was lying on a bed covered with a sheet, and people in white coats were talking. Yes, this must be the morgue.

I couldn't be dead—I just couldn't. There were sheets underneath me. The surface I lay on was soft. This wasn't the morgue. If I were in the morgue, I'd be on a stainless-steel table. This must be a hospital. *Think, Bernie. Think,* I commanded my brain, but it didn't respond. I felt myself drift again, for how long I didn't know.

The sound of another voice reached my ears. This one was deeper than the rest. It didn't whisper but spoke in a low, resonant tone, with a subtle Southern lilt. It was Buck! He had come to get me. *Thank you, God!* I still couldn't move or even open my eyes. I felt trapped inside my body, but I heard what they were saying.

"This is one lucky woman, Sheriff. She went through hell, but she came through it."

"Thanks for taking such good care of her, Doc. Sorry it took me so long to get here, but this snow is somethin' else. We had to wait for a break in the weather before we could land here."

"I can't believe you got here as fast as you did. I know the airlines are backed up with holiday traffic. Combine that with the bad weather, and travel is difficult right now."

"I chartered a private jet, Doc. Cuts down on delays. Can you tell me how she's doing?"

"She lost consciousness at some point during this ordeal and hasn't yet regained it. The human body has a way of protecting itself when it needs to. Hers has shut down for a while. I'm sure it's temporary. We're giving her IV meds and keeping her hydrated. The feeding tube will come out as soon as she wakes up. Her physical wounds are superficial—cuts, bruises, and bumps, but no broken bones. There's no internal damage that I can see. And she didn't lose the baby, which is a miracle in itself. The physical damage isn't bad, but we won't be able to assess the mental damage until she wakes." The doctor hesitated for a moment before concluding his assessment. "Sir, she was raped. I don't know if anyone told you."

"Yes, I was told," Buck whispered. He was quiet for a few moments before continuing. "Was there a head injury?"

"She was battered, but she didn't suffer a concussion. When I said, 'mental damage,' I meant we haven't been able to assess the extent of emotional injury and how it might affect her mentally. She's been through a terrible trauma. Sometimes emotional damage can take a while to heal. Do you understand?"

"Yes. I'd like to kill the bastard who did this to her."

"She beat you to it, Sheriff," a voice sounded from the doorway. "Nailed him right between the eyes." I recognized the voice. It was the chief.

"Sheriff Davis, I'm Paul Cleverdon, the chief of police. I'm the one who called you."

"Thank you, sir. I'm obliged to you for all you've done to help my wife."

"I feel this is my fault, Sheriff. This guy lived right here in this town, off and on, for twenty years. I knew him when he was a kid. He was always polite and helpful to me. I never had an inkling he'd do the things he did to your wife. He even sexually abused his sister. Hell, there may be more victims here. I just don't know."

"Gentlemen, I need to visit other patients," the doctor said, "so I'll leave you for now. I'll check back soon."

"Thanks, Doc. See you later," Buck replied. "Chief, tell me everything you know, even the things you think a husband shouldn't hear about. Bernie means everything to me. She's not only the officer of record in Sally Keith's murder case but also my wife. I need to know everything."

"Son, I'll tell you as much as I can. I pieced together some of it, but my theory probably isn't far from the truth.

"Your wife came here to investigate the murder of a girl who was as close to me as my own daughter. I gave her some background information and helped her get a court order so she could go up to the state mental hospital where Sally had been confined. I probably should have gone with her, but they aren't too fond of me up there, so I figured she'd get more information on her own. The night clerk at the Uplands Motel called me when your wife didn't arrive back there that night. I rousted the administrator of the mental institution out of bed, but he told me your wife left his office early that afternoon. I retraced her path to the hospital and found her rental car crashed in a stand of pine trees along the road. There was no trace of her. It was as if she had been spirited out of there.

"I suppose he saw her in town, figured she was getting close to him, and followed her to the mental hospital. I imagine he ambushed her, overpowered her, and took her to that basement room in his sister's house. I went through your wife's briefcase and handbag, which we found in Nadine's house. I found your name and called you, but I also found two photographs—one of Sally and one of Nadine—his own sister—tied to a bed, badly beaten, and God knows what else. It doesn't take a super sleuth to make the connection now, but I couldn't have done it before. I believe Mark followed Sally to Florida, stalked her, and killed her. I don't know if there's enough hard evidence to prove it, but it's clear in my mind.

"Son, I have another photo here in my pocket. I want you to know that I'm the only person on God's earth who's seen it. I'd just as soon burn it, but I don't want you to live the rest of your life wondering if it's in an evidence file somewhere with people ogling at it. It's a photo of your wife, and it's not pretty."

A groan escape Buck's lips, and then he was silent for some time. "At least it's over now. He won't harm anyone ever again. What was his name, Chief?"

"He was born Marcus Ritter Barnard, but his driver's license listed his name as Mark Ritter."

"Ritter?" asked Buck. "A guy named Ritter was the guard who called nine-one-one for Sally Keith's murder."

"You don't say? Mark often worked as a security guard. He wanted to be a police officer, but he was too high-strung for this kind of work. Mind you, I'm not offering this as an excuse for his behavior, but he had a lousy home life. His mother was a beautiful woman but as naïve as they come. She came from a very religious family; her parents died while she was still in school. Kids called her 'Crazy Margaret,' poor thing. She let men talk her into anything, and pretty soon she had a couple of kids; her boyfriend's gone; and she's trying to raise those kids by herself. Nadine—that's Mark's sister—was always a little slow in the head. Margaret wasn't quite right either, but it looks like Mark was the worst of the three.

"Most of the story I got from Nadine via Alice. She's Sally Keith's mother, my secretary, and a lifelong friend. She knew Margaret in high school and feels sorry for Nadine, so she looks in on the girl from time to time. Nadine was awakened by loud noises in the house. She saw her brother carry someone down the stairs to a room in the basement. She hid in her own room until she heard Mark moving around upstairs in the kitchen. Only then did she venture out of her room. It took a lot of courage for that poor girl to make that trip downstairs.

"Nadine watched Mark from a dark section of the basement. She said there was a noise upstairs. After Mark went out to investigate, a man came into the room. Ritter appeared shortly thereafter, shot him, and then went back upstairs to look for me. He figured I had accompanied the man. Nadine helped your wife unfasten the restraints so she was able to get to the man's backup piece and kill Ritter. That fellow is in a room down the hall. His name is Isaac McDuffie."

"What was McDuffie doing up here?" asked Buck.

I heard the soft whoosh of a door opening. A squeaking noise followed. The noise got closer and stopped somewhere in the middle of the room.

"I came up here to find Bernie—I mean Sheriff Davis. Sorry, sir, I meant no disrespect," said Ike.

"That's all right. I know you two go way back," said Buck. "Are you OK, Detective?"

"Yes, sir. They have me all bandaged up, and they make me sit in this wheelchair, but I just have a flesh wound in my arm. The other shots hit my vest and knocked me out. I'll be fine."

"Thank you for everything you did to help her," Buck said.

"I was too late, sir. He had already..." Ike's voice trailed away.

"She's alive. That's all that matters."

There was a long silence in the room.

"Take me over near her," Ike asked.

"Mr. McDuffie, you need rest. I should take you back to your room," a female voice suggested.

"Later. Take me over to her."

I heard the squeaking noise again and realized it was the wheelchair. It stopped near my bed.

"Has she said anything? Has she moved at all?" Ike asked.

"No," Buck said. "The doctor said it'd take her some time to heal."

Ike picked up my hand. He raised it to his lips and placed a kiss on top. "C'mon, Bernie. It's time to wake up. We need to get out of here." Then he placed my hand gently on the bed.

I wanted to say something to him, but no matter how hard I tried, I couldn't respond.

"What brought you up here?" asked Buck.

"I was working on some background checks. Responses were slow because people were out for the holidays. I finally received a fax from one of the companies listed on Mark Ritter's résumé. His hometown was listed as St. Peter, Minnesota, but he'd told us he was from Upstate New York. He also was using a slightly different name. It was too much of a coincidence that

St. Peter was Sally's hometown as well as the place where Bernie had gone. I had a bad feeling about it.

"Sheriff Davis had put me on desk duty. I couldn't go the condo to check on Ritter without disobeying her direct order, so I asked to use some vacation days and did some investigating on my own time. You won't believe what I found out there. That sick bastard had a little maintenance room at the condo building set up like some kind of a shrine. Pictures of Sally were plastered everywhere. There were photos of other women too. All of them had been beaten. I don't know if they're alive or dead. I didn't have time to find out. But I knew I had to get up here.

"A weird thing happened while I was there. Bernie and I interviewed a couple of different folks who lived on the fifth floor of that condo. I was standing in that little room of Ritter's when I realized I smelled something familiar. It permeated the whole place. I turned around, and a woman named Lenore was standing right behind me. Then I realized the smell was incense. She reeked of it."

"I've met Lenore," said Buck. "She's a member of the witch coven that congregates on the jetties each month."

"That's right. She says she's a good witch," Ike continued.

"What's all this about witches?" interrupted the chief.

Buck told him about the witches that met on the rock jetty near Sally's beach house.

"Sally told me once that she herself was a witch. I took it as an attention-getting rambling of a teenage girl."

"What else did she say, Chief?" Ike asked.

"Not much. She said she knew a powerful warlock who performed ritualistic sacrifices using animals. She said she was afraid of him. I asked his name, but she went silent after that. I nosed around a little but never took her too seriously."

"Any problem with missing pets around here?" asked Buck.

"A handful went missing several years back. Nothing recent, though."

"Psychopaths often abuse animals," Buck said. "They sometimes advance to abusing children or weak adults. Sally's warlock could have been Mark Ritter, or whatever his name is. Ike, did you find anything else in that maintenance room?"

"Some candles, a few posters of dark rock bands, some test tubes filled with powders. I figured the test tubes were drugs."

"Anything printed on the floor?"

"Come to think of it, there were some lines on the floor, but I didn't stay there long enough to do a detailed examination. Not after Lenore came in."

"What did she do?" the chief asked.

"Scared the shit out of me for starters. That woman can come and go without any sound at all."

"What did she say to you?" Buck prodded.

"She told me Bernie was in danger. Actually she said 'the beautiful sheriff' was in danger."

"In what way?"

"She said evil had followed her to Minnesota, and she needed my help," Ike said. "She gave me a little bag of stuff to wear that she said would help defeat the evil one. I figured she was loony tunes, but since I already had the feeling that Bernie was in danger, I headed to the airport."

"What did you do with the bag she gave you?" Buck asked.

"She tried to put it around my neck, but I didn't want her to touch me, so I put it in my pocket. Lenore said she had given an amulet—that's what she called the bag—to Bernie, who wore it around her neck, but the evil was very powerful and needed much good magic to defeat it. Did you ever hear anything so crazy?"

"Bernie had the amulet on her neck when she came home Saturday afternoon. Look. It's still there."

"Didn't help either of us very much, did it?" asked Ike.

"You're both alive," said Buck.

Silence filled the room. I almost could hear Buck's thoughts. Three months ago he would have dismissed Lenore's beliefs and actions as the rants of a crazy old woman. But our lives had become intertwined with a band of Gypsies from my past, and he had come to understand there were unexplained forces at work that affected us. Magic and spells weren't out of the realm of possibility, and now he was willing to admit these things existed.

Ike's voice broke the silence. "Well, anyway, it took me forever to get here. I tried to call Bernie several times at her motel but couldn't reach her. By the time I got to the house listed as Ritter's home, he already had her. At first I wasn't sure I had the right place. The house looked abandoned. There were no lights inside, in the yard, or on the porch. As I approached the front door, I saw a small, dark object lying in the snow near the walk. That's when I was sure."

"What did you find?"

"Bernie's hat."

"How in the world did you know it was her hat? She never wears hats. She only brought one here because she knew it would be so cold."

"I knew it was hers because I have one exactly like it," Ike explained.

"Oh," was all Buck said, but I heard the hurt in his voice.

"She learned to knit during Hurricane Donna in nineteen sixty. She didn't make complicated things—just hats, scarves, and mittens. It isn't usually cold enough to get much use out of those things in Sarasota. One winter she got on the school bus wearing a new knitted hat. She looked so cute with all that curly blond hair poking out from beneath that stocking cap. She sat down next to me, like she always did, pulled out another cap, and placed it on my head. They were exactly alike. She had used navy blue and white yarn because they were the school colors for Sarasota Junior High."

"I see," said Buck, and I heard a catch in his voice.

"We were twelve years old, sir," Ike explained.

"You both kept those hats for twenty-three years."

"Yes, and that's how I knew she was inside that house." Emotion choked Ike's voice as he continued. "When I saw her lying naked, strapped to that bed, I was so angry. Before I took two steps toward her, Ritter had me in his sights. I took one in the arm and two in the back. It's weird, isn't it?"

"What's that?"

"I came up here to save her, but in the end she saved me. I would've died on the spot if she hadn't hammered it into my head that I needed to wear a vest all the time."

"She knew you carried a backup piece too, Ike. Thank God you two stick to patterns." He paused for a moment. "You look tired. Why don't you let this pretty nurse take you back to your room now?"

"Yeah, maybe I'd better rest a little. I need to be strong enough to travel so we can get out of here. Will you tell me when she wakes up?"

"Yes, I will," Buck promised.

"You look a little tired yourself, Sheriff," said the chief. "She still has a room at the Uplands Motel. You could go there and sleep a little. I can sit with her."

"No, thanks, Chief. I want my face to be the first one she sees when she wakes up."

"OK, I understand," he said. "I'll see you later then. Please keep me posted on her condition."

Buck pulled a chair over to the edge of my bed. Before he sat down, he leaned over and placed a kiss on my forehead. "McDuffie's right, Bernie. You need to wake up. We need to get far away from here." He picked up my hand and held it against his lips. I felt the rough stubble of his beard on my skin. I also felt the wetness of his tears as they rolled down his cheek.

Chapter 32

Unknown Day

I'd lost all concept of time. I could have been unconscious for hours or days. My mind drifted through layers of fog. I thought I'd never break free, but finally I was able to lift my eyelids. The lights in the room had been dimmed, but sunlight peeped through the blinds. Buck was still holding my hand. From the growth of his beard, it appeared that he hadn't shaved in several days. He had laid his head on my bed, and the rhythm of his breathing told me he was asleep. My lips were cracked and dry; the inside of my mouth and throat felt like sandpaper. I tried to speak, but no words came out, so I squeezed Buck's hand. He woke with a start.

"Bernie," he said. "Welcome back, love." He reached for the nurse's call button and pushed it. Within seconds, a woman hurried into the room. "She's awake," was all he needed to say.

The nurse disappeared but returned with the doctor close on her heels. "I'm Dr. Cambridge, Mrs. Davis.

He looked at me with kind, smiling hazel eyes. He was young, perhaps in his late twenties. His body had the lean sinewy muscles of a runner. We're all *very* glad to see you're better. Mr. Davis, would you allow me a few minutes to examine your wife?"

Buck left the room while the doctor poked and prodded me. He ordered the removal of the feeding tube, and a technician came in almost immediately to perform that task. The nurse changed the dressing on my wounds, gently washed my face, and helped me drink some water.

"The next thing to go will be the saline IV and after that the meds," he told me. I nodded my understanding. "Do you know where you are, Mrs. Davis?"

Again I nodded. I formed the word *hospital* with my lips, but I couldn't make the sounds.

"Your voice will come back after you get more liquids into your mouth and throat. Don't worry. All things considered, you're doing very well. Your vital signs are good. You have no serious injuries, no broken bones, and none of your facial cuts will require plastic surgery. Most important, you're still pregnant, and the baby is unharmed."

My eyes filled with tears as I nodded once more. We both looked toward the door as a knock sounded. A commotion came from that direction. Buck was pushing McDuffie's wheelchair into the room. A look of relief covered Ike's face. Buck was smiling as our eyes met.

"Oh, I'm so glad to see your eyes open again, ma'am," Ike said. "We've been waiting for days."

"Doc, what'll it take to get her out of here?" asked Buck.

"She'll have to wait until she no longer needs the IV. She needs to be able to ingest food. She must be able to walk, and she must be strong enough to endure the rigors of travel."

"I have a private jet fueled and waiting to go at a moment's notice, so travel will be easy. If I carry her onto that jet, can she go?"

"Mr. Davis," Dr. Cambridge urged, "she still needs medical care."

"What are you doing for the Christmas holidays, Doc?"

"What?"

"Do you have to work here over Christmas?"

"No. This will be my first Christmas off in years."

"How would you like to spend your Christmas vacation in Florida?"

"What?"

"You heard me. If we can get her on that jet, we're outta here," said Buck. "You could come with us."

The doctor seemed to be quietly wrapped in his own thoughts for a few moments. "OK, yes, I'll go. Can my girlfriend join me?"

"The more the merrier."

"We were supposed to leave tonight for a ski trip, but the lodge had so much snow that the roof collapsed. They cancelled our reservation this morning. We'll have to repack for the warmer climate, but we can do it."

"Let's go."

"We can't just pick up and leave. Your wife may need—"

"What will help her more, being in her home for Christmas surrounded by people who care about her or being here in the town that holds such terrible memories?"

"Touché, Mr. Davis."

"Call me 'Buck.' McDuffie, are you ready?"

"I was born ready."

Chapter 33

December 23

I experienced what was probably the fastest hospital checkout in the history of medical science. Buck drove Ike's rental car. Ike and the doctor's girlfriend, Anastasia LaPointe, who happened to be Ike's nurse, were his passengers. I was loaded into the doctor's car along with cases of medical supplies and luggage. Chief Cleverdon had volunteered to go to my room at the Uplands Motel to gather all of my belongings and drive them to the airport. He also said he'd get my damaged rental car back to the agency and arrange for repairs. His brother-in-law owned the local car rental agency, so he'd square it with him.

After the drive to the airport, I was exhausted. Dr. Cambridge pulled his car onto the tarmac alongside the jet. Buck carried me out and onto the plane and settled me into a seat. It didn't take long for a crew to remove the snow and ice from the exterior of the plane. Minutes later we were in the air. I fell asleep as the wheels lifted from the ground and awoke when they touched down at the Sarasota-Bradenton Airport.

Collectively we had three cars at the airport—Buck's, Ike's, and mine. The doctor, however, wouldn't let Ike or me drive. Dr. Cambridge, Anastasia, and Buck transferred the luggage and medical supplies to the vehicles and caravanned to the ranch. By the time we reached the house, darkness had fallen, and I was beyond tired. I noticed that Buck and Ike's eyes were bloodshot and ringed with black circles. Only Dr. Cambridge and Anastasia seemed perky and alert. Buck insisted on carrying me into the house, though I probably could have walked. The house was ablaze with light, and delicious-smelling aromas greeted us.

Wiping his hands on a towel, Devereaux sauntered in from the kitchen. A long chef's apron covered his usual attire of jeans and a white T-shirt. The jaunty red bandana adorned his neck, and a smile of welcome adorned his swarthy face. "Maurice Devereaux, at your service. As we say on the bayou, '*Joyeux Nöel.*'"

My exhaustion slipped away as the sight of his happy, familiar face breathed energy into me.

"Everyone, come, come, all of you," he said. "Devereaux and the ranch hands will handle the luggage. All the weary travelers will rest and relax. Then you will all feast on Devereaux's special chicken-and-Andouille-sausage gumbo and crusty French bread, *oui*? Come, come, all is ready." He herded us into the great room.

I was astonished at how my home had been transformed. A twenty-foot fir tree, engulfed in tiny white lights, was the focal point. Shiny glass ornaments reflected the light, and strands of foil tinsel swayed with the slightest breeze. Boughs of cedar adorned the mantles, and swags of the same cedar draped the doorways. A hundred white candles had been arranged on every level surface of the room. Both fireplaces burned brightly, and the scent of cedar logs filled the air.

"Welcome home, *madame*," Devereaux said as he kissed my hand. Though his face smiled, I saw worry in his deep-black eyes.

"Thank you, Devereaux. I'm fine. Please don't worry."

"*Oui*, *madame*," he said with a wink.

Buck placed a tape into the cassette deck, and the soft sound of "Joy to the World" filled the room. Devereaux disappeared into the kitchen but quickly returned with a large crystal goblet filled with wretched milk and handed it to me with a smile. All the others were drinking cocktails from the bar. Buck moved close to me and raised his glass. "To safe returns," he said as he clinked his glass against mine.

"Hear, hear!" said the others in salute.

Dinner was a happy affair. As everyone relaxed, conversations were lively and filled with the warmth of the season. We ate in the formal dining room at the huge cypress table that easily could seat twenty. A heavy silver candelabra supported beeswax candles that filled the air with a sweet honey scent. Votives flickered on the buffet cabinet and windowsills. Potted poinsettias were tucked into every nook and cranny, and cedar boughs cascaded from the doorframes and the massive chandeliers.

We finished the meal of delicious gumbo and crusty bread with trays of cheese and fruit and individual servings of flan de leche, my favorite dessert. At the end of meal, Dr. Cambridge escorted his patients to their rooms.

I crashed as soon as my head hit the pillow but woke a few hours later. Buck wasn't in bed yet; I heard his voice coming from the direction of the great room. I was thirsty, so I pulled on my robe and made my way to the kitchen. I didn't mean to eavesdrop, but my ears tuned into the conversation just the same.

Dr. Cambridge was speaking quietly to Buck. "Yes, she's healing quickly on the outside, but it's the inside, her mind, that I'm worried about. During the holidays there will be lots of people around and plenty to do. After Christmas is over, life will settle back into familiar routines. She'll be here alone while you're working. She'll have too much time to think about and relive that traumatic event over and over. You know the effect these kinds of experiences can have. You must have encountered similar events in your line of work. She may become paranoid; she may withdraw inside herself; or she may have nightmares. She may shrink from your touch. The thought of intercourse may be horrific."

"But I'm not *him*," Buck argued.

"No, you're not, but that isn't the point. It's the act itself that may be repulsive. It happens."

"Well, I can live without it."

"No, you can't," Dr. Cambridge said, "but it's noble of you to be willing to try. I'm just suggesting she see a psychiatrist. Give her an unrelated party to talk to—someone she can tell about this."

"Seeing a psychiatrist could negatively influence her political career. She likes being the county sheriff. If the press finds out what happened in Minnesota, they'll have a field day."

"What's more important, your wife's mental health or her career?"

Buck was silent.

The doctor continued, "At least talk to her about it. Ask her gynecologist to suggest it if that would help, but get her to talk to someone."

"OK," Buck finally said.

I heard them rise from the couch, so I scurried back to the bedroom. Buck came in a few minutes later. I heard him undress in the walk-in closet before he slipped into bed. I was lying on my side with my back facing him. He carefully moved over close to me and encircled me with his arm.

"You're awake, aren't you?"

"Yes," I said. "How did you know?"

"Your skin is cold as ice." He shifted his foot to touch mine. "And your feet feel like Popsicles."

"I was thirsty," I said in explanation.

"So you heard what the doctor told me."

"Yes."

"Will you talk to someone about this?"

"We'll see."

Buck sighed. "That means no. Will you talk to me about it?"

I was silent for several long moments. I didn't want to talk to anyone about what happened. I didn't want to relive it. I didn't want Buck to know how terrified I'd been. It would just cause him pain. "I don't know," was all I could say. I lay awake nestled in Buck's arms. I felt so safe and warm there. He was snoring gently in a few minutes, but my mind was too active for me to sleep.

Was Buck right? Did I need professional help? I *didn't* want to see a psychiatrist. What could I do? A thought formed in my mind. The more I thought about it, the more plausible it seemed. Before long, I realized this could be a solution. Perhaps there was someone who could assist me, but his methods would be more than unconventional. Dukker, my Gypsy friend, could help.

Chapter 34

Christmas Eve

The next morning I awoke with a start to the sound of hard rain pelting the bedroom windows. A fierce north wind howled like a banshee. Laughter resounded from the kitchen, so I donned my robe and headed in the direction of the sound. I felt stiff from having slept in one spot, so my movement was slow. All eyes turned toward me as I entered the room. Buck quickly moved to my side to offer his support.

"It's good to see you up and about, Mrs. Davis," said Anastasia. Her smiling black eyes lit up her face. She was a beautiful French-Canadian with a soft French accent. I am sure that she and Devereaux would have much to talk about during the next few days.

"I'm so stiff and sore that I need to stay up and move around. Being in bed makes me stiffer."

"Me too," said Ike. "I was hoping to go outside for a while but not in this rain."

"The rain probably will be gone in an hour or so," said Buck. "It'll be beautiful for Christmas Day. Since our two invalids seem to be able to move around by themselves, the rest of us may be able to go out for a couple of hours this afternoon," he told Doc and Anastasia. "We have a stable full of horses if you're up for a riding tour of the ranch."

"That would be wonderful," said Anastasia. "I haven't ridden in years, but I haven't forgotten how."

Dr. Cambridge turned to Ike and me. "I'd like to examine both of you before we go off and leave you alone."

"We're both fine," said Ike. "Go and have a good time. We'll take care of each other."

Buck had cooked sausage and bacon, but he waited until I got up before he finished preparing breakfast. Before long we were devouring thick slices of French toast with warm maple syrup accompanied by the breakfast meats. My appetite had returned, and it felt good to eat. I gobbled down two helpings of everything.

After breakfast, Ike and I made our way to the living room and sat by the fire while the others headed for the barn. The crackle of the flames mesmerized me, and I found my mind drifting into sleep. I saw mountains of snowdrifts and felt myself spinning on an icy street. My eyes snapped open as I crashed into a pine tree.

"You OK, Bernie?" Ike asked softly. My head was resting on his shoulder as his arm held me tightly against his body. "You were crying in your sleep."

"I was dreaming," I told him. "Actually it was a nightmare."

"Would you like to tell me about it? It's after breakfast, so you don't have to worry about it coming true." He laughed at his own reference to the old wives' tale that dreams told before breakfast would come true.

"It's already come true."

"Tell me about it," he said softly. "You need to tell someone."

"Why does everyone keep saying that to me?" I snapped.

"Look, Bernie," Ike started, but his voice drifted away. When he stopped speaking, I looked up into his deep-blue eyes. He gently placed a beefy hand against my face, tilted my chin up, and bent down until our lips touched. His passionate kiss was sensuous and deep. I knew this was wrong, but I couldn't stop myself from kissing him back. My arms encircled his neck, and our bodies pressed against each other. The heat of passion burned between us.

When we separated, Ike said softly, "I had to do that, Bernie. I've wanted to for twenty years. Funny how a brush with death makes a man realize what is important in life."

"We won't ever talk about this, Ike," I whispered. "Chalk it up to emotional stress on both our parts. We need to forget this ever happened. I can't imagine how hurt Buck would be if he knew about this."

I wriggled out of his arms and moved to the opposite end of the couch. Hot tears pooled in my eyes. It was all I could do to keep from sobbing. I had betrayed Buck with that kiss. Pangs of guilt filled me, and my insides shook.

Ike watched my retreat. "It never happened, ma'am," he said. "You can trust me not to speak of it, but I'll *never* forget this moment."

We looked at each other but spoke no words for several minutes. Finally I broke the silence and changed the subject. "Do you think Jack is working today? It's Christmas Eve."

"He's there. With your being out of town, he probably slept there."

"I haven't checked in for days," I said. "He's probably a little peeved at me right now. I don't know if anyone called him at all. We have to tell Danny Dean that he's off the hook. Mark Ritter killed Sally; he admitted that to me. I can't go to Danny's in my condition, and neither can you. A phone call isn't appropriate for this. Jack can go see him, but he'll need to know the details. We'll also need to tell the state attorney's office to dismiss the charges. And we'll have to notify the press."

Ike's face appeared filled with emotion. He reached out to me but then thought better of it and withdrew his hand. "Bernie, I'm the only one who actually saw what happened up there. I saw you lying naked, strapped to the bed, in that hellhole. When the doctor and nurse go home, your husband and I will be the only ones here who know you were raped. Let's keep it that way. Don't tell the press the whole story. Please."

There was wisdom in Ike's words. We had enough evidence to release Danny and close the case without describing all the details of my capture. The psychopath who had killed Sally Keith had held me prisoner, and I'd been injured in the process. Ike had been injured trying to rescue me. The killer was dead. That would be enough.

"I'll call Jack and ask him to come out here," I said. "Then I'll take a shower and get dressed. I may try to cover up these bruises a little too, so I won't scare him."

**

An hour later Jack knocked on the front door. I had sent one of the ranch hands down to the gate to let him in. "Good God," was all he said when he saw Ike and me standing in the hall.

"I guess the makeup didn't help much," I said with a little laugh.

"Sheriff, McDuffie, what happened?"

"C'mon in, Jack. Sit by the fire. We have a story to tell you."

Ike and I relayed the events that had transpired, minus the fact that I'd been raped. I explained away injuries as being a result of the auto accident and the subsequent kidnapping. We described the murderer's fiendish habits and what he had done to Sally and his sister. Ike told him about the maintenance room in the condo and the wall of photographs portraying the suffering of many women. I told him the state's attorney had to be advised of the new evidence so formal charges against Danny Dean could be dropped and the cash bond could be released. I gave him a fact list that Tom could use to prepare written statements for the press. Jack and Tom would have to be the point men for information because I wasn't going to show up at the office until I'd healed. Ike would receive a commendation for his rescue attempt and for uncovering the information in the maintenance room.

"I know this is a lot to throw at you all at once, Jack," I said apologetically. "It's sort of the baptism of fire. But it won't help any of us for me to be seen in this condition. It would invite more questions that I'm not willing to answer. I'd like to tell Danny Dean in person that the charges are being dropped, but I can't do that either. Will you go by the Deans' house and tell him today? It might make his Christmas a little merrier."

"Sure, I'll go tell him. You're nicer to him than he deserves, you know."

"He's a jerk, but he isn't a murderer, so he deserves the courtesy of a personal visit. He'll want to know where I am and why I didn't come tell him myself. Just tell him I've been injured and can't go out, but I'll see him in a week or so."

"We'll send a team to the condo this afternoon. Any ideas where Ritter kept the women?"

"I didn't see anything in that room to indicate he'd held them there," said Ike, "but I didn't spend any time looking once I figured out that Bernie—I mean, Sheriff Davis—was probably in danger in Minnesota. I just threw some clothes in a bag and headed for the airport."

"You did the right thing, McDuffie," said Jack. "Are you OK? You look a little pale."

"I'm fine. I'll be back to work the day after Christmas."

"If the doctor releases you, you mean."

"Yeah, well, maybe."

Some noise in the hallway ended our conversation. The riders had returned from their tour. They were laughing and happy, and their faces were pink from the cold. I made introductions all around, and then Jack excused himself to go back to work.

It was Christmas Eve; my environment was spectacular; and I was safe in my home. Devereaux would soon serve a Christmas Eve feast to all of us. I should have been happy and smiling like the others, but instead I felt restless and agitated. I had an overwhelming feeling of dread that I couldn't seem to shake. I felt as if someone had sandpapered all my nerve endings. I had to fight to keep from sobbing. As Buck's eyes locked on to mine, he saw my inner turmoil. He suddenly stopped his conversation and wrapped me in his arms. The others drifted away, making excuses for needing showers or naps, and Buck and I were left alone in the grandly decorated room.

"I'm sorry. I can't help it," I sobbed.

"Shh," Buck whispered while maintaining a tight hold on me. "Let's sit down for a minute," he said, as he guided me to the couch in front of the fireplace. He propped his feet on the coffee table and pulled me onto his lap. I buried my face into his shoulder, and he held me while I cried. I dozed a little, and when I awoke, Buck was still holding me in his arms.

"I'm sorry," I began to apologize again, but he gently placed his forefinger on my lips to stop the rest of my sentence.

"Don't apologize to me for anything you do, understand?"

I nodded and rested my head against his chest again. He smelled of the outdoors, leather, and heady masculinity. Guilt flooded into my mix of feelings. This man accepted everything I did without question; yet a couple of hours ago, I had sat in this very spot kissing Ike. Would he understand that too? No. He would be so hurt.

Buck had known, and bedded, many women before we'd married. A friend once said his little black book was the size of the phone book. Many of them would rush to his side should he ask. Still I had no reason to doubt his loyalty to me. What was wrong with me? He trusted me, yet I had betrayed that trust today. Guilt and panic churned inside me, and I felt depression descend upon me. These emotional ups and downs weren't normal for me. I was exhibiting all the classic symptoms of a victim of kidnapping and rape. I did need some help. Now that I admitted it to myself, I once again knew what I had to do.

"Buck, will you take me to see Dukker? Not today but after Christmas?"

He stiffened slightly. Dukker was a powerful Gypsy with special powers. He could see into a person's soul, and he'd know how I felt without my telling him. He'd helped me before, and I felt he could help me again.

"If you think he can help you, we'll go."

"You know what he can do."

"Yes, I know," he whispered.

Chapter 35

Christmas Eve

Our Christmas Eve celebration was elegant. Devereaux had set the table with all our finest linens, crystal, and china. He had cooked the traditional Christmas foods of ham, roast beef, mashed potatoes, and candied sweet potatoes but had added Cajun specialties of dirty rice, mirliton gratin, and crawfish quiche topped with tasso sauce. He had set a buffet line using our best silver chafing dishes, and we served ourselves. Devereaux would dine with the ranch hands, in the bunkhouse. He had prepared the same fabulous feast for them.

Buck had given me an early Christmas gift, a red lounge set trimmed with antique lace and pearls. He had convinced me to put my hair up in a loose chignon. I added more makeup to my face in hopes of covering the bruises. In the low light of the candles, they were barely visible. Ike's sharp intake of breath as I entered the room on Buck's arm told me I looked good tonight. Dr. Cambridge and Anastasia smiled their approval. Each time I caught Buck's glance, I saw adoring love in his bright-green eyes.

After dinner we gathered by the fire with steamy mugs of hot, spiced cider. The others splashed rum into their mugs, but I stirred mine with a cinnamon stick. Full stomachs and the warm drink had us all yawning, so one by one our guests drifted off to their respective rooms. Buck and I extinguished the candles that burned throughout the house. When the last flame died, the house was dark and silent. The only sound was an occasional pop of wood in the hearths. As I turned to leave the room, Buck took my hand and led me to the arched opening that joined the hallway and the great room. He stopped and put his arms around me.

"You didn't notice the mistletoe up there, did you?"

In the darkness I barely could see the green sprigs with white berries that hung from the velvet ribbon above my head. Buck's big hands held my face gently as he placed his lips against mine.

"Merry Christmas, love," he said as we kissed. His hands drifted from my face to my shoulders then down my back to my bottom. As he held me tightly against him, I felt his passion come alive. When he wrapped me tightly in his arms and kissed me again, a surge of panic overtook me. I wasn't ready for this. Feeling trapped, I pushed him away to resist his affections.

"It's OK, Bernie," he said quietly. "I won't go any further. C'mon. Let's get some rest." He led me by the hand to the bedroom. We were silent as we undressed and climbed into bed.

"Can I hug you?" he asked.

"Yes," I whispered.

He moved closer to me and pulled me into an embrace. As always his warmth and strength comforted me.

"Buck, I'm so sorry…" I began.

"Shh," he whispered. "I should apologize to you. I know you aren't ready. I just can't help loving you and wanting you. Let's go to sleep so Santa will visit." He gently kissed my cheek and held me even more closely against him.

It wasn't long before I heard the soft, regular breathing that signified Buck was asleep. I usually drifted off the instant my head hit the pillow, but tonight my mind raced, and my conscience tore at my gut. Why had I been so willing to succumb to Ike's advances but panicked when my loving husband placed his hands on my body? Was I crazy?

I didn't remember falling asleep, but I awoke with a start. It was quiet and dark in the bedroom. I lay still while allowing my ears to search for any sound that could have awakened me. Buck was still sleeping peacefully beside me, and I carefully crawled out of bed so as not to awaken him. This was the perfect opportunity to sneak out to the great room to place gifts in the stockings we'd hung on the mantle. I had several small items for Buck's stocking. This morning

I had commissioned Devereaux to go to the jeweler's to buy watches for each of our guests. I placed the traditional orange and a handful of nuts in their shells in the toe of each stocking before adding the wrapped items. Several weeks ago I had ordered a hand-tooled Spanish leather saddle for Buck as his Christmas gift; it was well concealed in the bunkhouse. I had written a clue to the location of my gift on a slip of paper and wrapped it in a large gift box. I placed this box under the tree.

Most of the logs in the hearth had burned down, but a few embers still glowed red among the gray ashes. I sorted through the box of logs and selected some small pieces of oak to add to the fire. The wood was very dry, and the glowing coals soon ignited it. Gradually I added larger logs to create a roaring fire. I stood in front of the brightly burning hearth to warm myself before curling up in a large armchair near the hearth. I stared into the flames and allowed my mind to drift. As I remembered the Christmases of my childhood, a smile curled the corners of my lips.

My parents had moved to Sarasota in September 1950, two months before I was born. We lived in a small apartment complex owned by two wonderful people who, like my parents, had migrated to Florida from Pennsylvania. We became very close to Claire, William, and their children and spent most of our holidays with them. Christmas was a huge affair at the little complex named Attwood's Place. All the tenants and neighbors were welcome at the midday Christmas feast. Aunt Claire added leaves to her dining-room table, where she displayed and served all the food. Every chair in the house was used to accommodate all the guests. There was much laughter and conversation, some in English, some in Italian, with a few words of Polish occasionally slipped in.

After the meal, gifts were opened. For the children this was the best part of the day, as most tenants bought something for each child. Next came the group photo. Everyone would gather in front of the house, and Uncle William would snap a few shots with his box camera. Extra copies of the Christmas photos would be made at Norton's Camera Shop and distributed to each tenant.

Tears gathered in my eyes as I thought of my parents, the Attwoods, and the other elderly tenants, all of whom were gone now. I wished my parents could have known the man I loved and the children we would bring into the world. Depression was gripping me again. It was so bad that it hurt deep inside me. If I hadn't been pregnant, I would have been holding a big tumbler of bourbon. Instead I sat in the chair and cried.

A movement at the doorway caught my eye, and I glanced up to see Buck. He made his way to my chair and bent over to kiss the top of my head. "Missed you," he whispered.

"I just…" I sobbed.

"I know," he said, as he settled down on the floor next to my chair. He rested his head in my lap, and I absent-mindedly stroked his hair. Little sparkles of tears reflected the firelight. "The ghosts always get to me on Christmas Eve too," he said quietly.

I'd been wallowing in so much self-pity that I hadn't even considered that Buck's family was all gone too. He was feeling the same sadness I felt each Christmas, but this year I was adding to it.

I rose from my chair and held his hand. "Let's get some sleep before we greet Christmas morning."

We walked silently back to bed and spent the rest of the night wrapped in each other's arms.

Chapter 36

Christmas Morning

The day dawned bright and chilly. My curly blond hair snapped with electricity as I brushed it. *This will be a perfect day*, I promised myself. Buck had gone into the kitchen ahead of me to brew coffee, the elixir of the gods. I found myself humming Jingle Bells as I headed down the hall in the direction of the good-smelling brew. Feeling much better today, I smacked Buck on the bottom as I passed him. He grabbed my wrist and pulled me in close for a Christmas kiss. We separated as Ike cleared his throat to announce his presence.

"Sorry to interrupt, but I didn't want to stand here like a peeping tom."

"Merry Christmas, Ike," I said as I kissed him on the cheek.

"Merry Christmas," Buck echoed as they shook hands.

"Breakfast will be ready in a few minutes," I said as I began to gather ingredients for cherry-nut muffins. Under normal circumstances, I would've made yeast coffee cakes and Grammie's raisin bread, but this year we'd have hot muffins, cold ham, cheeses, fruit, and of course orange juice.

As I mixed the muffin ingredients, the scent of the melted butter, sugar, and nuts filled my nostrils and carried me back to my mother's kitchen at Christmastime. We always had enough money to live but never any extra, which made funds tight during the holidays. Each year, as Christmas approached, my mother began to use a little of the weekly grocery allotment to buy extra baking ingredients to use for Christmas cookies. The most expensive ingredients were real butter and nutmeats. She began to collect those items in November and stored them in the freezer to keep them fresh for her baking week. The week before Christmas, evening meals were simple affairs because of short funds and the cleanup required for a multicourse family meal. We ate, washed dishes, and put everything away quickly to have time to bake.

Mom selected recipes that were favorites among our friends. She made little pound cakes with candied fruit, rum balls, Mrs. Hale's snicker doodles rolled in red or green sugar, Chinese tea cookies with blanched almonds on top, Granny Fisher's sesame cookies, butter spritz cookies in the shapes of Christmas trees and holiday wreaths, and of course kolaczki, Polish cookies made to look like baby Jesus in swaddling clothes. When each batch was finished, we placed them in Tupperware containers and stacked them in the dining room. On Christmas Day we visited our closest friends and took boxes of assorted homemade treats to each family.

I wished I'd been able to do those things on my first Christmas with Buck. I'd hoped to resurrect some of the traditions from my childhood, share them with him, and perhaps make them traditions for our own family. Instead we would remember the horrors of my experience each year at Christmas. To hide the tears that welled in my eyes, I walked into the pantry to put away the items I'd used for the muffins. I wiped my tears on my sleeve, put on a happy face, and joined Buck and Ike in the kitchen.

When Dr. Cambridge and Anastasia joined us, we filled our plates and carried them into the great room. Buck lit the fire and illuminated the tree lights even though sunshine seeped through every window. There was much laughter and camaraderie as we ate the simple meal, sipped warm mugs of coffee, and opened gifts. Our guests were surprised and delighted to receive the watches. My gift from Buck was a gorgeous earring-and-necklace set made of pearls and blood-red rubies. He smiled as he read his clue, and we all donned our coats to follow him on the hunt for his gift.

Devereaux met us at the door of the bunkhouse. "*Joyeux Nöel, mes amies*. It is a lovely day, *oui*?" His deep-black eyes sparkled with delight. "You come to see old Devereaux to wish him well, no?" He laughed at his own joke, knowing we'd come in search of Buck's hidden gift. My clue had been written in French; the English translation was, "Where our good friend sleeps." Buck knew where to look. He headed for Devereaux's bedroom and opened the closet doors. In the back corner was a huge box that he hauled into the living room. He smiled when he pulled the intricately tooled, black saddle from the box. Artisans had hand crafted and stitched the exquisite leather into a work of art. Swirls and flourishes had been pressed into the body of the saddle and soft fleece covered the underside.

"It's beautiful, honey," he said with a grin. "Thunder won't know how to act with such a fine saddle on his back." He hoisted the saddle over his shoulder and led us toward the barn. "I'm going to put this in his stall for now. He'll have a couple of days to smell it before I put it on his back." When the black stallion nuzzled against him, Buck affectionately ruffled his mane and patted his flank.

Dr. Cambridge and Anastasia asked if they could take a ride around the property, and Ike wanted to go inside to watch football, so Buck and I took a walk. The sun shone brightly from a cloudless sky, but the wind was brisk. I pulled my camel's hair coat tightly around me as we strolled down a familiar path. We soon found ourselves on a ridge that overlooked acres of rolling pastureland. Barbed wire separated pastures, but here a wooden fence had been erected to form a small corral. Buck helped me up onto the fence, and we sat quietly looking out over the land—our land.

"Do you remember the first time we sat here, Bernie?"

"Of course I do."

How could I forget that night? Just three months earlier, I had asked Buck for help on a murder case involving my childhood friend. Circumstances were dangerous, so Buck asked me to stay at his ranch until things stabilized. We'd sat in this exact spot to watch the sun set across the vast acres of pasture. As darkness settled in, my body had slipped into Buck's warm embrace, and we'd shared our first kiss.

"That was when I knew I loved you, Bernie. Do you remember that you described a painting you wanted to do for me? You wanted to capture the sunset and silhouettes of the trees."

"Yes. I remember."

"I remember how you described the technique and how excited you were at the prospect of painting that scene. I know you haven't painted in years, but, I'd like to see you start again."

My body stiffened. Buck was suggesting a therapeutic hobby to me.

"No, I'm not," he said.

I was taken aback that he'd read my mind. "You're not what?"

"I'm not suggesting painting as therapy. I want you to do it because you enjoy it."

My skepticism clearly was transparent. Buck laughed, and amusement shone in his eyes. "You're not so difficult to read, you know."

"I guess I'm not," I admitted with a soft chuckle.

"I've been thinking about this for a while, Bernie, and I'd like to tell you about what has come to my mind."

"Oh." I was worried again, and panic rose inside me. Was Buck planning to do something to manipulate me, or was I just being paranoid? Insecurity filled me. Was I losing my grip?

"Bernie, are you in there? You sort of zoned out there for a minute. Do you want to go back to the house?"

"No, I'm all right," I said quietly.

"Let's see what you think of this," Buck said happily. He looked like a little boy who was about to describe how he'd taught his puppy to shake hands. How could I have doubted the sincerity of his intentions?

"You know we have jobs that don't adhere to regular business hours," he began. "And you know the baby will be here in six months." He paused and looked at me lovingly. "I'd like to hire a full-time nanny who'll live on the property with us. I'd like to add a wing to the house for her and also a nursery that could be accessed from the nanny's rooms and the main house. That way we'll still have some privacy. At the same time, since we'd have a construction crew here, I'd like to build an artist's studio for you. Of course I don't want to destroy the integrity of the house, so we'll need an architect to design the addition. Come to think of it, we might consider adding a garage. Sure would be easier than parking in the barn. Whatcha think?"

"That's a great idea, Buck," I said with a smile.

"Will you be able to meet with an architect next week? Your murder case is closed now. Can we schedule a time?"

"Of course."

Buck jumped down from the fence. He put his hands on either side of my waist and lifted me as I stepped down. When my feet touched the ground, he held me close. Then he placed his hand gently under my chin, tilted my face upward, and kissed me, just as he had done the first night on the ranch.

Chapter 37

Boxing Day

Everyone rose early the next morning. Ike insisted he was ready to go back to work and promised to adhere to light-duty rules. I called Jack to advise him of Ike's duty status just to be sure he stuck to it. Dr. Cambridge and Anastasia were booked on a commercial flight, so Buck and I took them to the airport. After seeing our guests onto the plane, we headed south on US Highway 41, locally known as The Tamiami Trail, then turned east toward a small trailer park called "The Gypsy Rendezvous."

We sailed through Elliot's Four-Way, a tiny community centered around a four-way stop intersection, and entered the parking lot of the Caravan, a quaint little roadhouse bar. From the lot we turned onto a dirt road that led to the park. The narrow road wound its way through a wooded piece of land. Pine trees and live oaks grew close together amid a tangle of vines and underbrush. Wispy pieces of Spanish moss fluttered in the breeze made by our passing car.

A cement-block building sat on the right side of the road behind the park entrance sign. A painted placard indicated this was the office, and we parked in front of it. Before I could knock on the door, it opened, and David, the trailer park manager, appeared. This gentle giant easily measured eight feet tall and had been part of a circus sideshow in his younger years. Now retired, he managed the park that was occupied by many former circus performers as well as a band of Gypsies with whom Buck and I were well acquainted. The man's bearded face smiled as he recognized us.

"Greetings. The old one told me you'd be visiting today. He waits for you in the wagon."

"Merry Christmas, David," I said as he bent down to hug me. He shook hands with Buck then guided us to Dukker's dwelling.

We stopped in front of a spectacular wagon. It resembled a covered wagon of the Old West but was made entirely of wood. Bright-yellow curtains were visible through the small windows that dotted each side. In front was a driver's seat that was backed by a large hinged window. Polished brass lanterns hung on either side of the window, and a matching set flanked the back door. The body of the wagon was painted a dark green. The window trim, wheel spokes, shutters, and rafters had been carefully painted in bright reds and yellows.

Buck and I entered through a Dutch door in the back. The top and bottom halves of the door were hinged separately and opened independently, but today both pieces were tightly closed to keep out the cold. David's massive height kept him from entering the wagon, so he waved his good-bye.

The interior of the wagon was outfitted in a fashion similar to the cabin of a ship. Every inch of space was used to maximum efficiency. The beds, stove, refrigerator, sink, and bathroom were nestled together amid an amazing number of storage cabinets. Dukker sat at a wooden table that was attached to the wall with hinges. Two wooden benches provided seating at the table. He smiled warmly and gestured for us to join him.

Buck occupied an edge of the bench opposite the old man, and I squeezed past him and sat next to the wall. He moved slowly in the close confines of the wagon, as his height made it difficult for him to stand up straight. There were many low-hanging obstacles on which he could bang his head. He sat gingerly on the bench with his long legs stretched out toward the kitchen. A pot of coffee, along with cream and sugar, sat on the table. I poured hot, spiced brew into the mugs Dukker had placed in front of us.

I smiled broadly as I gazed at the old man. He looked very much the same as when I'd known him as a child. His old-style clothing had been fashioned in Eastern Europe. His shirt had a high, straight collar that was richly embroidered with gold and red thread. Full, bloused sleeves covered his arms, and the cuffs were embroidered in the same detail. A leather vest had been added to his wardrobe for warmth. A peaked felt hat, resplendent with a long black feather, sat on the table next to him. The old

Gypsy's hair hung in soft salt-and-pepper ringlets down to his shoulders. His complexion was swarthy, and his eyes were as deep and dark as pools of swamp water. His eyes and lips were smiling at us today.

"Merry Christmas, Dukker," I said as I leaned across the table and placed a kiss on his weathered cheek.

"You flatter an old man, Tshilaba," he said affectionately. He never called me by my given name but used the nickname he'd tagged me with many years ago. It meant "seeker of knowledge."

A stack of tarot cards sat on the table. The old man reached for the cards and placed them in front of me. I smiled at the familiar routine. I cut the deck then placed five cards on the table between us. One by one I turned the cards over.

"What do you see, Dukker?" I leaned across the table to hear his response.

"You know the lovers card indicates an intense bond between two people, little one," he said as he touched the first card. "The empress represents motherhood. The wheel of fortune is the destiny card. Fate has taken a hand in things. The ace of swords indicates triumph, victory, and strength. It is the card of great determination and mental clarity. The king of cups represents the completion of an emotional time." After the reading he placed the cards back in the stack and moved the deck to the far edge of the table against the wall.

Next Dukker took my left hand and uncurled the fingers. He placed my hand faceup on top of his palm. Then he quietly traced my lifeline with his finger. He examined the fate line and the creases on the side of my hand. "The lifeline is still long, and the fate line is not broken," Dukker related. He was quiet for a moment but peered deeply into my eyes. I felt his mind search my thoughts; I felt him feel my pain and experience my fear. I closed my eyes to break his hold on my mind. When I opened them again, he gazed kindly at my face.

"Do you know why I've never read your right hand, my dear?"

"No, I don't."

"The right hand shows the past. It already has taken place and cannot be changed. We could not stop the danger, Tshilaba. The evil one had much power. The witch was able to work her magic, however. True?"

"She gave me this," I said as I pulled the amulet from inside my blouse, "but it didn't stop him."

"Oh, but it did, my child. It stopped him."

"No, it did *not* stop him," I said in a voice louder than I'd intended. "He captured me and beat me and raped me." I heard the terror build inside me again. Tears poured from my eyes, and I sobbed uncontrollably. Buck made a move toward me, but Dukker held up a hand to stop him.

He took my hands in his gnarled ones and held them tightly. "Listen to me, my child," he began. "The witch's magic was very strong. She's the magical superior of her coven. No one could have done better."

"She didn't stop him," I whispered slowly.

"She stopped him from killing you, my dear, and the life inside you still flourishes. That is what really matters." His powerful mind invaded my thoughts again. As he spoke, the melodic drone of his voice almost lulled me to sleep.

Chapter 38

Boxing Day Afternoon

The next thing I knew, Buck and I were back in the car. I barely could hold my head upright. I felt drugged and woozy. Could there have been something in my coffee? Dukker was skilled in the use of magical herbs. We rode home in silence. Buck glanced at me from time to time, but he made no move to start a conversation. In concentration, his brow was creased with worry lines, and his lips were pressed into a straight line. When he pulled the Range Rover into the barn, I jumped from the front seat without waiting for him to come around to open my door.

"Buck, I need to go for a walk," I said. "Alone," I added. I saw the hurt in his eyes when I spoke that last word.

The path behind the barn led through a copse of cabbage palms and palmetto scrub. Beyond lay a small creek that ran toward a stand of live oaks. I followed the path of the water into the majestic trees. The branches of the largest of the oaks spanned fifty feet. Long limbs covered with moss and ferns dipped almost to the ground and rose skyward again. It was cold under the cover of the trees, so I moved toward the end of a long branch that was bathed in sunlight and sat on it. I arranged my body among the leafy branches and lay back. It was almost like lying in a leafy green hammock. Had I not been pregnant, I would've climbed the tree and wedged myself into a notch in the highest branch.

As a child I had learned to climb trees and had spent many afternoons reading and snoozing in the topmost branches. There were no oaks on my parents' land, but they had several Brazilian pepper trees that served nicely. Across the street from our house stood a large mango tree where I'd built a makeshift tree house. During the construction process, I'd discovered that every nail I pounded into the tree drew huge globs of sticky brown sap. I had to be very careful not to get the gooey mess on my clothing because it was almost impossible to remove. I often wondered why no one had thought to make mango sap into glue.

I smiled at the childhood memories. I had come out there to think and hopefully plan how I would overcome the horror I'd experienced. Dukker had helped me before when trauma had numbed my feelings, but he had just told me to use the powers and strengths I already possessed. In the wagon I had heard him speak to me inside my head. *Use the power in your mind, little one*, he told me, though his lips had uttered no words. *Draw strength from what you know.*

What do I know? I asked myself. *I know I'm honest and decent. I'm good at what I do. I like being the county sheriff. I've been happiest when I've immersed myself in work. But things have changed over the past few months. I have different responsibilities now. My life is no longer just about me; it's us: me, Buck, and the baby. I've loved, and I've been loved in return. I've felt the most comfortable and the safest in Buck's arms. I've drawn my strength from him. He's the one who can support me and steady my emotions. And it was him I pushed away when I walked off.*

Tears trickled down my cheeks. Sobs shook my body as pent-up feelings poured out. I cried myself to sleep, and fog enveloped my brain. I heard Dukker's voice all around me as he said, *Draw strength from what you know.* Again

I found myself spinning on an icy road. Terrifying images flashed before me—a pair of cold blue eyes, a metal framed hospital bed, the muzzle flash of a pistol, and blood on the floor. I felt blows to my face and the terror of captivity. Then a tall figure emerged from the bank of fog. He was broad shouldered, with a lean abdomen and long, muscular legs. He grabbed my wrist and pulled me from the horrors of the nightmare. When I opened my eyes again, deep purple and grays of dusk covered the land. Something had awakened me. I was immediately alert. Predators roamed at night. I was unarmed and alone.

I jumped down from my perch and retraced my path through the stand of oaks, but a rustle of underbrush stopped me dead in my tracks. Something was heading in my direction. I looked around for some sort of cover, but the palmetto scrub offered little protection. Wild boar roamed the wooded areas, and they could be vicious. I looked at the nearest tree, decided my best escape option would be upward, and hoisted myself up to the nearest limb. I hoped the intruder wasn't a Florida panther. The cat could follow me aloft. I was halfway to the top of the tree when I heard the unmistakable crackle of a two-way radio. I stopped my ascent and listened more intently. The jingle of a bridle reached my ears. A horse and rider were near.

I worked my way down the branches and jumped to the ground from the last limb. My sudden appearance startled the horse, which reared up on his back legs. A whinny of fear escaped the animal's lips.

"Bernie, is that you?" Buck's voice sounded from atop the horse. In a moment he had calmed Thunder. I breathed a deep sigh.

"Yes, I'm right here."

"Thank God. We've been looking for you for an hour."

"I'm sorry. I fell asleep. I guess the time slipped away from me."

Buck jumped down from Thunder and pulled me into his arms. "You're shaking with cold," he said as he removed his heavy suede jacket and wrapped it around my shoulders.

He pulled a two-way radio from the pocket of the coat and keyed the microphone to talk. "I've found her, Devereaux."

"Is she all right?"

"Yes, she's fine, but she's practically frozen. We'll spend the night in line shack number four. It's only a couple of hundred yards from here.

"*Oui, monsieur*. See you in the morning."

"We'll call if we need anything. Over and out."

Buck lifted me onto the broad back of the stallion. He walked through the oaks, leading the horse behind him. I held on to the saddle horn and gripped the animal with my knees, but my feet didn't reach the stirrups, so I didn't have a firm hold. I was glad the ride to the shack took just a few minutes.

Buck opened the door, disappeared inside, and reappeared moments later. He lifted me from the saddle and carried me through the door. The fire he had started in the hearth was already warming the small room. He deposited me in a chair near the fire, made his way to a door in the corner of the room, and started to run the water in the bathroom.

"I turned on the water in the shower to warm the bathroom," he explained. "I'm going to settle Thunder in for the night. I'll be right back."

True to his word, he returned a few minutes later, his cheeks red from the cold.

"I'm still wearing your coat," I said. "Sorry. I didn't realize it. It wasn't very nice of me to let you go out in the cold without it."

"Doesn't matter. I'm fine," he said as he warmed himself by the hearth. "C'mon. Let's get you into the warm shower. I'll get a blanket for you to curl up in. Give me your clothes so I can warm them by the fire." He followed me into the bathroom, gathered my clothing, and headed back to the living room.

The warm water felt good as it cascaded down my neck and back. My hands had been so cold they were aching, but the heat eased the hurt. I felt as if all my cares and woes were washing down the drain. I dried off with a fluffy towel then wrapped my hair in it.

Steam had completely fogged the full-length mirror that hung on the back of the door. I took a hand towel from the rack by the sink and wiped off the moisture. I glanced at my figure in the glass. The cuts had healed, the bruises were fading, and my legs looked good again. I placed a hand on my protruding abdomen and thanked God once more for the life that still grew inside me. As I looked at my face, I saw resolve and sparkle in those ice-blue eyes again. I stood tall, with my shoulders square and erect. A confident smile turned the corners of my lips. I removed the towel from head, arranged my wet hair across my shoulders, and pulled open the door.

As I stepped from the brightly lit bathroom into the semidarkness of the main room, I stopped to let my eyes adjust. The bathroom was the only other room in the shack. A small kitchen occupied the space next to the bathroom; a bed was centered on the opposite wall; and the living room was arranged around the fireplace. The line shacks were only used when bad weather kept one of the hands from returning to the bunkhouse or during a roundup. They were functional but not elaborate.

Buck drew his breath in sharply when I appeared at the hearth, and his eyes wandered up and down my body.

"Here. Wrap up in this, honey," he said as he offered me a heavy blanket.

"That's wool, Buck. If I even touch it, I'll break out in hives."

"You can't sit around like that," he said, smiling. "I'll see what else is in the cupboard."

"Why can't I sit around like this?" I teased.

Buck pursed his lips and exhaled loudly. "Because I'll have to go somewhere else. It's too cold to sleep outside with Thunder. You're beautiful, honey," he said with a loving look in his bright-green eyes.

I walked to him and unbuttoned his shirt. One by one, pieces of clothing hit the floor. Buck picked me up and carried me to the bed.

"I thought you were lost to me, Bernie," he whispered.

"I don't believe you'll ever be rid of me."

"Oh, that's wonderful," he said as our bodies melted together.

Chapter 39

Friday

Buck woke me with a steaming cup of cowboy coffee. He had used an old-fashioned stovetop percolator to brew it. Boiling water rose up a metal tube and trickled down through a basket of grounds. Cooking time was judged by the color of the brew, or as the ranch hands described the consistency, "until a horseshoe will float in it." Buck also heated a can of evaporated milk to mix with the thick coffee. The fire had gone out during the night, and the room was cold. I drew the bed covers around me as I savored the warm drink.

"Damn, it's cold," Buck said as he slipped under the covers with me. "There's frost on the grass."

"Are the oranges damaged?" I asked? My voice was laced with concern. A freeze that could destroy our entire crop would cause us a substantial financial loss. Many ranchers and grove owners were land wealthy and cash poor and counted on the winter citrus harvest to make ends meet. We were lucky because we had two salaries and other investments to keep us afloat during hard times, but a loss would still hurt.

"No, it's just a frost, not a freeze. There's no extreme cold in the forecast so far. Everything's fine."

I smiled at his reassuring words. He obviously was trying to keep me from worrying, yet I knew he checked the weather several times a day during the winter. As my mind drifted back to Danny Dean's case, I slowly slipped the coffee. There was something I still had to do.

"How does my face look?" I asked Buck.

"Beautiful," he said as he gently touched my cheek.

"No, I mean really. The cuts are healed, and my eyes are no longer swollen, but are any of the bruises still visible?"

"There's a little yellow on one of your cheekbones," he said, as he peered closely at my face. He kissed a spot on my cheek, as if to assist in the healing process. Then he kissed my lips and my neck and my breasts.

He grinned. "Everything looks OK to me."

"Just OK?"

"Actually, it all looks fantastic and you know it. It's good to have you back, honey," he said in a serious tone.

"It's good to be back."

"What happened out there last night, Bernie?" he asked. "What did you do?"

"I drew strength from something I knew I could count on."

"What's that? What do you mean?"

"You. I put my faith in your love. It's a great comfort to know I can count on that."

"But you've had my love all along."

"I know," I told him with a smile. "All I had to do was realize how much I can count on that. I know you love me, and I drew strength from that knowledge. The mind is a powerful thing. Dukker told me my mind could heal itself if I'd just allow it to happen."

"He didn't tell you that, Bernie. I was with you the entire time. He didn't say that."

"Dukker's lips didn't speak the words, but he told me just the same. You know the power he possesses. His mind spoke to mine without the need of words."

"Jeez," Buck said.

"I know you don't like to hear about his powers, but he really can do things that are outside the normal range of human ability. You have to admit that. You've witnessed what he can do."

Buck was silent.

I decided it was a good time to change the subject, so I asked him a favor. "I'd like you to go with me to Danny Dean's house as soon as my face is completely healed. I need to tell him a few things, and I need to look my best to see him."

"I'll go," Buck said. "Just tell me when."

Chapter 40

Monday Evening

Three days later the last traces of the bruises on my face had vanished. Makeup hid any remaining evidence of the beating. My strength had returned, and it was time for me to return to work. The first item on my agenda was visiting the Dean home. I told Buck why we were going to his home instead of visiting his office. What I needed to discuss with Danny was very sensitive and couldn't be overheard by prying ears. In fact no one would even know I'd been there unless Danny or Kelly released the information. I was dressed in my business attire when Buck arrived home after his day's work.

"Are you sure this is the right time to go to the Dean house?" Buck asked as we drove down our long driveway.

"Yes. I have to discuss this with him privately, and he might not be there during the day."

"How do you know he'll be home?"

"He remarried his ex-wife last week and moved back into the house. He won't stray too far from her for a little while. He'll be there."

The Dean home was ablaze with light. Christmas trees covered in twinkling lights appeared in several windows. Palm tree trunks were wrapped in coils of colorful bulbs. Boughs of fir draped the front portico. Life-size nutcracker figures stood guard on either side of the massive double doors. Kelly Dean answered our ring with a bright, plastic smile on her face, but when she recognized me, the smile slipped away, and her eyes hardened.

"What do you want?" she asked, spitting the words at me.

"Mrs. Dean, I'd like to speak with your husband."

"I bet you would. He's married to me again, you know."

"Yes, ma'am. I know you were remarried. Congratulations. I still need to talk to him."

"No, you don't need to talk to him."

"This is an official visit, Mrs. Dean," I said as I stepped past her into the hall.

She raised her hand as if to slap me, but Buck grabbed her wrist in midair. "I don't believe you understood, ma'am. This is an official visit," he said sweetly.

Her eyes softened a little when she saw Buck. She seemed not to have noticed him until that moment. "Well, now," she said, as her eyes wandered up and down his tall frame. "You're much better looking than the one she brought with her the last time. Maybe you can keep me occupied while she talks to my husband. He's in the library." She tossed the words in my direction as she led Buck toward the living room. Her honey-coated words plied him with compliments as she attempted to work her charms on him.

I walked down the hall, away from the sounds of their voices. A dim light seeped underneath a door that led from the hall, and the muted sounds of a television came from behind it. I took a deep breath and knocked.

"What do you want, Kelly?" Danny's voice called from within. I pushed the door open and quietly entered the room. Danny was staring at the television screen. "What do you want, Kelly?" he repeated, annoyance in his tone.

"I need to talk to you, Danny," I said.

At the sound of my voice, his head snapped away from the TV, and a smile spread across his face. "To what do I owe this honor, Bernie? C'mon in. You want a drink?" he said as he raised his glass.

"No, thanks. Danny, we need to talk," I said as I closed the door behind me.

"Ooh, baby. Behind closed doors, no less. Kelly will scratch your eyes out if she sees this." He laughed, and then he laughed again.

"She's in the living room with my husband. She's entertaining him."

"You're a trusting soul, Bernie."

"In this case, yes, I am," I said with a little smile.

"You're not here to arrest me again, are you?" he asked with a note of alarm in his voice.

"No. You didn't kill Sally. I'm positive of that. That's why the charges were dropped."

"Then why the visit?" The confusion showed on his face. "And come to think of it, why didn't you come out here earlier to tell me the murder charges were dropped? You sent your minion. That's not like you."

"The officer who called on you was my chief deputy. He's hardly a minion."

"He wasn't you, Sheriff. I'm County Administrator Danny Dean. You should have come out here yourself," he said smugly.

"Let me tell you what I've done in the past couple of weeks, County Administrator Dean," I began. "I paid a visit to Sally Keith's hometown of St. Peter. I spoke with her mother, some acquaintances, and one of her teachers, a Miss Corrigan. I think you might recognize her name. I spoke with the chief of police, who told me about Sally's traumatic childhood and her confinement in a mental institution. He also told me about a family who hired Sally to care for a child, a family named Dean, as I recall. The chief helped me gain access to Sally's records, and I learned even more about her.

"What I didn't know was that Sally's killer had followed me to St. Peter. He kidnapped me and held me captive there. I'm only just now able to venture out of my home, where I've been recuperating. That's why I sent my *minion*, as you put it, to tell you that the murder charges against you had been dropped. I wasn't able to get here myself." My voice had risen to a level I'd promised myself it wouldn't reach. This pompous ass was so aggravating that I was finding it difficult to keep my temper in check. I took a deep breath to calm myself. He was *not* going to goad me into losing my professionalism.

"Sorry to hear all that, kid." His lack of sincerity was unbelievable, but he was still the county administrator. As much as I would have liked to punch him, I wasn't going to do that.

"Danny, can you turn off the TV? There's something we need to discuss, and we don't need the distraction. I need your full attention."

"Sure, sure, baby, whatever you want," he said as he pushed the power button. "What's so damned important?"

I reached into my purse and pulled out an envelope. "While I was in St. Peter, I met a young woman. She was another victim of the psychopath who killed Sally and who held me captive. She had suffered for years at his hand. She was the man's sister."

"Yeah, so?"

"Their mother's name was Margaret, Danny. Do you remember anyone in that town named Margaret?"

"I grew up in St. Peter. I knew lots of people there. I imagine I knew someone named Margaret. What of it?"

"Do you remember anyone with the nickname Crazy Margaret?"

"Yeah. There was a girl we called Crazy Margaret. Cruel to call someone by that name, but kids are cruel, you know."

"Think a little harder, Danny. How well did you know Margaret?"

"I knew her as well as all the other kids in my class."

"You're a terrible liar, Danny. One would think you'd be really good at it by now, since you do it so often."

"I resent that comment, Sheriff." With an indignant expression, Danny sat upright in his chair.

"Save it, Danny. I already know the truth."

I opened an envelope, removed a yellowed page of onionskin paper, and handed it to him. He glanced at the paper but made no move to read it. "Don't have my glasses in here, Bernie. You tell me what it says."

"These are adoption papers. Sally Keith was adopted by Alice and Sam Keith."

"I knew Sally was adopted," he said. "That's no secret."

"Do you want to know who her parents were?"

"What difference can it make? She's dead. No one cares now. Can I turn the television back on? I have a big bet on this football game."

The man's shallowness was unbelievable. "Sally's biological mother was raped, Danny. Her name was Margaret Barnard, or Crazy Margaret, as you called her. Her biological father was you, Danny. You raped Margaret, and the child born as a result of that rape was Sally. She was your daughter, Danny."

A low moan escaped Danny's lips as my words registered in his brain. It escalated into a primal scream. Over and over he screamed. I heard footsteps in the hall, and Kelly burst into the room, followed by Buck.

"What the hell is happening in here?" she yelled.

Danny was hunched on the floor crying. He was a pitiful sight, but I had no pity left for him. His evil deeds had come back to haunt him in the worst possible way. He had been in love with his own daughter and had even fathered a child with her. The child, mercifully, had died with Sally, so the horror he had started so many years ago had ended with the death of the unborn child.

"Your husband can tell you the story," I said as I walked past her into the hall. Buck followed me as I headed out of the house.

"Are you OK, honey?" he asked quietly.

"I'm fine. I had to do that, Buck. The truth was hidden all these years. It had to finally come out. He raped Margaret, and the trickle-down horror spanned thirty years. If he hadn't done that, Margaret might have lived a happy life instead of the wretched existence she endured. She might not have given birth to a sadistic murderer. Sally and Nadine's tortures might never have happened. A madman might not have touched our lives. The chain of horror could have been stopped before it started. It started with Danny, and now it ends with him."

"Are you going to research the possibility of prosecuting him for rape? The chief may want to do that."

"It's not worth it now. It would harm the living without giving justice to the dead. Danny created his own punishment. That's the only justice. As Dukker has told us time and again, one can't escape one's destiny once the cards are dealt."

Buck was silent for several minutes. "Yeah, you're right, honey. Let's get out of here."

Epilogue

Danny Dean never recovered from the realization of what he had done. Kelly divorced him again, was awarded most of their worldly goods, obtained custody of their three children, and moved back to Minnesota. He was forced to resign as county administrator. Two of the county commissioners—Ruskin and Torrino, the same two who had posted his bail—arranged to have him committed to the mental institution in Arcadia under the provisions of Florida's Mental Health legislation, known as the Baker Act. There was some scuttlebutt flying around about shady real estate deals Danny had been a party to with the Sherlocks and the same two county commissioners, but with Danny declared mentally incompetent and under wraps, so to speak, nothing could be proven.

Ike bought Sally's house from Mrs. Keith. He and his cat, Skitzo, lived there happily among the skyscrapers. Real estate agents constantly pestered him to sell the property, but he always gave them the same answer—not "No" but "Hell, no."

I shoved the horror of my experience into the deepest recesses of my mind. It only surfaced in my nightmares, and eventually those became less frequent. Life settled into a wonderful routine once again. That's not to say it wasn't without ups and downs, but Buck and I could handle anything fate could dish out. As Dukker had said, we were destined to be together.

Made in the USA
Lexington, KY
17 December 2014